OTHER BOOKS BY IAN A. O'CONNOR

FICTION

The Twilight of the Day

The Seventh Seal

The Barbarossa Covenant

The Wrong Road Home

Point Option

The Pegasus Directive

NON-FICTION

Co-author:
SCRAPPY: Memoir of a U. S. Fighter
Pilot in Korea and Vietnam

"God, I hate to go to Texas," JFK said to his friend, Dave Powers,
earlier that week in November 1963, adding that he had
"a terrible feeling about going."

The Week ™ —Paul Brandus, January 8, 2015.

———————————

Directive – noun – something that serves to direct, guide, and
usually impel toward an action or goal *especially*, **government:** an
authoritative order or instrument issued by
a high-level body or official.

A presidential directive. *Merriam-Webster*

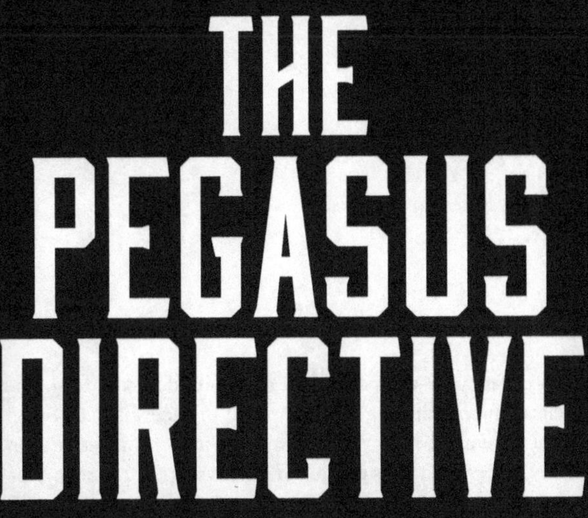

THE PEGASUS DIRECTIVE

THE TOP SECRET KENNEDY ASSASSINATION FILE

An International Thriller

IAN A. O'CONNOR

Pegasus Publishing & Entertainment Group

Pegasus Publishing & Entertainment Group – USA.
First Edition: June, 2023

LIBRARY OF CONGRESS CATALOGUING-IN-PUBLICATION DATA

Library of Congress Control Number: 2023901430

O'Connor, Ian A., 1944-

THE PEGASUS DIRECTIVE – The Top Secret Kennedy Assassination File
Fiction - Novel
Thriller – Political – Mystery – International Intrigue

ISBN-13: 978-1-7374229-2-1 – Hardcover edition
ISBN-13: 978-1-7374229-4-5 – Trade Paperback
ISBN-13: 978-1-7374229-3-8 – ebook edition

Cover & Interior Design by Glen M. Edelstein, Hudson Valley Book Design.

Visit the author at: www.ianaoconnor.com
Contact the author at: ianaoconnor@ianaoconnor.com
This is a work of fiction.

Printed in the United States of America
LSC-C

1 3 5 7 9 10 8 6 4 2

This book is for my wife and best friend,
Candice Myers O'Connor.

ACKNOWLEDGMENTS

I owe a particular thanks to Margaret Datzman O'Connor who undertook the task of editing my work.

A very special thank you to my friend of over fifty years, John Siniscal, of Carlsbad, California, for his invaluable advice, suggestions, and corrections in getting the final copy of this thriller into print.

PRESIDENT LYNDON JOHNSON'S THOUGHTS ON THE POSSIBILITY OF AN INTERNATIONAL CONSPIRACY THEORY

During a filmed interview with CBS journalist Walter Cronkite at his ranch in Texas in September, 1969, President Lyndon Johnson was asked whether he was satisfied there was no international conspiracy in the Kennedy assassination:

" I can't honestly say that I haven't been completely relieved of
the fact there might have been international connections . . .
I don't think that me, or anyone else, is absolutely sure
what motivated Oswald or others."
A Documentary Film – *Kennedy: A Legacy In Blood*

GOVERNOR JOHN CONNOLLY'S THOUGHTS ON THE CONCLUSIONS OF THE WARREN COMMISSION REPORT

Texas Governor John Connelly who was in the limousine with President Kennedy the day he was assassinated, said during an interview in 1982:

"I do not for one second believe the conclusions of the
Warren Commission." Pressed as to why he had not spoken
out at the time, Connelly replied, "Because I love this
country . . . and we needed closure at the time."
A Documentary Film – *Kennedy: A Legacy In Blood*

CONTENTS

THE PRESENT

"Hello, *Orion*. This is *Pegasus*."

Justin Scott froze. *Pegasus*? It was a name and a voice from fifty years earlier. A lifetime ago.

But Pegasus has been dead for years! he told himself, heart racing, eyes glued to the computer screen and a still-life rendering of the winged horse from Greek mythology.

"Because you're now listening to this message, *Orion*, it means I'm dead."

Justin hit the pause button on the CD drive and sat back, his mind overloading on memories. *But Pegasus has been dead for years*, he told himself again, then silently added, *hasn't he?* After a few minutes, he was ready to resume. He pressed start.

The voice continued. "I will explain everything in due course, but first, I need you to make sure you have three discs and a key. That key is important. Guard it with your life."

Justin heard the garage door opener engage, signaling his wife was home. He stopped the disc and shut down the computer, as much to take time to further gather his wits about him as to greet Paula. His thoughts harkened back to earlier in the day.

"Excuse me, are you Justin Scott?"

Startled by the unexpected sound of a woman's voice coming from so close behind him, Justin Scott wheeled to confront the unknown. The UPS driver smiled, her familiar brown uniform crisp and professional looking, her "package car" with its large brown and gold shield logo idling at the curb. She held an overnight envelope.

"I'm Justin Scott. You caught me by surprise," he added sheepishly, holding up his iPhone. "Trying to text my golfing buddies to tell them I'm running late."

As he reached out, she brought up her other hand holding an Apple Tablet. "I need your signature, you know, to verify receipt."

Justin did the honors, thanked her, took the padded envelope and studied it for a long moment, noting the return address in Washington, D. C. He shrugged, turned back to the house and entered through the open garage door.

"Honey, it's just me," he called out. "I'm leaving a delivery package on the kitchen counter. Don't know who it's from, but I'll open it when I get back from golf. See ya."

Five hours later, Justin was in the kitchen with a cold beer close at hand to celebrate another lousy golf score when he spied the overnight envelope. Lying atop was a hastily scrawled note from his wife saying she had gone shopping and would be back before dinner.

Justin tore open the envelope's perforated flap, thinking the contents were rather light. He reached in and pulled out three CDs encased in separate white paper sleeves, each clearly marked 1,2, and 3. He then held the envelope facedown and gently shook it. A small key tumbled onto the quartz countertop. *This is getting interesting*, he thought, his curiosity piqued. He began walking over to his wife's computer station by the pantry but stopped, gave a quirky little shake of his head, pivoted, and instead, headed down the hall to his own office computer.

Justin put the disc marked 1 into the open CD slot, punched the start button and listened as the soft whirling sound intensified, signaling the disc's imprinted information was being transferred to his hard drive. Two minutes later as the screen came to life, he found himself genuinely startled for the second time that day.

"Hello, *Orion*. This is *Pegasus*."

"No wine with dinner tonight?" Justin's wife asked, surprise evident in her tone. "Not feeling well?"

"No, no, I'm fine. I've got some work to do later, and I'll need a clear head."

"Does the work have anything to do with the package that came this morning?"

Justin nodded. "Yeah, and it's right out of the *Twilight Zone*," he said, "because from what little I know so far, it's about something going back to my days in the Nixon White House when I was still a newbie FBI agent."

"Well, no need to help with the dishes," Paula said, rising from the table. "Sounds like something interesting, hon, so have at it, but don't stay up too late."

Ten minutes later Justin was seated in front of his computer, eager to uncover the disc's remaining information. The earlier screenshot had been replaced with a video of *Pegasus*, the man. He was propped up by multiple pillows in what appeared to be a hospital bed and tethered to several machines with blinking lights, intravenous drip lines, and an untold number of wires disappearing beneath blankets.

Justin unconsciously leaned closer to the screen for a better look. His boss of fifty years ago was a markedly changed man: unrecognizable really. *Pegasus has got to be well into his eighties by now,* Justin thought, and although he indeed looked frail, the voice was surprisingly strong and unchanged with the passage of time.

"Justin," he began, "as you well know, this year, 2023, marks the sixtieth anniversary of the assassination of President Kennedy. Most of the last of the classified files held in the *Kennedy Assassination Records Collection* at the NARA Archives at College Park, Maryland were released by President Biden in December 2022, and the world was told at the time, that's it; there are no more, for now. At the same time, we were reminded that *The Warren Commission Report* is still the definitive document on the subject, just as it was when first published in September 1964." He paused, and Justin watched as the man struggled to cough. It was heart-wrenching. An arm appeared on-screen and gently wiped the patient's mouth. After a few seconds, *Pegasus* waved the arm away, took several shallow, preparatory breaths, and began speaking again.

"You are now the only man left alive who knows what really happened in Dallas that terrible day in 1963, and how the *Warren Report* got it so wrong in their orchestrated rush to judgment. Had the truth come to light at the time, or even in the years immediately following, it would have in all likelihood triggered World War III.

"The cover-up must finally come to an end. Sixty years ago the American people had a God-given right to know the truth and the information on the three discs will do just that."

Pegasus closed his eyes. After watching the recumbent figure for almost three minutes, Justin saw his friend shudder, open his eyes, then stare into the camera lens.

"What you are about hear, *Orion*, will awaken memories of the information we uncovered from the three major players during those dark, desperate days in May 1972. And you will also see that all of our original recordings have been faithfully copied onto the third disc.

"I never told a soul that I made duplicates of everything before depositing the originals in the Roosevelt Presidential Vault at Fort Knox, on orders from President Nixon. I labeled that package *The Pegasus Directive*, and now, I'm handing-off this electronic copy to you. Good luck, *Orion*, and I'll speak for the last time at the end of disc number three with my final instructions."

As Justin pressed the stop button, he was struck with an epiphany-like moment. Something his long-ago mentor had said made him realize he should not listen to the discs alone, but with the one person he trusted implicitly to give him the sound advice he knew he would need when finished.

Her name was Paula.

CHAPTER 1
WASHINGTON D.C.
MAY 8, 1972

ANDREW ST. JAMES nodded a silent greeting to the Secret Service agent on duty as he stepped through the doorway and into the Oval Office. A visibly impatient President Richard Milhous Nixon beckoned him forward with a wave of his right hand, while holding out a single sheet of paper in his left.

"This just came from Ottawa," the President said. "It was sent to Mel Laird at the Pentagon, and he forwarded it to me over that newfangled ARPANET gadget."

St. James took the message that had him dropping everything to report post-haste to the President.

FLASH (Z) TOP SECRET
FROM: Canadian Intelligence Service Ottawa 8 MAY 1972
TO: U.S. Secretary of Defense Melvin Laird
MESSAGE: Soviet defector en route to Ottawa from London.
Requests meeting on landing with American code
named Pegasus. Seeks asylum in the U.S. in exchange
for information he claims critical to America's immediate
security. End message.

St. James was visibly stunned. *How is it possible an unknown Soviet walk-in knows about Pegasus?*

"You think this defector might hold the answer to our prayers?" his titular boss, Dr. Henry Kissinger, wondered aloud, in his distinctive monotone.

"I do; but then again, he could be a Trojan horse," cautioned St. James. He turned to the President. "We don't have a choice, sir, I must follow-up."

"How will you determine that he's legitimate?"

"I'll know within seconds with his correct answer to just one question. If he is indeed the real deal, then I'll need your authorization to bring him home."

Nixon replied by plucking a fountain pen from inside his jacket and writing rapidly on a sheet of White House stationery. Finished, he scanned it once, nodded a silent approval, added his signature, and handed the note to St. James.

"This presidential directive is all the authority you'll need," Nixon said. He rose and held out his hand. "Good luck, *Pegasus.*"

St. James shook the proffered hand. *Pegasus* was a name given him three years earlier by the only person from whom he took orders: this President of the United States.

St. James stopped by his office in the bowels of the White House long enough to retrieve his red diplomatic passport, then sprinted to the parking area. Within five minutes he was headed to Andrews Air Force Base, where a flight suited major stood waiting on the ramp. St. James held up his White House security badge for inspection. "No luggage, but possibly a passenger on our return. The flight plan filed?"

"We're cleared direct to Ottawa, sir."

St. James fell into step beside the major. To this officer—or anyone else—St. James was just another government worker toiling for Dr. Henry Kissinger. Invited to sit in the cockpit jumpseat of the T-39

Sabreliner, he followed with interest as the two-man crew worked their way down the checklist through engine startup to taxiing. The tower cleared them for takeoff; and after reaching their assigned altitude, St. James retreated to the cabin, plopped himself into a large leather seat, and promptly fell asleep.

The next thing he knew he was being nudged awake by the copilot. "Time to buckle up for landing, sir."

Seven minutes later they were parked in front of a Canadian Forces hanger. Two men in civilian clothes introduced themselves as Canadian Security Intelligence Service inspectors from the covert division. "The subject will be here in ten minutes," said the taller man.

After the jet from London landed, and a mobile ramp affixed to its forward door, the Canadians climbed up followed by St. James who had asked them to say nothing that could identify him to the Soviet citizen. He wanted to see if he would be recognized without prompting.

He did not have long to wait. There were four passengers seated together in the center of the spacious cabin. A rumpled figure heaved himself up and lumbered forward, his eyes riveted on St. James. He thrust out his right hand. "So, I finally get to meet the mysterious *Pegasus,*" he said in English, while sizing up the American.

Late thirties, early forties, athletic, but not muscle-bound. About six foot, lean, maybe one seventy-five, good-looking, used to making important decisions, and doing so on the spot. He carries with him an aura of self-confidence, that certain something often described in a military officer as having a command presence. Not a person to be trifled with.

St James likewise took inventory. Early fifties, average height, stocky build, hair more gray than black, and colorless eyes exuding as much warmth as the Arctic Ice Pack.

St. James ignored the outstretched hand and answered in flawless Russian. "I will ask you one question. If you give me the right answer, then I'm authorized to take you to Washington. You will reply in Russian. Understood?"

"*Da.*"

"I'm interested in a specific, unique piece of film. There are only two people in it. I want you to tell me who they are, and where and when it was shot."

For several seconds the Soviet said nothing, his unblinking stare boring into St. James. Slowly, a hint of a smirk appeared. "I congratulate you. You obviously know more than I would have dreamed possible. As for the film in question, it shows your then-Vice President Lyndon Johnson and my Ambassador Anatoly Dobrynin. It was shot inside our Soviet Embassy in Washington on November 18, 1963."

"And that same Washington will be our next stop," replied a stone-faced St. James.

Thirty minutes later they were flying south in a cloudless, azure sky. The Soviet was fast asleep while St. James remained awake, his mind a million miles away as he stared down at the earth, reminiscing on the journey that had taken him to this moment in time.

When anyone asked what he did for a living, he would parrot that he worked for Henry Kissinger as an intelligence analyst, then immediately assure the questioner that his was a wholly unglamorous existence, and quickly change the subject.

But that was where fiction parted company with fact. St. James was not an analyst. Rather, he and his elite six-man team were a brotherhood of handpicked, covert agents answering solely to the President, and their *raison d'être* was known to only a handful of executive level officers at the CIA, the DIA, and the FBI.

The Soviet citizen slept through engine shutdown, and when St. James shook him awake, he appeared startled and confused, but only for a moment. Wordlessly, he followed St. James off the plane and into a waiting unmarked sedan with darkened windows.

"The Quarter Deck," St. James said to Justin Scott, the driver, code-named *Orion*, his most senior agent, and currently on loan from the FBI. Their destination was a residence in a fashionable, Alexandria, Virginia, neighborhood. It was a reinforced, electronically guarded fort capable of holding invaders at bay long enough for help to arrive.

"We're going to our safehouse," he said to the Soviet defector, while glancing at his watch. "It's now almost four. I suggest you have a bite to eat then grab some sleep." St. James let loose a small, self-pitying sigh. He would be up half the night preparing for the many debriefings with the still-unknown man seated beside him.

Minutes later, they entered an impressive three-story, red brick Colonial on Buchanan Circle. St. James led the way to the second floor and into a suite at the end of the hall.

"You'll find shaving gear, toiletries, and pajamas in the bathroom," he said, motioning with a cocked thumb. "As for street clothes, you'll be outfitted tomorrow, but don't expect anything fancy because you won't be going anywhere for a while."

The Soviet shrugged.

St. James looked him squarely in the eye. "I have to inform the President who it is I picked up in Ottawa, so what do I tell him?"

The man drew himself erect. "Tell President Nixon you have in protective custody Major General Mykel Alexei Zakharov, First Deputy Chairman, and Deputy Director of the Committee for State Security. In that capacity, I am also responsible for the First Chief Directorate."

St. James was dumbfounded. Standing before him was the second most powerful man in the Soviet Union's infamous KGB.

CHAPTER 2
WASHINGTON D.C.
MAY 8, EVENING, 1972

President Nixon and Dr. Henry Kissinger were marking time when St. James entered the Oval Office and came right to the point. "Our walk-in claims he's Major General Mykel Alexei Zakharov, deputy chairman of the KGB, and the guy in charge of running the infamous First Directorate."

Nixon arched a questioning eyebrow as his mouth fell agape in a rare display of surprise. St. James held up a cautionary finger. "The operative word is *claims,* but I'm leaning strongly towards believing him because there's no doubt in my mind he's seen the film footage that's been giving us fits. So before coming up here, I stopped by my office to check out our rogues' gallery of *Who's Who in the Kremlin,* and guess what? The only mugshot missing from the lineup was his. His name and position are posted correctly, but there's no photo. I was puzzled by that, so I contacted the CIA and asked for updated file pictures of all the major players in the First Directorate. I didn't want to set off alarm bells by singling him out for specific scrutiny."

"Does anyone else know who he is?" Nixon asked.

"He says he didn't tell the Canadians, though they probably guessed he was someone top-tier. But my gut tells me no."

"Then let's keep it that way. I don't want any direct FBI or CIA institutional involvement, at least not yet."

"When do you plan to start the debrief?" Kissinger asked.

"This evening."

Nixon drummed his fingers in a nervous tattoo on his desktop. "Andrew, I've got to know whether President Johnson has been fully truthful or not with me before I meet Secretary Brezhnev in Moscow two weeks from now."

"Understood, sir," St. James said, taking his cue that the meeting was over. "I'll need a working copy of all of President Johnson's recordings that we made with the two of you, and I'll also require copies of the pertinent sections from Edgar Snow's China diaries delivered to the safehouse. That way I can work without having to run back and forth, but I can come here every day and brief you."

Nixon shook his head. "It's not necessary you give me a daily update. You decide what's important and when I need to know it."

St. James left the Oval Office and headed downstairs. Three of his six-man team were on duty, so he took the time to bring them up to date. He turned to Justin Scott.

"Make up a duty roster covering the next month for the safehouse and pencil me in, too. I'll be moving there until further notice. Also, make me a duplicate of President Johnson's March 11 tape recording of his meeting here in the White House with President Nixon, and lastly, run off photocopies of Edgar Snow's diary excerpts. Bring everything to me before dinner."

Arriving shortly after seven, St. James found Zakharov seated in the dining room sipping tea and reading *The Washington Post*. He could hear the house staff preparing dinner.

Zakharov rose. "Good evening, Mr. St. James."

"Good evening, General," St James replied in Russian. "Sleep well?"

"Thank you, yes."

St. James realized they were both being correct to a fault, each trying to finesse the other as if searching for some infinitesimal advantage. It couldn't continue.

"General, please sit. Now, let's both relax, shall we? You and I are going to be spending a lot of time together, so I suggest a little less formality is in order. And if it's OK with you, I would like to start our first debriefing after supper." St. James took a seat and unfolded his napkin. "You've been with the Canadians and us for about forty-eight hours now, correct?"

Zakharov nodded.

"Then tell me, what's your best estimate on how long it'll be before the KGB realizes you've turned?"

Zakharov flashed a wintry smile and shook his head. "The KGB thinks I'm dead. The Canadians have already taken the necessary measures to convince them of this, and I daresay those measures will be accepted as true, unless, of course, you choose to tell my government otherwise."

"Then don't give me a reason to tell them," St James said, picking up his knife and fork.

After desert, coffee, and cigarettes, they retreated to the living room where Justin had already set up a sophisticated reel-to-reel tape recorder. St. James tested it by recording a couple of sentences then playing them back. He repeated the procedure a few times until he was satisfied.

"Ready?" St James asked, conspicuously switching to English for the first time since entering the house.

"Ready," the Soviet replied.

"My name is Andrew St. James. The date is May 8, 1972, the time is nine twenty-seven p.m., and I am recording this conversation somewhere in Washington D.C. This is an official, on-the-record debriefing of a citizen of the Soviet Union. Please state your full name, date of birth, nationality, and occupation."

"My name is Mykel Alexei Zakharov, but I go by Alexei. I was born on January 5, 1919. I am a Soviet subject and a major general in the Soviet KGB. Until a short time ago, I was the First Deputy Chairman of the KGB, but also responsible for the Soviet's external intelligence department in the First Chief Directorate. You in the West know it as the Thirteenth Department."

St. James remained pokerfaced. "Responsible for "direct actions" such as assassinations, and sabotage. I thought the deputy director of the First Directorate was Vladimir Kryuchkov. When did you replace him?"

Zakharov gave a shake of his head. "I didn't replace him. However, unless you are bluffing, I can see now the West knows nothing of this change. Director Fyodor Mortin has been terminally ill for a couple of months now, so the Politburo promoted Vladimir to the post of co-director last December. He supposedly runs the day-to-day activities, which will make for a smooth transition when Fyodor dies. But I am really his boss, at least I was until a couple of days ago."

St. James was satisfied with the answer and moved on. "General, tell me in your own words how you came to defect and how you managed to come in contact with the Canadians. Also, you said earlier the KGB thinks you're dead. Please explain. Then tell me your motive for defecting to the West."

A look of annoyance flitted across Zakharov's face. "Mr. St. James, I will tell you in good time why I defected, your choice of a word, not mine. However, I do not care to tell you about any of that just now. I have my reasons."

St. James shrugged. It could wait.

Zakharov lit a Marlboro, inhaled deeply, blew a long stream of smoke toward the ceiling and continued. "Mine was no overnight decision, but rather one that had been on my mind for almost two years. I bided my time and waited for just the right moment. It came late last year when our spy network in England was exposed, and the

British government expelled ninety of my agents and detained fifteen others. However, one man defected to the English rather than return home, and he did so very publicly. His name was Oleg Lyalin. Of course, I had to assume he was talking his head off. This was very, very bad. My worldwide spy network was now in serious jeopardy, and I had to act fast. I ordered our most important agents home and, I assure you, the abrupt disappearance of several dozen prominent Soviet embassy officials around the world was noticed. But of course, you know all this," he said in a matter-of-fact tone.

"I do but tell me anyway."

"In order to get my spy network up and running again—not just in England, but around the world—I needed new agents, new codes, new recognition signals, new job assignments, new everything. This was our biggest intelligence setback since the end of WWII. My directorate worked non-stop throughout the winter and into spring, and by early last month, we were ready." Zakharov paused, stubbed out his butt, then continued.

"Because of the importance of the task at hand, the KGB director decided I should oversee the entire operation from London. This was a bold move which required the approval of the Politburo. Some members were openly skittish about letting me out of the country. It was not a matter of trust, they insisted loudly, but rather it was about my irreplaceability in the event of an accident. Of course, the real reason was that I knew too much. Anyway, after a lot of back and forth, approval was begrudgingly granted, and I left for London this past April 6, traveling under the name Frantz Webber, a citizen of West Germany. There were no problems."

As he listened, St. James found himself remembering attending CIA briefings with Nixon and Kissinger on the Soviet's intelligence troubles. Now he was learning firsthand just how bad things had really been.

Zakharov winced, moved into a more comfortable position, lit another Marlboro, and continued. "Every Friday I would fly into a different European city, meet with a contact from headquarters and report to him. Director Andropov insisted he wanted it done this way, but I'm sure he was instructed to do so by the Politburo. I never met the same contact twice, and I was always photographed.

"Anyway, on May 5 an evening meeting was scheduled for Palermo. I left London's Heathrow on an Alitalia DC-8, and despite some inclement weather, we landed in Rome for a short stopover. My stomach had become upset during the flight and there was nothing on the plane for me to take, so I asked one of the stewardesses if I had time to deplane and buy some medication. She said we would be on the ground for thirty minutes and told me to listen for our departure information on the loudspeaker.

"Well, if you've ever been in Leonardo da Vinci Airport you know what a crazy place it is. I found a chemist shop and got the woman to understand what I was looking for. I returned to my gate to discover that my plane was gone! There had been no loudspeaker announcement whatsoever. So typically Italian."

Justin inwardly smiled as he pictured the scene.

"Well, here it was already nine o'clock, and I had a meeting in Palermo at eleven. I ran to the ticket counter, only to encounter lines five abreast and fifty people deep. I decided there was nothing I could do but sit and wait, reasoning that once the lines had thinned, I could explain what had happened and get my ticket changed. Ninety minutes later, I heard a loud commotion. A teenage boy was yelling in Italian and broken English that a plane had just crashed. It took a half hour to get the complete story. My plane had crashed and burned on impact in the mountains surrounding Palermo, killing everyone. Frantz Webber's name was on the manifest. That was me! I was now officially dead, and my luggage was still aboard. It was perfect.

"I jumped into a taxi and directed it to the Canadian Embassy because it was the only one I had the address for. I told them I was a Soviet agent, that I wished to defect to America, and explained that I was listed as a passenger on the plane that had just crashed in Palermo.

"The Canadians took my Frantz Webber passport and assured me it would be found in the wreckage. The TV stations were now all reporting how the plane had exploded and that the passengers had been burned beyond recognition. From firsthand experience, I can tell you this: it's impossible to identify with one hundred percent certainty a badly burned body.

"Anyway, I was quickly issued a Canadian diplomatic passport and flown to London. Then they flew me to Ottawa. At no time did the Canadians learn my identity, and not once did they push me to reveal who I was. They were all remarkably professional, and that's how I'm here with you now."

"Eventually, people will realize you're missing. How will the KGB explain that away?"

Zakharov stared at St. James for an extended moment. "The KGB has a long history of not explaining such things, and the people have a long history of not asking questions. I can be turned into a nonperson overnight. It could be over a perceived slight, or something more ominous. Our past is littered with such happenings. No, I assure you, I will not be missed."

St. James turned off the recorder. There was a lot in Zakharov's story that needed to be verified. A couple of points came to mind. Had anyone come to claim Frantz Webber's body or his luggage? Had the Canadians actually been able to place his passport at the crash site? The wall clock told him it was eleven-thirty. Time to call it a day.

As Zakharov shuffled up the stairs to his room, St. James retreated to the basement and stood in front of a solid steel door. He picked up a red phone on the wall and uttered a one-word recognition signal. It was answered in kind.

"Justin, I need into the vault."

There was a humming sound, and the door swung open to reveal a room he had long ago nicknamed the "coffin": a fireproof, climate-controlled, lead-lined vault filled with communications gear and floor-to-ceiling storage racks.

Its construction had been his idea. The door could only be opened remotely from his office in the White House; a safeguard in the unlikely event the house was ever overrun. And should a staffer accidentally lock himself inside, there was a phone extension he could use to summon help.

He entered the chamber, placed the just-finished tape onto a color-coded rack and checked to confirm that President Johnson's Oval Office tapes and Edgar Snow's China diary excerpts had arrived. He stepped out.

"OK, Justin, close her up, then I've got a job for you."

"Fire away, Boss."

"I need you to check with the CIA about that Italian plane crash in Palermo back on the night of the fifth. Find out what happened to the bodies and personal effects. Ask if any corpses are still unidentified. But in particular, see if anyone came to claim the body of a Frantz Webber, a citizen of West Germany. Tell Langley the President wants this kept low key. Frantz Webber is the name our Soviet guest was traveling under, so we don't want the word getting back to the KGB that the American Intelligence Community is interested in the guy."

"Anything else?"

"Yeah. Ask the Canadians what they did with Frantz Webber's passport."

A thunderstorm woke St. James at six-thirty. At eight o'clock he was ready for Zakharov.

"Yesterday in Ottawa I asked you about a piece of film that was shot in Washington in November 1963. You correctly confirmed it was of then-Vice President Johnson and the Soviet Union's Ambassador Anatoly Dobrynin."

Zakharov nodded.

"I want you to tell me everything about that film. Start with the planning, tell me how the actual filming took place, and explain what it was the KGB hoped to accomplish."

Zakharov waited as if gathering his thoughts before speaking. He let loose an audible sigh of surrender. "Yesterday I told you I was surprised to learn you were even aware of the film's existence. That meant Mr. Johnson must have talked, something the KGB never anticipated."

St. James shook his head. "Not only have I seen the film, but I've spent countless hours studying it."

Zakharov let loose a derisive laugh. "Now that's not true, Mister St. James, because only one copy was ever made, and it's been under lock and key inside a vault in the Kremlin since 1964." After several moments of silence, Zakharov leaned forward, his demeanor suddenly belligerent. "Don't ever think that you can bluff me, *Mister Pegasus* . I have been a chess player since childhood, and I would rank myself to be among the best. You will never be my equal upon this particular global chess board, even if you live to be a hundred." His tone turned condescending. "No, you must conjure up something more believable than an amateurish feint meant to test me over some film you have never seen."

St. James's eyes turned to ice as he silently counted to ten. "Then respond to this amateurish feint, *Mister Chessmaster,*" he replied, his voice as hard as diamonds. "Your film is printed on sixteen-millimeter Kodak Ektachrome, Type 7270 stock. In case you don't know it, that's a reversal print film which was first used in 1960 but is scheduled to be discontinued later this year. The running time is exactly six minutes. Johnson and Dobrynin are clearly seen sipping expensive Remy Marin brandy as they go over their last-minute plans for President Kennedy's assassination, and subsequent scapegoating of the Chinese to make it look like they are the culprits. Their discussion ends with a recounting of how they intend to divide the world into two spheres of influence after Mister Johnson becomes President. Do I have to continue?"

Zakharov's face melted as he listened to a factual recitation of the impossible. He sank low into his seat. "It seems I have badly underestimated you, Mister St. James."

"First, yes you have badly underestimated me; and second, I tell the truth. You'll do well to remember that. But now, I want to hear in your own words how these sordid events unfolded, and I need you to start at the very beginning. I expect your story to emerge over many sessions, but that's OK, because I have all the time in the world. And come to think of it, so do you."

Zakharov was about to light a cigarette but changed his mind and laid it carefully atop the hinged Marlboro box. When he began to talk, his voice and manner were subdued.

"When we set out on this venture ten years ago, I never dreamed it would take us as far as it did. We achieved all of the goals we believed at the time were indispensable to our national well-being. Khrushchev and Brezhnev were adamant in emphasizing that the assassination of President Kennedy was not an end unto itself. Far from it. No, it was to be the first step in a carefully thought-out plan to destroy America." He shook his head. "When I think of all those innocents who insist history is merely happenstance, I must counter with two words: how naïve. Nothing of importance is ever left to chance: nothing. You say you know the whole story, Mr. St. James? "Well, you don't," Zakharov said in a now-lowered voice. "Not by a long shot. However, after you hear what really happened that November day in Dallas in 1963, you will want to shoot me."

CHAPTER 3
MOSCOW – SEPTEMBER 1963
NINE YEARS EARLIER

The last of the three Zis limousines crunched its way on the hard pack gravel past the metal barricade guarding the entrance to a dacha forty miles northwest of Moscow. The ranking Soviet Army sergeant in charge dropped his salute and dialed up the residence to let Colonel Zakharov know the guests had arrived.

The three men arriving in separate cars were: Leonid Ilyich Brezhnev, Chairman of the Presidium of the Supreme Soviet; Alexei Nikolaevich Kosygin, also a member of the Presidium; and Anatoly Fyodorovich Dobrynin, Soviet Ambassador to the United States.

This would be their fourth and final meeting where they would put the finishing touches on an audacious plan to change the course of history.

Brezhnev was the first to enter the large study. He readily admitted to a fondness for this villa and often used it as a working retreat. City living annoyed him in general, the walled fortress of the Kremlin in particular, and he took advantage of every opportunity to escape for even a few days to the quiet of the country where he enjoyed fishing and hunting.

Marshal Lavrentiy Beria, head of the People's Commissariat for Internal Affairs, (NKVD) had built this villa in 1947 with forced labor from German prisoners of war, and there was no denying that any Western capitalist would find himself hard-pressed to build one finer. It sat on six hundred acres of rolling land, well-timbered, and stocked with game and fish. In Beria's day it had been protected and staffed by his dreaded NKVD agents, but in 1956, three years after Secretary Nikita Khrushchev absurdly claimed to have personally blown Beria's brains out, the villa was put at the disposal of members of the Presidium, its upkeep tasked to the Red Army. Khrushchev had not used the place in five years, and rarely had any other members of the Presidium, so by default it become known as Brezhnev's retreat.

Brezhnev's mind was abuzz with thoughts of what lay ahead. A steward, busily fussing over an ornate silver tray holding several glasses, a pitcher of ice water and a bottle of Stolichnaya vodka in the center of the conference table, spotted Brezhnev and snapped to attention.

"Once Mr. Kosygin, Mr. Dobrynin, and Colonel Zakharov come downstairs, I don't want to be disturbed for any reason. If I need something, I'll ring."

Five minutes later the trio arrived, and when all were seated, Zakharov locked the massive oak door and took his place alongside the others.

Brezhnev's hooded eyes swept the table. "Gentlemen, Colonel Zakharov will again join us," he said, stating the obvious. "We have much to finalize, and I need not remind you that all of our futures depend on a successful outcome."

Kosygin cocked his head and leaned closer, as if he was having difficulty hearing. His dour look spoke volumes. "If we don't take matters into our own hands, and soon, then Secretary Khrushchev will destroy everything that's taken the Party forty years to build. And to think that I used to be one of his most ardent supporters. How could I have been so stupid?"

Brezhnev shrugged rather than answer the rhetorical question, then turned to Dobrynin. "What's the mood in Washington since President Kennedy's return from Europe?"

Dobrynin's ever-present public façade of bonhomie faded. "'*Ich bin ein Berliner.*" "I am a Berliner,'" he began, parroting the words spoken in June by the American President to an adoring crowd in Berlin. He could not hide his contempt. "That man can do no wrong in the eyes of the masses, and sad to say, we badly underestimated him. However, the situation is far from lost, thanks to Vice President Lyndon Johnson, soon to become America's next President."

Colonel Zakharov was hanging onto every word.

"Orchestrating the transition from Kennedy to Johnson will not be an easy feat," Kosygin said, "and the part that you must play, Anatoly, will test every skill you have learned as a diplomat. Mr. Johnson may be many things, but a fool he is not. So when the time comes, your task will be to convince him beyond all doubt that what you tell him is the absolute truth."

Brezhnev placed his beefy hands on the table. "But getting rid of President Kennedy is only the first of many hurdles," he began. "All the follow-on tasks will be just as important, including our ever-growing Chinese problem which must be solved and fast. Then there's the matter of persuading Mr. Johnson to do our bidding once he becomes President. And lastly, we will have to remove Nikita, something that should have been done years ago."

Back and forth the comments and suggestions flew until midnight, when a yawning Kosygin suggested adjourning until morning. He turned his watery gaze on Zakharov. "Will you be ready to present us your finalized plan for doing away with President Kennedy when we meet in the morning, Colonel?"

"I will, Excellency."

After spending a restless night and checking his watch every half hour, Zakharov surrendered by tossing back the covers and climbing out of bed. The luminous hands showed six o'clock. Ten minutes later, he was off on a solitary walk around the villa's manicured grounds. Fall was most assuredly in the air.

The Chinese have become a monster of our own creation, he thought, with more than a twinge of regret. Kosygin, who was considered the Kremlin's expert on all matters Chinese, and his rapport—such as it was—with Chairman Mao, Premier Chou En-lai, and Marshal Lin-Biao, had made possible what little high-level contact there had been between the two governments.

After stopping to light a cigarette, Zakharov continued down the pathway while allowing his mind to reminisce over the Soviet's troubled history with China.

Stalin had never trusted them, yet here was Khrushchev—against all advice to the contrary—insisting that their future should be irrevocably entwined with China's. It was madness. But Khrushchev refused to listen to any contrary opinions and continued turning a deaf ear to those who warned of the day that would come when the hand holding the carrot would be snapped off at the wrist by an ungrateful Eastern beast. Khrushchev insisted that America was the problem whose goal it was to destroy both the Soviet Union and China. He had used that premise to press for their continued collaboration on a joint nuclear program. Zakharov crumbled his cigarette butt between his thumb and fingers, tossed the remnants to the ground, and shook his head in disgust at the pigheadedness of such a position.

As his booted heels crunched atop the graveled path creating the only noise in an otherwise still morning, his mind harkened back to the historic day in June when the Presidium had voted against Khrushchev for the first time. It had been a watershed event.

Zakharov was seated in a row alongside the wall, his chair directly behind Brezhnev's. From this vantage point in the opulent Kremlin hall, he had an unobstructed view of Nikita Khrushchev, the Secretary General of the Communist Party of the Soviet Union. For two hours the members of the Presidium had been arguing about China, and the consensus finally reached was they adopt a policy of gradual withdrawal of their economic aid, but all nuclear assistance to Peking's Lop-Nor facility would be halted immediately.

Khrushchev was having none of it. He slammed his fist down. "All of the projects will continue—economic and nuclear. That is my final say, and my voice is the only one that counts here."

Brezhnev snapped. He hoisted himself out of his chair, strode the length of the conference table, and came to a halt beside Khrushchev. In the suddenly silent hall, he bent over until his mouth was an inch from Khrushchev's right ear and said in a loud voice, "This is the one time you will listen to the advice of the Presidium, and you will follow that advice. You stand alone on this. Only a madman would continue to give atomic assistance to the Chinese. Well, it's over. We will withdraw our technicians immediately and hope it's not too late. We have warned you repeatedly that the Americans could easily one day preemptively attack us and China simultaneously because of your insane nuclear policy, yet you have continued to ignore our advice. Your reasoning has been clouded ever since President Kennedy's defiant drawing of a line in the sand regarding removing our ballistic missiles from Cuba last October. He called your bluff, and you blinked. You underestimated him then, and your continuing intransigence on this matter will spell ruin for us all now."

An enraged Nikita Khrushchev flew out of his chair. He pushed Brezhnev away with both hands and lashed out with a booted foot. "Have you gone mad? Have you forgotten what I did to Beria? I shot the bastard! And now you dare stand over me and tell me what I will or will not do?" Khrushchev was shaking with anger. Flecks of spittle landed on Brezhnev's tie.

Brezhnev's reply was to grab Khrushchev's lapels with powerful hands and fling his nemesis back into his chair.

The silence in the room was epic.

Again, Brezhnev leaned over to within an inch of Khrushchev's cropped head, his onyx eyes filled with fury. *"You dare threaten me with a fate similar to Beria's?"* he screamed. "You who's been marching to the beat of a drummer heard only by yourself? General Batitsky shot Beria, not you! Listen to me you senile fool. You no longer enjoy any support among the Presidium, so you'll damn well do as you're told if you treasure life itself."

Brezhnev swung to face Kosygin, the erstwhile ally. "Alexei, prepare a memorandum right now outlining our official position." Turning back to Khrushchev, he roared, "*And you will sign it!*"

Khrushchev staggered to his feet, held a steadying hand on the table for a few seconds, then lurched out of the hall without a backward glance.

Within a week, Soviet nuclear scientists began leaving China, their exodus causing the rift to widen dramatically.

What a mess, Zakharov thought as he left the hall an hour later.

★　　★　　★

At a few minutes past nine, the four were ready for their second meeting. Brezhnev wasted no time getting to the point. "Shortly after my confrontation with Nikita last June, I asked Colonel Zakharov to finalize the plan to rid ourselves of President Kennedy. He will now tell us what he has accomplished."

Zakharov stood out of deference to the three and began without notes. "An assassination as consequential as this one—and make no mistake, gentlemen, that's exactly what we're talking about here— demands the utmost in planning, right down to the smallest detail. My overriding challenge has been to make sure no one will ever be able to point an accusatory finger at the Soviet Union, at least not with any degree of certitude. I also concluded that this particular assassination be carried out in a very public manner so that the finality of the act must be beyond question. The reason is simple. We do not want an injured President Kennedy. We want a dead President Kennedy."

Zakharov could see he had their undivided attention. *So far so good*, he thought. "How does one carry out such an assassination?" he continued. "How does one ensure that the assassin escapes, while convincingly laying the blame at someone else's doorstep?" He let loose a short, mirthless laugh, then hurried to answer his own questions. "We know that everyone will immediately want to accuse the Kremlin, at least they will at first, but for my plan to work we only need to convince one man that we had nothing to do with it. And that man, of course, is Lyndon Johnson. He must be made to believe right down to the very depths of his being that it's the Chinese who are responsible for the dastardly act."

Zakharov paused to search through a sheaf of pages, found the one he wanted, picked it up and began reading aloud.

"Starting with the premise that China must be held responsible for the killing of President Kennedy, the Soviet Union will provide irrefutable proof to support what Ambassador Dobrynin will convey to Mr. Johnson in confidence. The Vice President will be informed of several disturbing events which will have already taken place, and then told of rumors and whispers that our intelligence services have been hearing from several sources about an attempt to be made on President Kennedy's life. To ensure that Mr. Johnson believes what Ambassador Dobrynin tells him, I'm recommending we take the following drastic, but absolutely necessary measures. I must use field assets from the Thirteenth Department to eliminate three of our own spies in various countries and do so within a very limited timeframe. Then we follow that with the assassination of a well-known puppet head of state mere days before President Kennedy himself is killed."

"Eliminate three of our own spies?" Dobrynin asked, his puzzled look suggesting he didn't understand.

"Execute," a stone-faced Zakharov replied, "and it's already started, sir."

"I see," Dobrynin finally managed, his voice hushed. He removed his glasses and began a vigorous polishing of the lenses, as if such physical activity would somehow wash away the shock he obviously felt.

Zakharov studied the ambassador with a hard look, wondering if perhaps the other two had badly misjudged him. Because without Ambassador Dobrynin, he had no plan.

Brezhnev seemed to read Zakharov's mind and quickly weighed in. "Anatoly, because you've been busy in America for the past few months, Alexei and I had to approve the implementation of the first phase. We could not wait for your concurrence. Two weeks ago a KGB agent named Konstantin Zimin, stationed in Copenhagen as second vice consul died suddenly . . ."

"But the cable traffic spoke of possible Chinese . . ."

"Yes, Anatoly," Brezhnev replied, "and the same messages you received in Washington went out to all of our embassies and consulates worldwide, and for a very good reason." Brezhnev continued. "Think back for a moment, and you'll remember the original communiqué was transmitted in the *sigma* code group. That should have tipped you off. We've known for a year that *sigma* has been compromised by American and British Intelligence, but they don't know we're on to them. They will have read our cables and believe we think the Chinese killed Zimin. That was Colonel Zakharov's brainchild. Ambassador Chertov officially reported to the Danish Foreign Office that Zimin had died of a heart attack, and that we would be replacing him shortly. You need to know all of the facts about what really took place in Copenhagen, Anatoly. In reality, Mr. Zimin was shot in the embassy by the military attaché who was given an order for a 'direct action' signed by both me, and Politburo Secretariat member Yuri Andropov. He was told Zimin had been flipped by the Chinese, that he was a traitor, and had to be eliminated. We were able to keep Nikita in the dark about all this. That's how tightly we controlled the matter. But in order to make the ruse work in convincing the Americans and the British that what they had learned from our *sigma* intercept was valid information, the body was flown home, and Zimin was given a very public hero's burial."

Brezhnev sat back and waited to see if Dobrynin had any further comments. After a few seconds, he nodded for Zakharov to continue.

"The plan calls for the next two executions of our agents to be highly visible wet affairs, and again, *sigma* will be used to inform our embassies we are convinced the Chinese are responsible and that all personnel should take extra precautions. Then a few hours later, we'll continue to use *sigma* to say we're getting reliable information from several sources that the Chinese are upping the ante and will begin targeting American agents as well. I want the CIA to become genuinely alarmed on hearing that news."

"You spoke moments ago of assassinating a head of state a few days before Mr. Kennedy is to be killed . . ." Dobrynin began, but Zakharov cut him short.

"President Diem of South Vietnam, Mr. Ambassador. We intend to make it look as if he was killed by disgruntled junior army officers acting on command from Peking."

Dobrynin spent several seconds digesting all he had just heard. Finally, a hint of a smile crossed his face. "It's brilliant. Diem is known to harbor a rabid hatred of all communists, especially those from China. Of course, the Chinese would want to see him dead."

Kosygin jumped in. "But we don't want South Vietnam to collapse. We want the Americans to commit themselves to that wretched country with a single-minded purpose. With Diem and Kennedy dead, we expect President Lyndon Johnson to boldly march into Vietnam fueled by the idea that he'll be following the Kennedy Doctrine of containing communists everywhere, but especially the ruthless Chinese."

Zakharov waited politely while the three conferred amongst themselves, but after a few minutes, he discretely suggested they move on to other matters. He turned to Dobrynin.

"I've given a lot of thought to the suggestion you made some months ago that you favor the idea that President Kennedy should be eliminated while away from Washington D. C. I didn't think it important at the time, but I do now. What do you know of his travel plans for the rest of the year?"

"The American President's travel schedule is not a secret; in fact it's publicized weeks in advance, but subject to change. According to the White House Press Office, Mr. Kennedy will be traveling frequently between now and December," Dobrynin said. "However, during a trip he'll be taking in late November would be my first choice. Could you act that quickly?"

Brezhnev raised a questioning eyebrow. "Why late November, Anatoly?"

"Because it's been common knowledge for some time that Mr. Kennedy will be going to Texas along with Mr. Johnson on what American politicians call a fence-mending campaign. It seems things haven't been going well for the Democrats in Texas, and the party leaders want the President to spend a couple of days there to bolster the morale of the faithful, and to raise money from the rich cattle barons and oil millionaires. Texas also happens to be the state Mr. Johnson calls home, so it's the perfect place for him to be suddenly *"elected"* president. And when I tell him in confidence mere days before that how we suspect the Chinese have something sinister planned for President Kennedy, he will see I was right. But to have the deed take place in his home state of Texas, well, this should be more than enough to make Mr. Johnson a true believer in what I will tell him."

"But also, if for no other reason than to draw even a whisper of suspicion away from himself," Zakharov added, while carefully placing two 8 x 10 color photographs in the center of the table. "Gentlemen, permit me to introduce you to two very special KGB agents. They have been given the code names *Romulus* and *Remus*, and that is how they will be spoken of, and written about from today forward."

Romulus and *Remus* stared blindly back at the four pairs of eyes studying their images. The older man appeared to be about forty. He was slim, wore his blond hair cropped close to his skull, and his blue eyes bespoke of a competent, confident individual. His partner was younger, slightly pudgy, but seemed to exude an innate charm often found in those who enjoy life. Neither was so remarkable looking as to attract attention, and thus be remembered for being in a certain place at some later date.

"Both are fluent in English and French, and they're extremely resourceful," Zakharov said, digging again into the pile before him and finding another photograph. He placed it between the twins. "This is a Paillard Bolex H16mm film movie camera, the kind used by many TV film crews in the West." Zakharov smiled briefly. "Well, not quite," he corrected, "because what you are really looking at is a one-of-a-kind sniper rifle, highly modified by our KGB Weapons Institute, and specifically designed for this singular mission. When the 100mm zoom lens is in position, it becomes a barrel capable of firing high velocity bullets with pinpoint accuracy up to a range of five hundred meters. It holds only two rounds, and as each bullet is fired, the spent cartridge is not ejected, but remains inside the camera housing. That feature ensures no one will find evidence of our twins ever being at the scene. The Zeiss viewfinder becomes the sniper scope. Now, this rifle masquerading as a camera can be either shoulder-mounted or placed on a tripod for maximum stability. Muzzle flash is non-existent, and the gun is almost silent. And even as it's being fired, it is still capable of filming through another lens. All in all, a remarkable bit of engineering.

"Now, immediately after the job is done, the entire camera apparatus will have to be destroyed on the off-chance authorities at the scene confiscate all film and still photos from the TV crews and newspaper photographers. And because we do not want the slightest chance of *Romulus* and *Remus* coming under suspicion, I will have a third person whose job will be to fire a regulation rifle from a nearby location at the same time our agents fire. His shots will be loud and heard by lots of people but discharged harmlessly into the air. Under no circumstances will he actually aim and fire at President Kennedy. He is to be an expendable decoy, nothing more."

"I must admit, Colonel, you make it all sound so doable," Dobrynin allowed. "Can you tell us more about your decoy shooter?"

"*No, absolutely not!*" Brezhnev interrupted in a loud voice, startling Dobrynin. "Anatoly, the less you know of any American involvement in this, the better. You cannot be put in a position where you could ever be compromised."

Zakharov nodded his agreement. "I can tell you this much, Mr. Ambassador," he replied. "There are several to choose from. Two are "sleeper agents" already in Texas, but they have only been told in the vaguest of terms that there might be a special job for them. A third is a fringe operative code named *Gemstone*. He's older, more experienced, and could be a big help getting *Romulus* and *Remus* out of Texas. He knows nothing about the mission; all he's been told is something important is being planned, and he might be called on to help. So, as soon as you can tell us which day President Kennedy will be in Texas and also his itinerary, then our American assets will be notified and given instructions."

Brezhnev asked, "Anyone have objections, reservations, or suggestions?"

Kosygin and Dobrynin shook their heads in unison.

CHAPTER 4
CHINA
NOVEMBER 1970–FEBUARY 1972

THE DAY WAS NOVEMBER 8, 1970, and St. James was in an early morning meeting with Kissinger when a courier arrived from the French Embassy with a sealed envelope. Kissinger read the note inside, and wordlessly handed the single page to St. James. It was from President Charles De Gaulle of France. Neither knew what to make of it, and President Nixon was equally puzzled when shown the letter that afternoon. De Gaulle had written that the Chinese were interested in a high-level meeting to discuss a matter of supreme importance to America.

Twenty-four hours later, on November 9, a bulletin from Paris flashed around the world stating that the seventy-nine-year-old de Gaulle had just died at his home in *Colombey-les-deux-Églises*. The news threw Nixon into a quandary. What should he do with De Gaulle's letter now?

President Nixon decided his best course of action would be to wait for some signal from Peking, or from another corroborating source. It came a month later when the world-renowned American author, Edgar Snow—a personal friend of Chairman Mao Tse-tung—arrived at the White House bringing a message from the Chairman to a surprised President.

☆   ☆   ☆

At three o'clock in the afternoon of Wednesday, December 23, 1970, President Nixon and Edgar Snow met in the Oval Office. Nixon introduced Snow to Henry Kissinger, White House chief of staff Bob Haldeman, and a political analyst named Andrew St. James.

"Mr. Snow, I'm glad to have this opportunity to meet you. I've read most of your books and found them fascinating and informative. Tell me, how would you describe China today? And, please, don't feel rushed. We know so little about that country, yet it's home for almost one-third of the world's people."

"How right you are, Mr. President," Snow replied. Here was President Nixon making him feel at home, something wholly unexpected. If truth be told, he had been nervous at the prospect of this encounter. He had heard from several sources that Nixon was a cold fish and not one to engage in small talk. Yet, here he was putting him at ease.

"China has changed more in the last two decades than in her entire history up to 1949. The China I first saw in the 1930s defied description. The disease, filth, poverty, and squalor was such that I will remember the smell until my dying day. This was shortly after Chairman Mao's celebrated "Long March", when Generalissimo Chiang Kai-shek's army had soundly thrashed the Communists. Mao was finished as far as Chiang was concerned.

"It was now back to business as usual," he continued, "and of course, throughout the war years China had suffered greatly. Untold hundreds of thousands, maybe millions, perished either from starvation, disease, or at the hands of the Japanese. And also at the hands of their own government too, I might add. Things were so bad that when Mao went on the move again after the war, the people rallied behind him simply because he stood for change, and any change was better for the majority than the conditions they found themselves living in under the Nationalist Government of Chiang. Mao finally emerged the victor, and the Generalissimo fled to Taiwan. Mao knew he had a job of immense proportions on his hands in somehow moving

China into the 20th century. Only one country supported him—the Soviet Union. Of course, Stalin was in it for what he thought he could squeeze out of China, and his biggest mistake was believing Chairman Mao was nothing more than an ignorant peasant.

"Anyway, China definitely profited in those early days of the nineteen-fifties at the expense of the Soviets. Mao proved to be not only an able administrator, but a master of impossible tasks too. Just imagine, Mr. President, the job confronting him. It would be like trying to unify all fifty of our states into a simple union when you have fifty separate languages to deal with, fifty different cultures, and fifty different leaders, or warlords, to bring into line. Although the commoners were solidly behind Mao, the rich mandarins, the other privileged classes, the capitalists who controlled the entire economy, all these people strongly opposed Mao and his communist ideas. It was an undertaking any ordinary man would have thrown up his hands against and run away from."

Snow held center stage for almost a half hour, the President spellbound by his summary of China's recent history.

"Needless to say, Mr. President, there were many measures taken by the Chairman in those early days that were none too agreeable, and I've said as much to him on more than one occasion. He was harsh, even ruthless, with those who opposed him; and again, I would venture to say hundreds of thousands lost their lives. A staggering number also died from starvation, but the Chairman understood unless the land was worked, and quickly, even he would fail, and China would be at the mercy of the Soviets who were like vultures on the sidelines, waiting for the easy pickings. Until about 1955, three quarters of the people were sent into the fields, Mao's emphasis being on land reform and agriculture, but once he saw that enough food was being produced, he then introduced a series of five-year plans to industrialize the economy. Comparing these plans, beginning with the famous "Great Leap Forward" to the industrialization process taking place inside the Soviet Union would be folly, but at least China had started to build a fledgling manufacturing base, no matter how crude."

"And now?" Nixon asked.

"And now it's an entirely different country," Snow replied. "No matter how much you and I will disagree with the Chairman as to how he accomplished the change, the changes have been effective. There is virtually no hunger now; everyone is clothed; there is universal education, universal medical care, and adequate housing. The cities and the countryside are spotless; there is no longer that smell of death and decay. Chairman Mao has truly accomplished the impossible in a relatively short time, and that is why he is so revered."

"And the Cultural Revolution, what was its effect?" The question came from Dr. Kissinger. "Is it over as we've been told, and what exactly did it accomplish?"

"Good questions," Snow replied. "I still don't understand it, and I was in China at the height of the revolution. The best I can tell you is it was a power struggle between Mao and Party Vice-Chairman Liu Shao-chi, just one in a long line of ever-changing successors to Mao. Liu is dead now, so it's safe to say Mao and his followers were the victors. Normalcy and stability has returned, and I don't think we will see a repetition of those years, at least not while the Chairman is alive."

"Which brings us to the purpose of your visit today," said Nixon.

"Yes, Mr. President. I was informed by the Chairman that General de Gaulle had written you saying that Mao is interested in normalizing relations between China and the United States. Sadly, we all know he has since died."

"Well, de Gaulle emphasized how a meeting between me and the Chairman would be beneficial to the United States and my Presidency," replied Nixon. "It was his phrasing that still has us puzzled. The General was vague, stressing only that such a meeting would be in our best interest. Can you shed any further light for us, Mr. Snow?"

Snow waited a few seconds before replying, taking time to carefully choose his words. He could reference the film, as the Chairman had suggested, but only in passing.

"Mr. President, I was tasked by the Chairman and the Premier to convey the same message Monsieur de Gaulle did. Chairman Mao asked for my help, simply because we are old friends, and he hoped my request coming on the heels of one from the French General would lend added weight and credence to the sincerity of the message. I can further say, Mr. President, that while I am privy to some of the reasons for the Chairman's unexpected request, I was specifically instructed not to divulge those reasons, other than to say China is in possession of some Soviet film that should be of grave concern to the United States. At the appropriate time, the Chairman will show you it himself, but until then, I can say nothing more. And even though I'm a friend of long-standing, I'm still a foreigner. I can reaffirm what President de Gaulle has stated. In my humble opinion, it is indeed in the best interest of the United States and the Presidency that you accept the Chairman's proposal for a face-to-face meeting at a time mutually agreeable. I cannot emphasize that point enough."

"You do not feel as a patriotic American that you have a deeper obligation to your country to divulge all you know, Mr. Snow?" said Bob Haldeman, speaking for the first time and surprising Snow with his bluntness.

"Sir, I am not a diplomat, but I do understand that discourse among nations would be impossible if the messenger could not be trusted to follow instructions, as I now find myself. Right or wrong, I am following instructions. My loyalty as an American has never before been questioned, and I strongly protest your inference now." The righteous anger shown on Snow's face was evident to all.

"You're right, of course, Mr. Snow," said the President, hastily. "We are grateful you've relayed the Chairman's request. You have done your country a great service. Please accept my heartfelt thanks."

"And I apologize, Mr. Snow. I did not mean to question your loyalty in any way. My choice of words was in poor taste."

Snow smiled, letting Haldeman know his apology was accepted.

"In closing, Mr. President, let me just add that knowing the Chairman as I do, he will give you another signal at some future date. I cannot say how or when it will be delivered, but I recommend you act with dispatch when it arrives. Meanwhile, I have been given permission from Chairman Mao to leave you copies of entries from my private China Diary which divulge the many history-changing events as they occurred over the past decade. And I think they will answer the many questions you no doubt have regarding that society."

The President nodded as he rose from his chair. "Thank you, Mr. Snow," he said, shaking hands. "It's been a rare pleasure meeting you, and I hope we have the opportunity to get together again sometime in the future. We will look for the signal you speak of, and I assure you, we will act favorably when it arrives."

On April 6, 1971, the signal came. The Chinese premier, through the leader of the Chinese ping-pong team playing in Japan, invited the United States' ping-pong team to Peking. The State Department received the request via telephone from the American Embassy in Tokyo. Within four hours, the President responded by having the Secretary of State make the necessary arrangements.

The ping-pong team remained in China for a week, and on their last night, Premier Chou En-lai hosted a banquet in their honor where he informally remarked that the Chairman would welcome a visit by Mr. Nixon. The accompanying press contingent picked up on the story and headlined it throughout the world the next morning.

Secret negotiations followed, until it was agreed that Dr. Kissinger would meet clandestinely in Peking with the Premier to pave the way for the President's visit. His accompanying party would be minimal. Included was a State Department China expert, and a White House political analyst named Andrew St. James. The list was approved by the Chinese government.

"Can you think of anything we've not covered? Anything at all?" President Nixon was addressing his question to both Kissinger and St. James, even though he was looking directly at the former.

They had been in the Oval Office for most of the day, painstakingly preparing for Kissinger's and St. James's upcoming trip to China. Time and again, the President nervously stressed the need for secrecy, and each time was assured that the two understood. It was now pushing midnight, and their itinerary, along with all the other arrangements had been exhausted.

"We're as ready as we'll ever be, Mr. President," said Kissinger. "There are less than fifteen people outside of China who know about this. I have every confidence it will proceed as planned."

"Well, I hope so, Henry," the President replied. "This could well change the course of history," he continued, visibly excited at the prospect. "No peace in Vietnam is possible without the direct intervention of China on our behalf. We know that now. The Soviets have been nothing but a hindrance for years, and we can only expect more of the same from that quarter. But China, if we can just secure their cooperation, then indeed the peace that's eluded us for so long will become a reality."

Nixon rose from behind his desk, walked to the center of the spacious room while continuing to speak. "I will casually announce at the press conference tomorrow your departure on a factfinding swing through Vietnam, Thailand, India, Pakistan, et cetera; a trip that will take . . . oh, let's say . . . ten days. I won't dwell on it, so no suspicions should be aroused in the press." He paused, and looked around. "Well, that about wraps things up." He shook hands with Kissinger. "If the world forgets everything else about Henry Kissinger, they will remember you as the man who opened China for a second time in Western history. You're my Marco Polo."

Kissinger smiled at the reference. "I hope I don't find I'm persuaded to stay the same seventeen years as my predecessor did."

"Good Lord, Henry, I should hope not either," said Nixon with a laugh. "I've got a few more jobs for you to do before you embark on a vacation of that sort. Good luck." He turned to St. James. "Keep your eyes and ears open while you're there, *Pegasus*," said Nixon, a sly reminder that he was talking to St. James as an intelligence operative.

"Needless to say, we're all counting on your keen observations to details." He shook St. James's hand warmly. "Ah, hell, Andrew," he added with a huge grin, "I'm glad you're going along to take care of the good doctor."

The clock on the mantelpiece chimed midnight, signaling the last day of June 1971.

Their first seventy-two hours were spent in Saigon, South Vietnam, conferring with allied officials. From there, it was on to Bangkok, Thailand, for two days, followed by the next leg of the journey which took them into India, and then Pakistan.

Kissinger conferred with President Yahya Khan of Pakistan on the afternoon of July 8, ostensibly for conducting a review of relations between the two countries. This was not the case. Khan knew the secret; indeed, he was to provide the plane for Kissinger's flight into China. They finalized the arrangements and agreed that Kissinger's absence would be explained by issuing a joint communiqué saying he was ill with a minor stomach ailment and would be resting in seclusion for a few days.

The Chinese had agreed in the early planning stages that the leader of Pakistan be asked to help arrange the historical meeting, and Khan took his role seriously. He had been explicit in explaining the need for secrecy to his few aides who were informed. If anyone leaked the information, they would be shot, he had warned, and there would be no appeal for clemency.

The next morning, Kissinger and four aides boarded a Pakistan International Airlines jet and flew to Peking. They were met at the airport by ranking Chinese officials and whisked away to meet with Premier Chou En-lai. From the onset, both men were at ease with each other. Each seemingly saw in the other a reflection of himself: a deep-thinking, hard-bargaining individual, one not easily hood-winked or swayed to abandon a position for some transitory gain.

They spoke through interpreters, one Chinese, the other American, even though Chou En-lai was fluent in English, and passably well-versed in German, Kissinger's native tongue.

During the second day, they reached a tentative agreement as to a date for the President's visit: the following February, but if unforeseen developments precluded that from becoming a reality, then the visit would be rescheduled for no later than May 1972.

Between meetings, Kissinger was taken on a tour of the Forbidden City, the home of China's Emperors.

On the last morning of the visit, July 11, the two met for the final session. Kissinger requested having St. James sit in, and the Premier graciously gave his approval.

Chou opened the discussion. "We have accomplished much in our short time together, and I for one, hope it marks the beginning of a cordial relationship between China and America." His face grew serious as he leaned in closer to the American. "I must now tell you of certain events that have become known to the leadership of China. These events have been at least eight years in the making, quite possibly longer." Chou paused, but continued looking steadily at Kissinger. "It is not my intention to divulge all the information on this subject which I possess at this time. I believe such a strategy is followed in the game of poker in your country. We have already agreed that you should return this October for another meeting to draw up the final preparation for Mr. Nixon's visit. I will impart some of that information now, in exchange for concessions from you. However, I will not be as presumptuous as to assume you are empowered to make policy for your government, but I do suspect you can influence the President regarding my proposition."

"That is a purpose for my being here, Excellency," Kissinger replied.

"Then let me preface my remarks by saying this: America's greatest threat lies not with China, or even to some extent with the Soviet Union. No, her greatest enemy at this moment is an internal one. I say quite candidly that your President has enemies in the most unlikely of places. Motivated by greed and a lust for power, these men will destroy America, and I do not speak idly when I say this. From the time of Mr. Kennedy's death, not much has gone right in the United States. You have found yourselves immersed in a war which seemingly has no end. Your erstwhile allies abroad now treat you as one would a leper, and your cities and universities are no longer safe. I do not recite such activities out of a sense of glee, but rather, only to point out precisely how things are. What I am also most emphatically implying is that fate has played no hand in this. Your country has been sold out by a single greedy man."

"And you have proof of what you say?" If Kissinger was startled at what he heard, his voice betrayed no emotion. He too was a poker player, and a good one.

St. James sat still, listening to their every word. It appeared that indeed Edgar Snow had been right when he had told them in the Oval Office that it would be in the President's best interest to meet with the Chinese. But what the Premier was now saying had nonetheless come like a bombshell.

"I have the proof, and I intend to divulge everything when you return in October."

"And until then . . . what are you suggesting?"

"Simply this. Tell Mr. Nixon that he has enemies. Not just political enemies who would see his administration's agenda defeated simply because he is a Republican President trying to pass legislation through a Congress controlled by a party of another persuasion. No, I speak rather of enemies bent on destroying not only the Presidency, but the very system of government that seems to have worked so well in America for the past two centuries. You're going to have to ferret out those enemies and destroy them before they destroy you. More than that, I will not tell you, but come October, I will unveil the proof of what I say."

"Your warning will be transmitted to the President," said Kissinger. "but until you reveal the proof in October, your words imply you want a concession from the United States before then. That is understandable. What is it you seek?"

"Something which is rightfully ours," replied Chou. "We want to be recognized as a legitimate country among the family of nations.

The United States alone has made that recognition impossible for more than twenty years."

"United Nations membership?"

"United Nations membership. Only your government can make this a reality. I truly believe that Mainland China would be recognized within the next five years regardless of your country's continued objection, but I do not see what will be accomplished by waiting that long. Further delay on implementing that which is inevitable serves no useful purpose." Chou sat back, folded his arms and waited for Kissinger's response.

"For years I've advocated that China be recognized in the United Nations," Kissinger said. "Your conditions for temporarily withholding the proof of what you charge is acceptable to me, and I think I can safely say that the request will be met with approval by the President."

But Chou had an ace to deliver from up his Mandarin sleeve. "We are the legitimate government of China, not Taiwan. They must be expelled, and not even be allowed to remain in the General Assembly. The Chairman is adamant on this issue."

"I accept that," replied Kissinger, after several moments of thought. "When we meet again in October, you will already know Mr. Nixon's decision by his deeds."

On July 15, 1971, President Nixon addressed the nation on television and announced to a surprised country that Doctor Kissinger had just returned from a secret visit to China, and that he himself was planning on making such a trip to that country sometime before May of the following year.

On October 16, 1971, Kissinger and St. James departed from Andrews Air Force Base with Peking, China, their final destination. This time, there was no secrecy, so they traveled in one of the presidential planes, accompanied by the personnel necessary to help arrange for the President's trip, now firmly set for the coming February. They flew west, with intermediate stops in Hawaii and Guam, then on to Shanghai where they would take aboard a Chinese navigator for the final leg into Peking. While the technical experts made arrangements with their Chinese counterparts, Kissinger and Chou En-lai met in private, this time with only a Chinese interpreter present. Kissinger later recounted to St. James what took place.

He first relayed to the Premier the news that the Administration would support China's bid for entry into the United Nations this year, but for appearances sake would request that Taiwan retain membership in the General Assembly, something Kissinger did not expect would actually happen. Chou was pleased. St. James knew he had waited for such an announcement for so many years, and the fruit of final victory must have been sweet tasting indeed.

"Now, as I promised last July, I will show you the proof that will give credence to the warning I gave at that time." Chou gestured towards a motion picture projector. "What you are about to see has only been viewed by one other Westerner, and it shocked him to his core, so be forewarned Dr. Kissinger." He signaled the interpreter.

Though steeled for the worst, Kissinger was left speechless at what he saw. He asked that the film be run again.

"We've had this in our possession since early 1967," Chou said when the lights were turned back on. "We came by it through an agent of ours in Albania. It's my belief that the Kremlin has no idea we have this copy. As I stated, only one Westerner has seen this footage, and that man, of course, is Edgar Snow. He's been deeply troubled, yet he kept the secret well. There was nowhere to turn for help in America while Mr. Johnson remained in office, and Mr. Snow has suffered greatly having had to keep such information bottled up inside of him. Chairman Mao assured his friend that when the time was right to release this information, it would be done. Well, that time is now. General de Gaulle knew of this film although he never saw it, and he too felt that the time had come to make it known to the current American President. That is why he wrote to Mr. Nixon almost a year ago about the need for our two countries to open an avenue of discourse between the leaders. We agreed with the General's wisdom, and that too is why you are here today."

Kissinger found his voice. "I'm sure you have given strong support to the possibility the film is a fake, manufactured by the Soviets and deliberately "leaked" to your agent?"

"Indeed we have," replied Chou. "Our experts have carefully analyzed it, and concluded it is authentic. But remember, Doctor, history validates for us all that the film is genuine. Moments ago, we saw Mr. Johnson conspiring with Mr. Dobrynin to assassinate President Kennedy. That indeed came to pass, just as they said it would. And in Texas no less. So too has the rest of what they plotted that day. It has to be accepted for what it is."

"Can I have a copy?" Kissinger asked.

Chou shook his head. "We are still playing American poker," he replied. "A copy cannot leave China, at least not yet. This is the only print, no others have been made, nor will we make more. I do not know how many copies the Soviets have in their possession, but this is our only one." He took a sip of water and continued. "Dr. Kissinger, if the President and the Chairman can reach agreement on the many pressing problems facing our countries, then the Chairman will turn this film over to Mr. Nixon to do with as he wishes. We are not attempting to blackmail America. If that were our purpose, we would have done so long ago. But we will use it as leverage to bargain with, nothing more."

"I see," replied Kissinger. "You've shown me a most damning piece of film, and if it were ever made public, there's no saying what the repercussions would be. The possibility of the American Congress voting for war against the Soviets would not be out of the question. It could precipitate WWIII. Americans loved their President Kennedy. They are frustrated to the breaking point now, and if this film was ever shown, it could well put them over the edge. But seeing the film makes me think the future for Mr. Johnson looks more than just bleak, even though he's no longer the President. I shall tell Mr. Nixon about it as soon as I see him and prepare him for the worst."

"You know our position," said Chou. "There is much Mr. Nixon can accomplish during his visit in February. However, he should be at ease knowing that China poses no threat to America. Indeed, it never has. As for the Soviets, well, you know where you stand with them without having to be reminded by me."

The Nixon Administration was true to its word. On October 25, 1971, the Peoples Republic of China was admitted to the United Nations as one of the five permanent members of the Security Council. The Taiwanese delegation was voted out, the United States offering only token resistance.

The explosive information Kissinger brought home from China was the nexus for St. James to place his entire team on high alert. If the film Kissinger had seen in China was legitimate, then St James realized he had to wonder how deep the conspiracy went. It was entirely possible there were spies burrowed deep inside the White House, the National Security Council, and even the Pentagon. At this point it was impossible to know with any degree of certitude, so he began planning for the worst.

All through those trying days, Nixon prepped for his upcoming meeting with the Chinese. His most pressing issue was to get a solid commitment from Peking to help bring the war in Vietnam to an honorable end. Kissinger advised the President to keep his expectations low, but as a realist, he knew Nixon's political future could well rest on this one vital issue.

By early February, Nixon was ready.

☆   ☆   ☆

The day that so many had been preparing for had finally arrived. At eleven-thirty a.m. on the morning of February 21, 1972, Peking time, President Nixon descended the stairway of Air Force One in full view of television audiences around the world and shook hands with an awaiting Premier Chou En-lai. A Chinese military band played both countries' national anthems, and a contingent from each of China's military services provided an honor guard. The ceremony was brief, but correct.

Two hours later, President Nixon, Dr. Kissinger, and Andrew St. James were taken to the Chairman's residence for their first and only meeting. They were accompanied by the Premier and one female Chinese interpreter. On President Nixon's expressed orders, Dr. Kissinger's special assistant, Winston Lord, was included in the group. St. James had argued that Lord did not have a need to know about this film just yet, and should not attend even though he had been present during both meetings Kissinger had held with Mao in the past. Kissinger had strenuously objected to St. James' stance, but Nixon stood his ground, and overrode St. James' professional assessment.

The Americans met the Chairman in his cluttered study and shook hands while two Chinese photographers recorded the historic occasion. The principals exchanged pleasantries for a few moments, but as soon as the photographers left the room, Mao got down to business.

"I welcome you, Mr. President, on behalf of the people of China," Mao began. "I am sure you join me in hoping that the rift between our two great nations will start to heal as of today. It is up to you and me to do what is right, so that all mankind can benefit from the fruits of our labors. Our task is great, but equaled only by our determination to succeed."

"I agree, Mr. Chairman," Nixon replied. "For too long China and the United States have suffered due to a lack of communication. I accept my share of the blame, and because of this, the whole world has felt the ill effects. The time has come to open up all possible avenues of discourse, and in the doing, I am sure we will discover that our mutual problems are not as unsurmountable as we have believed so readily in the past."

With the translation completed, the Chairman nodded to the young interpreter who rose and proceeded to set up a projector and screen.

"I know you're anxious to view the film that Dr. Kissinger has told you about."

Without another word, the projector was started and the group stared in silence at the screen for the next six minutes. When it was over, Nixon sat still for several long minutes, obviously stunned. Finally, he asked for it to be shown again. It was worse than he could ever have imagined.

After the second viewing and the lights were back on, Nixon turned to the two Chinese leaders.

"I can fully appreciate your apprehension and concern after seeing that," Nixon began, first looking to the Chairman, and then the Premier. "I would be less than candid if I said I'm not deeply affected by what appears to be an unbelievable conspiracy. And yes, the events those two men conspired to commit indeed came to pass. And here, for the first time ever, we finally know the truth behind the who, the why, and the how President Kennedy was assassinated. All I can say is if this is an ongoing conspiracy, then I intend to find out. But meanwhile, I want to stress to you both that America wants peace with China, and that's the main reason I am here today."

"China also wants to live in peace with all of her neighbors," replied the Chairman, smoking his third cigarette. "I am sure you can readily see how difficult the past few years have been for us with the Soviets and Americans entrenched on our very doorstep with their powerful armies. Indeed, because of that film, we have had to accept as true the fact that both countries have been acting in concert to exterminate us completely. China is no match for such enemies, and we have had no illusions as to what our fate would be."

"Mr. Chairman, it is not America's intention to impose its will on the people of China. That is not the policy of my administration, nor did I ever believe for a moment it was a goal of my predecessor. But in light of the film I have just seen with Johnson and Dobrynin conspiring to first kill President Kennedy then carve up the world between them, I can understand how you could doubt such a statement coming from me, even now. But that's the second reason for my being here today: to allay your fears. I want peace for America," Nixon repeated, "indeed, I want peace for the entire world."

"But as long as you choose to remain in Vietnam, you shall not have that peace," the Chairman reminded the President.

Nixon let loose a loud sigh. "Mr. Chairman," he began, "Vietnam has been the one area of foreign affairs to which I've devoted my greatest efforts, hoping to find an honorable peace. We have asked every major power to help us find a solution agreeable to us and to the leadership in Hanoi. As you know, since becoming President, I've reduced the American presence in the region to only a fraction of what it was in January 1969. America is tired. We want all countries to live in harmony with their neighbors, but we will not stand idly by and let any one country impose its wishes on another through military might. We only ask that South Vietnam be allowed to determine its own future without interference from Hanoi, China, the Soviets, or any other power.

"Dr. Kissinger has spent months negotiating in secret with the North Vietnamese representatives in Paris, and as they finally agree to one point, they bring up another, then another, and another. There is no end to their demands. We are willing to withdraw all of our remaining forces from South Vietnam, subject only to Hanoi doing the same, and to release of all of our prisoners of war. We will not accept less."

"And you would want Peking to intercede on your behalf?"

"We would welcome help from any government, Mr. Chairman," replied Nixon. "China has great influence with Hanoi. You could make our position clear. Tell Hanoi that we want peace, but we want that peace to come with honor."

Mao nodded. "China is prepared to explain your position, but we are not prepared to impose our will on any other government," Mao said. "Both China and Vietnam have felt the yoke of imperialism. It sat no softer on our shoulders than it has on the shoulders of our brothers. Hanoi rightfully distrusts Westerners because she has been lied to by Western governments for centuries. We in China also want to see an end to the war that has enveloped you both for so long. It is in China's interest to let your case be known, so we will intercede, and do what is in our power to help resolve the conflict."

Mao rose unsteadily to his feet. "And now I must ask you to excuse me, as I have many things to do. I fervently hope that your discussions with our Premier and his deputies will be most fruitful." He shook hands with his American guests, including St. James. "You shall have the film to take with you, Mr. President. It serves no useful purpose to China any longer. What it will mean to your relationship with the Soviet Union . . . well, that's another matter entirely."

The Premier escorted the Americans from the Chairman's residence. "Chairman Mao has been deeply affected by the recent death of his dear friend Edgar Snow," Chou explained, as the group waited for their cars. "If he seemed brusque, please forgive him."

The President and Kissinger murmured that they both understood. They too had heard the news Edgar Snow had died of cancer at his home in Switzerland on February 14, mere days before the start of their trip. St. James thought it was beyond ironic that the two men who had done so much to bring about the historic meeting had not lived to see it become an accomplished fact.

"We owe a great debt to General de Gaulle and Mr. Snow," acknowledged President Nixon. "Neither man will ever be forgotten."

Premier Chou En-lai merely nodded.

Back at the Government House set aside for President Nixon's visit, the President, Dr. Kissinger, and St. James huddled to discuss the impact and implications of the film, carefully choosing their words, knowing the room was in all likelihood filled with electronic bugs.

The President summoned Secretary of State Bill Rogers and briefed him on events for the very first time.

"It looks bad, Bill," Nixon said in summary. "You'll see it when we get home."

"And you don't think it's a fake?"

"I wish I could flat outright say yes, it's garbage, but I can't. But I can tell you this. I'm going to have the CIA go over it inch by inch, because if in fact, it's a phony, I need to have absolute proof. As you all are so keenly aware, we're going to Moscow for a summit with Brezhnev in May, and I sure as hell need to know where I stand before then."

"Mr. President, I suggest President Johnson be confronted with this evidence," said Kissinger. "Frankly, this should prove to be our best course of action if we want to get to the bottom of the problem in the shortest time possible."

Rogers snorted at the proposal. "If Johnson did have such a meeting, or more likely, a series of such meetings with Dobrynin, do you really think he'll admit to it?"

"No, I don't," replied Kissinger in his controlled monotone. "Regardless of whether President Johnson is guilty or innocent, he most certainly is going to be shocked when confronted with such evidence. And if he is innocent, then his help will be invaluable in proving the film is nothing more than the cleverest piece of Soviet propaganda ever manufactured. Which means we must neuter its value before they have a chance to use it."

"Well, I want this resolved before we go to Moscow," said the President. "One way or another, I intend to confront Mr. Brezhnev with it, and let him know we're onto any scheme he might have had for blackmailing America."

CHAPTER 5

WASHINGTON D.C.
MARCH 11, 1972

AT ELEVEN-THIRTY A.M. on Saturday, March 11, 1972, a limousine glided to a stop under the porticoed entrance of the White House. Ex-President Lyndon Johnson and his wife, Ladybird, stepped out to be greeted by the smiling Nixons. After posing for the White House photographer, the four withdrew to the private quarters on the second floor for lunch. Fifty minutes later, the two Presidents descended to the Oval Office and joined a waiting Henry Kissinger and Andrew St. James.

As the four settled into comfortable seats around the fireplace, St. James took the time to study President Johnson. He was genuinely shocked at how much the man had aged. Instead of sixty, Mr. Johnson looked a decade older, and his six-foot-three-inch frame was noticeably stooped. It was a chilling sight.

As was customary in the Nixon White House, this conversation would be secretly recorded, something known only to a privileged few—including President Lyndon Johnson. In fact, St. James remembered Kissinger telling him that the current taping setup had originally been Johnson's idea.

Nixon took a moment to introduce President Johnson to St. James, explaining he was the Soviet expert on Kissinger's staff. Then he got straight to the purpose of the meeting.

"Lyndon," he began, "when I was in China last month, I was shown a disturbing piece of film. I had heard of its possible existence several months prior, so I thought I was prepared for what I was about to see. I was wrong. Nothing could have prepared me for what I saw."

Johnson let loose a frightful, strangling sound, bolted upright, staggered out of his chair, and began gasping for air. Nixon dashed over to his desk to summon help, but Johnson stopped him with a raspy, barely audible, "No, Dick, wait."

Five minutes later he was breathing easier, but his face was ashen, and he was still shaking. Finally, able to focus his still-watering eyes on Nixon, he asked in a whispered, "How in the hell did the Chinese get ahold of that film?"

Nixon looked floored. "*You knew about the film?*"

"I've known about it since the day I met with Premier Kosygin in Glassboro at the Summit Conference back in June of sixty-seven after the Israeli War. I've lived with that nightmare all these years."

"*You're saying you knew about the film?*" repeated an incredulous Nixon.

"That film more than anything else was the reason I decided not to run for reelection. Sure, Vietnam was an all-consuming issue, and sure, it alone could have caused the party to dump me. Now, I don't rightly know that for fact, and probably never will, but I can tell you this: That son of a bitch Kosygin threatened to blackmail me with a piece of phony film the Soviets had supposedly shot in their embassy just days before Jack Kennedy was assassinated. I had met Dobrynin there for some kind of diplomatic function in late November 1963—at his invitation I might add, and which is all a part of the public record—but it seems our talk was filmed and recorded. Anyway, Kosygin told me while the two of us were taking a walk in the garden with only his Soviet interpreter present, just how this film had been painstakingly taken apart frame-by-frame over the course of many months by experts in Moscow, and how it now showed me conspiring with the Soviets to kill Jack Kennedy. He said the film further went on to show Dobrynin and me plotting Khrushchev's overthrow, as well as my agreeing to begin squeezing the living shit out of China to the point it would soon be rendered impotent. Kosygin assured me that miserable day in Glassboro that the Kremlin was prepared to go public with the film should I not accede to their demands regarding Israel. He was furious at the disastrous shellacking his Arab buddies had suffered at their hands. I told him to piss off and release his damn film. I said no one would believe such a shitass, obvious, blackmailing ploy. He smugly felt otherwise. He pointed out quite correctly that President Kennedy was indeed dead; that Khrushchev was also gone; that China was now surrounded and isolated by American and Soviet forces, and that everything in that film would be believed by whoever saw it, if for no other reason than they would want to believe. I knew—or at the very least, I hoped—that should the Soviets release it, I could somehow prove it wasn't genuine. But deep down in my gut, I also knew if it was as good as Kosygin claimed it to be, then delivering that proof would take time, and time was the one commodity I didn't have going for me into the spring of 1968. I was the most hated man on earth, and my enemies would have immediately branded me a traitor, an opportunist, a murderer, or what have you. I could protest my innocence, but I would have been ignored. Just remember the mood of the country back then."

"Who else knew about this?" Nixon finally asked. "There must be someone out there who can corroborate what you're telling us now."

Johnson shook his head. "There was only one other man who had maybe learned the truth, but I never knew for sure. I'm talking about Bobby Kennedy. Dobrynin assured me during our meeting in the embassy that he had alerted both Kennedys two days earlier about what the Chinese were supposedly up to, but I'm now thinking the son of a bitch lied to me about that too." After a pause, Johnson asked in a small voice, "Do you have a copy?"

"Yes," Nixon said. "It was my intention to show it to you, and you'd then tell me no such meeting ever took place. As soon as I got back from China I assembled a crackerjack team of photographic experts at the CIA to discover the proof I'll need to show to the world that it's nothing more than a Soviet forgery. But they're telling me that will take time, and I'm telling them I must have it before meeting with Brezhnev in Moscow in May."

"I see," said a visibly glum President Johnson.

Nixon forged ahead. "Lyndon, here's what I think we should do. I want you to tell us everything you can remember about that meeting in the Soviet Embassy, plus anything else you think is important. And I'd like your permission to record what you say. After you've finished telling us what you can remember from nine years ago, the four of us will watch the film together. Only a handful of people at CIA have seen the film, and I intend to keep it that way. They have each been sworn to secrecy, and I trust every one of them to remain silent on the subject no matter what pressure might ever be placed on them in the future. Also, this is the only copy. The original is still in the Soviet Union, and Chairman Mao insists the Chinese have no other copy. I would like to believe him, but I really don't know."

St. James saw the relief on Johnson's face. He had finally rid himself of the burden he had carried alone for so long. The years seemed to disappear. "Let's get started," he said, rubbing his hands together, then added, "and promise me, Dick, you won't be recording any of this on your secret taping system stashed under the desk."

"You have my solemn word," Nixon replied, then turned to St. James. "Andrew, would you set up the necessary equipment for us?"

Five minutes later a relaxed President Johnson began recording. He spoke nonstop for five hours, recalling events from 1963 to 1968.

Driving home that night, St. James asked himself the million-dollar question: *How in the hell did the Chinese get ahold of that footage; and how could it be so totally at odds with what President Johnson had told them took place in the embassy that November evening?*

The answer eluded him.

CHAPTER 6

WASHINGTON D.C.
1963

"Mr. Vice President, this is Captain Seymour, a presidential military aide at the White House," said the voice on the phone. "Sorry for the early hour, but the President is inviting the NSC (National Security Council) Executive Committee over for a working breakfast at seven forty-five. He apologizes for the short notice. "

"I'll be there."

President Kennedy was ten minutes late when he entered the Cabinet Room.

"Gentlemen, thanks for coming. There's no emergency, so everyone relax." Kennedy eased himself into his padded chair and nodded to Defense Secretary Robert McNamara to open the meeting. Vietnam was an ongoing problem, so the group spent the next fifteen minutes discussing its deteriorating political situation. The current regime had long ago lost what little popular support it had ever held, and the Buddhist population through rebellion and self-immolation had all but ground the corrupt government to a halt. Back-alley whisperings of a military coup were now regarded in Washington as more than idle chatter.

"Keep me posted, Bob," Kennedy said, then for the next several minutes other members of the committee took turns briefing items of interest. The last to speak was John McCone, Director of the CIA.

"We've got something of a puzzle in the making, Mr. President," McCone began, "and as of this morning, we don't know quite what to make of it. The Soviets are in some kind of a flap. It seems that over the past several weeks three, or maybe more, of their agents in various parts of the world have been killed. In fact, murdered would be the better word. Two of the killings were particularly wet affairs, and intercepted message traffic from the Kremlin to their embassies tells us they're genuinely alarmed. The Soviets seem convinced the Chinese are responsible, but we have not been able to corroborate this independently. However, we have confirmed that the dead Soviets were all seasoned agents. Some of my field assets have been approached on the Q. T. by their opposite numbers asking if they know anything. They don't. We're as much in the dark on this one as they are. It could be a Chinese grudge thing, but that's only speculation."

"How about our British friends? Have they got anything?"

McCone shook his head. "Nothing. MI6 is in the same boat as us."

"Interesting," said the President, rising from his seat. "Stay on top of it. Thanks everyone for coming."

The quiet on the international scene was shattered on November 1, 1963, when U.S. Ambassador Lodge cabled Secretary of State Dean Rusk from Saigon with confirmation that the army had overthrown the government of South Vietnam. The next day he cabled that President Diem and his brother-in-law had been shot in the Saigon Cathedral by army officers, unknown, and the country was now in the hands of the generals.

Vice President Lyndon Johnson learned of the coup one hour later.

"Don't forget, seven o'clock tonight, a reception at the Russian Embassy," Vice President Johnson's secretary said as she helped him into his suit jacket. Hers was a common mistake, referring to the Soviet Embassy as the Russian Embassy, but old habits die hard.

"What?"

"The Russian Embassy, you're expected there at seven. Today. Monday. November 18. 1963." She laughed at the look on his face. "You accepted two or more weeks ago, I guess. It's to introduce their new cultural attaché to the rest of the diplomatic corps. I can double-check your appointments calendar if you want, but a secretary from the ambassador's office called earlier today with a gentle reminder. She said Ambassador Dobrynin was looking forward to seeing you again."

"And you're sure I said OK?"

"Positive. You'll be the ranking guest, which means you can put in a quick appearance and leave. Protocol says no one leaves before you, so show your smiling face, say your howdy-dos, and scoot. That way no one can possibly be offended." She smiled. "Go, on, enjoy yourself, sir."

At seven o'clock sharp, Vice President Johnson was escorted through the large entrance of an impressive, four-story mansion situated among other equally gracious buildings on Embassy Row. A valet took his coat, and as he turned to check his appearance in a floor-to-ceiling mirror, he found himself face-to-face with a smiling Ambassador Dobrynin.

"We're honored, Mr. Vice President, and welcome," the ambassador said in perfect English, the smile genuine, his hand outstretched.

"The pleasure's mine, Mr. Ambassador," Johnson replied in his best Texas drawl.

"And permit me to introduce our new cultural attaché, Yuri Chernenko," Dobrynin said.

The attaché bowed deeply in old-world fashion, smiled, and shook hands.

"I'm honored to meet you, Mr. Vice President, and I am equally honored to be in your wonderful country."

"Glad to have you with us. You'll find America fascinating, and her folks friendly."

"Thank you."

"Excuse me, but duty demands I greet my other arriving guests," Dobrynin said politely. "I'll join up with you as soon as possible."

Johnson followed an aide who had seemingly materialized out of nowhere, down a carpeted hallway and into a large public reception room. There were already forty or so guests milling about, mostly members of the diplomatic corps. Tuxedoed waiters glided among the assembled carrying trays of hors d'oeuvres and flutes of champagne. Along the back wall were food-laden tables, their dazzling white linen tablecloths holding priceless silver and delicate plates, mute testaments to artisans long dead. Ten feet away a string quartet softly played chamber music.

Secretary of State Rusk, his wife, and several others began moving toward Johnson, all intent on paying their respects. Twenty minutes later, he excused himself and headed toward the food. As he was filling his plate, Dobrynin appeared alongside, and in a quiet, but serious voice asked, "Could I impose upon you for a few minutes of your time? I need to speak with you regarding a matter of some importance. I apologize for the interruption, but after you hear what it is, you will appreciate my concern."

"You mean right here, right now?"

"No, no," Dobrynin answered smoothly, "I suggest we meet in my study on the second floor. It will only take a few minutes. I will have an aide show you the way after you've had a chance to enjoy some of this excellent food." The ambassador turned to a woman on his left and asked brightly how she was enjoying the evening.

Twenty-five minutes later Johnson was shown into Dobrynin's study.

"Thank you, Mr. Vice President," Dobrynin said, closing the door behind them. He gestured toward two brocade-covered wing chairs flanking a table holding a bottle of *Rémy Martin* brandy and two Waterford crystal balloon snifters. The intimate grouping was centered atop an imposing stone hearth, the fireplace's façade an inlay of mirrored tile bordered by a richly veined travertine. A crystal chandelier cast a clean white light to the corners of the room. Johnson, seated on the right side of the table, spotted his reflection in the glass tiles. He subconsciously squared his tie, flashed his French cuffs, and finished by dabbing at his hair.

"Please, join me here and make yourself comfortable," Dobrynin said, pouring a generous splash of brandy into both snifters. Each took the obligatory sip.

"What I am about to tell you, I do so at the behest of my Politburo. Then, I have been instructed to extend all possible assistance to you and your government."

Johnson's brow furrowed. This didn't sound good. "Maybe you should be talking directly to the President, or possibly the secretary of state about whatever it is that's bothering your government." He began to rise, signaling the meeting was over.

Dobrynin raised a supplicant hand, a pleading gesture asking him to wait. "Please allow me to give you a brief background as to what has blossomed into a cause for grave concern in Moscow," he rushed on in a beseeching voice.

Johnson lowered himself back into his chair.

"Let me begin by saying that for some time now, Secretary Khrushchev has been granting vast sums of monetary aid and technical nuclear assistance to Peking. The Presidium vehemently opposed him on this, especially the nuclear assistance part. But then, last June, his policies were finally reversed by unanimous decree of the Presidium. The meeting was acrimonious, but the majority prevailed. Our military and economic aid has since been reduced to a trickle, and all of our nuclear scientists are now home. However, we believe the Chinese will soon have crude, but effective, nuclear capability, and that worries us greatly.

"Of course, the Chinese did not take kindly to this change," he continued. "To them, saving face is everything, and we made them lose a lot of face. Our agents in Peking told us that the Chinese Government believed Washington and Moscow had reached a secret accord to restrict their capacity to wage war. We were also told they planned revenge. Well, that revenge has started. They have now murdered three of our diplomats in the last few months. The killings have been particularly vicious but made to appear random. However, we needed more solid information before we could plan an appropriate response."

Johnson studied his reflection in the fireplace tiles, nodded woodenly, and waited for Dobrynin to continue.

"A break finally came when we uncovered a weak leak in a Chinese spy network. We learned that their terror campaign for revenge was really a two-stage affair. The first targets were to be Soviets; the second, you Americans. To initiate their campaign of attacks against America, they assassinated a man they saw as a puppet of Washington. Of course, I'm speaking of the late president of South Vietnam, Mr. Diem, and they did so by convincing some junior army officers that such a move was in their country's best interest. And with a vacuum of leadership in South Vietnam, the Peoples Liberation Front will unite the country under North Vietnam, an open satellite of Peking. Their intention is to drive you Americans first out of Vietnam, and eventually from all of Southeast Asia. They have become most fearful of President Kennedy's newly acquired interest in the region."

Dobrynin paused and took another sip of brandy, and Johnson followed his lead.

"But let me tell you what has truly alarmed my government," Dobrynin continued. "We now have proof that the Chinese have finalized plans for the assassination of two American diplomats; and for the finale, the aim is to kill President Kennedy."

Johnson jumped up. "*Stop right there. That's just bullshit!*"

"Mr. Vice President, please sit. I beg you, just hear me out."

"Look . . ." Johnson began, then stopped. He made a concerted effort to restrain himself. He tugged on his left earlobe, his mind racing. The look on his face said he was struggling to digest what he'd just been told. He downed a short swallow of brandy, saying nothing until the snifter was back on the table. "Dammit, why are you telling me this, and not the President? Look, every man who has ever held that office has enemies somewhere, and Mr. Kennedy is no exception. Also, may I remind you the President is keenly aware of the possibility that he could be assassinated at any time. When a man accepts that job, he also accepts the risks that go with it. But now you come to me speaking of a plot to have the President killed by the Chinese? Well, my next question should be obvious. When is this supposed to take place?"

"Mr. Johnson, let me put your mind at rest right now by telling you President Kennedy has already been informed," replied Dobrynin in a firm, but low voice.

That snippet visibly surprised Johnson. "*And?*" he asked forcefully.

"And, his attitude was one of disbelief. I personally told both the President and his brother, the attorney general, two days ago during a meeting in the Oval Office."

"And?"

And, the President said that if every threat by every unhinged person was taken seriously, a president would be forced to remain a prisoner of the White House, unable to govern the nation. I then told him our information suggested the attempt would come during his proposed Asian tour early next year, but his attitude remained unchanged. The attorney general, however, voiced an even stronger opinion. He bluntly told me to keep all such rumors to myself and said that if such sensational charges should find their way into the American Press, then I would be declared persona non grata and expelled from the country. I found his attitude to be supercilious, and blatantly hostile. I refrained from making a reply."

"And?" Johnson repeated for the third time. Dobrynin took note of the slight upward shift in the line of his mouth, a subtle indication that Johnson agreed wholeheartedly with his opinion of Robert Kennedy.

"I informed my superiors of the meeting, and this afternoon was instructed by Moscow to apprise you of all the facts. Even though President Kennedy does not seem to be alarmed or to take the threat seriously, my government *is* alarmed, *and* it takes the threat very, very seriously. It was decided, Mr. Vice President, that if such a terrible thing actually happened, then as the constitutional successor to

President Kennedy, you at least should be aware of what had truly taken place."

"During the President's spring trip to the Far East you say?" Johnson again raised a hand to his left ear and began tugging at the lobe in earnest. He managed a momentary, mirthless laugh. "I can sure picture your reception with Bobby; I've been at odds with the man myself on more than one occasion. And I'm not giving away state secrets when I tell you there's no love lost between me and the attorney general." He then asked, "And you say the President did not take kindly to your warning?"

"The President was courteous, but unconcerned. In contrast, the attorney general was cold, hostile, and impolite. The younger Kennedy said that American Intelligence was capable of finding out on its own whatever information they needed, then hinted rather smugly that Soviet squabbles vis-à-vis the Chinese was something the Americans had no intention of being dragged into. He ended by saying that the Secret Service was fully capable of protecting the President, either at home or abroad." Dobrynin allowed just the right amount of concern and worry to show. "I fear your attorney general has let his personal dislike for me cloud his thinking, and for that I am truly sorry."

"Does Robert Kennedy know you've been instructed by your government to inform me of this matter?"

"No, sir, he does not. As I stated a few moments earlier, I was only given my orders a couple of hours ago to make you privy to the facts. The attorney general was explicit in his warning that I speak to no one about what I had told him and the President. He is right about one thing, however. Given time, your CIA will uncover the same information we have, but I fear it could come too late."

"I'm aware of your country's troubles as far as some of your diplomats being murdered," Johnson said, as if deciding to be candid in a *quid pro quo* gesture. "I'm also aware that the Chinese might be behind those killings. But taking the life of the President of the United States is an entirely different matter. He can't just be murdered like the average man on the street. And anyone attempting to kill a

President would be signing his own death warrant. Hell, even if he were somehow able to escape from the scene of the crime, he would be subjected to the greatest manhunt in history. The only way it could be done would be by a fanatic, someone like those monks in Vietnam who've been setting themselves ablaze." He paused as if reflecting on what he had just said. "But from what little I know of the Chinese, there's no shortage of fanatics over there, either."

"How much you were already aware of about what I've just told you, I don't know, but whatever knowledge you do possess, you must see that I'm telling you the truth, and that is why I am justifiably alarmed. My government stands ready to help in any way possible. I know we do not see eye to eye on many of the important issues of the day, Mr. Vice President, but at least we Soviets strive to solve our differences through diplomacy. The Chinese on the other hand, are disdainful of the diplomatic community, and their innermost thoughts are known to none but themselves. But should they succeed in this most foul undertaking, and I truly hope they don't, then you as the new President must be aware of who your true enemies really are."

"Can they be stopped?"

"We're doing everything possible," replied a glum faced Dobrynin. "However, we must assume that they can succeed, and so must you, Mr. Vice President."

"What are Secretary Khrushchev's feelings about all this?"

"The mood in the Presidium is that he is responsible for a lot of our woes over the past few years. His dangerous, obstinate stance over our missiles in Cuba, his blind commitment to the Chinese nuclear program, and his many other blunders have forced the rest of us to question his capacity to govern. My suspicion is that he will be replaced shortly before he can do further damage. The Soviet government will be taking a more robust hardline against China in the months to come. Their newfound nuclear capability, coupled with their starving millions, presents a specter of nightmarish proportions. Their only direction for expansion is westward into Soviet lands, and my government believes that such a move will be attempted in the next few years. Not a pleasant thought, Mr. Johnson. There are more of them than there are flies. We must take steps to contain them now, and that is precisely what we intend to do. I tell you this only because you could soon find yourself President. Though we have our differences, the Soviet Union has no plans of upsetting our avenues of communication and mutual respect. We want to coexist peacefully with the West. Our troubles lie to the East."

"East is east and west is west…" Johnson said, almost to himself, then hoisted his brandy snifter and drained the contents.

"Ah, the English poet, Rudyard Kipling," Dobrynin replied. "Now there was a man who understood the mind of the *Asian brown.*"

Johnson stretched his arm to look at his watch. The gesture clearly said: *Time to wrap things up.* "Should I find myself President, Mr. Ambassador," he began in a firm voice, "and I find that possibility to be remote, understand that I would continue President Kennedy's policies regarding the Soviet Bloc. Any attempted expansion or encroachment into Western Europe would be met by force. A new President does not mean new ideas. I wholly support Mr. Kennedy's foreign policy because it is sound. He has made his feelings known when it comes to maintaining the integrity of Western Europe. Encroachment by the Soviets will not be tolerated."

Dobrynin listened in silence, his face a mask.

Johnson continued. "The United States stands behind the policies outlined in the NATO Treaty documents, and I would go to war to honor our commitments. I speak of Article 5 specifically. The strength of that alliance rests on the premise that the United States will protect Europe. However, we have no obligation to defend a member country embarking on a war with a neighbor, then turning to us for support. That was not the founding purpose of NATO. Under a Johnson Administration, Western Europe can rest assured America's military might stands ever ready to defend its freedom. The Soviet Union and the Warsaw Pact nations would have nothing to fear from me as long as you do not try to expand your holdings in Europe or anywhere else that we have treaty obligations to uphold. That is my clear statement of the facts, Mr. Ambassador. I trust you will so inform your friends in the Kremlin."

"I understand, Mr. Vice President. You have your sphere of influence and we have ours. What takes place inside our borders is our affair, something which was well understood by General Eisenhower regarding Berlin and Hungary. Likewise, that which takes place in the West is not our concern, and we would not interfere. Peaceful coexistence works."

"Who else in your government knows about Khrushchev?" Johnson asked. "I mean, specifically regarding his ouster?"

"Other than a select few members of the Presidium; none. I was authorized to tell you so that if you suddenly find yourself President, you will be aware that you will not have to deal with a senile and irrational old fool. Your job will be difficult enough without Secretary Khrushchev agitating you."

Johnson again looked at his watch. "Mr. Ambassador, I've been here about eight minutes, and that's long enough. Thank you for the information. I will be telling the President of this meeting and will express my hope that he takes those added precautions necessary to protect himself in light of what you've just told me. I am inclined to believe you and will convince him to also take the warning to heart." Johnson stood. "Present plans call for him be a guest at my ranch in Texas this coming weekend, so I'm hopeful the opportunity should present itself then."

"I understand, Mr. Vice President," Dobrynin replied, walking his guest to the door. "I trust your judgment. Please assure President Kennedy that our government stands ready to help prevent such a horror from taking place. I know the attorney general will be furious with me for having spoken to you about this, and I realize I could find myself expelled should he decide to follow through on his threat. However, I see that as a price worth paying should it save President Kennedy's life."

CHAPTER 7

WASHINGTON D.C.
MAY 9, 1972

"How did you happen into this line of work, Mr. St. James?" Zakharov asked, pushing back his plate. Lunch had been a somber affair; both of their thoughts still lingering on the unsettling revelations of the morning's session.

St. James lit a cigarette and took two long pulls before answering. "The simple answer is I fell into it, but now I can't think of anything I'd rather be doing." He tapped an ash onto his saucer. "You sure you're interested in hearing this?" He had decided on the spur-of-the-moment to be forthcoming, reasoning that providing a glimpse into his personal life would have a positive effect on Zakharov's own continuing candor.

"I've read everything in your KGB file. The only reason you have one is because you work in the White House, you speak Russian, and you're a political analyst. There is no listed current connection between you and any intelligence service, and as I mentioned earlier, the KGB is completely unaware of , or who you really are. That was a secret known only to me, and possibly one or two non-governmental folk, but one I discovered quite by accident. I guarded it well. But you've already proven in the short time we've been together just how one-dimensional and dry such files really are. So, tell me only what you care to," Zakharov said, then added with a hint of a smile, "and I'll promise not to repeat anything to the KGB."

"My father always wanted me to follow in his footsteps to our military academy at West Point," St. James began. "He had graduated with the class of 1929. I was born in 1935 while he was a first lieutenant stationed at Fort Riley, Kansas. My childhood was the same as thousands of army brats everywhere. We lived on two different posts before WWII started and I did what children do, I guess. One thing though that separated me from the others was my fascination with airplanes. I was building wooden models for as long as I can remember. Dad didn't think much of planes, or the people who flew them, and saw this as just a passing childhood fad. He believed nothing would ever be more important to America's security than the infantry.

"My sister Peggy was born two days before Pearl Harbor was bombed in the Sunday morning Japanese sneak attack, and on the following Wednesday, father left for Washington and eventually Europe, leaving mother and us to fend for ourselves at Fort Leavenworth, Kansas. He rode off to war wearing captain's bars and came home with a brigadier general's star on his collar. That was four long years for us, four short promotions for him. But one week before Christmas 1945, the Army bumped him back down to his permanent grade of lieutenant colonel. This really, really rankled him, especially when he heard that several of his classmates and some of those behind him who had opted for careers with the Army Air Corps had kept their promotions. One was even a major general, and here he was, a light colonel again, and a rather junior one at that."

"I feel his pain," Zakharov said.

"We moved twice in the next four years. I attended three different schools, excelled in none, which aggravated both my parents no end. They were convinced I was destined for failure. Then the Korean War came without warning in 1950, and father was soon over there in the thick of things. He served two tours, and for the second time in his career returned home from a war as a brigadier general. This time the Army let him keep his star. Meanwhile, I had managed to get into the University of Kansas and graduated in four years with a degree in political science and a minor in Russian. That was the summer of 1956, and because I didn't have the academic chops necessary to garner an appointment to West Point, then the least I could have done to redeem myself in his eyes was enroll in Army ROTC. But that didn't pan out either. I was tossed out of the program during the first semester of my junior year—I think I went to three drills in four months—and the Army decided I was not a serious candidate for a commission. But two months after graduation, I shocked him with the news that I'd been accepted into the Air Force and selected for pilot training. He was speechless. You see, he still didn't understand my lifelong captivation with everything to do with airplanes and my wanting to actually fly the things."

Zakharov was hanging on his every word. "And did you?"

"I did. In fact, I graduated from pilot training at Williams Air Force Base in Arizona in August 1958, and dad was there to pin on my wings. He was a lieutenant general at the time—a three-star—and I was a brand new second lieutenant. I saluted him; he returned my salute, then shook my hand and mumbled under his breath, 'Maybe I've been wrong about you, Andrew.' Anyway, to speed things along, my flying career ended abruptly eighteen months later when I was involved in a midair collision with another F-100 over Central France. I managed to eject, but the other pilot wasn't so lucky. They found me in a field an hour later, badly banged up and unconscious. I was flown back to the States where I spent the better part of the next year in the hospital. To pass the time, I enrolled in some extension courses through the University of Maryland Graduate School in political science and was well enough to attend my last semester in residence. So now I had a master's degree, but no career. You see, I was taken off flying status and told that I was to be medically grounded, permanently. The year was 1961, and I decided that if I couldn't be a fighter pilot, then the Air Force and I should part company. I resigned my commission."

"What did you do then?"

"My folks were living in Washington D.C. at the time, my father having retired the year before. His prodigal son was home again, but with no plans for the future.

"A month later I happened to tag along with a friend who had a job interview with a recruiter from the CIA. He had no interest in working for the government; he only wanted to use the interview as a dry run for landing a plum job on Wall Street. The day ended with the CIA hiring me instead. I remained with the agency as a political analyst for five years, then was vetted to a special hush-hush assignment outside the country for the next three. That's where I really learned to speak Russian fluently, which led to my present job in 1969 with Doctor Kissinger as a part of the Nixon White House transition team. End of story."

"And you never had time to get married?"

"Not true. Fact is, I was married from 1962 to 1967, and have two fine young boys, Kevin and Christopher. Somewhere along the way, my wife decided she hadn't planned on a life with a part-time husband, and we divorced. It was amicable. She met someone else a couple of years ago and is happily remarried. We share custody with our sons."

"Our profession does not lend itself to having a normal home life," Zakharov said with a faraway look. An inner voice cautioned St. James not to disturb him. For two minutes neither man spoke, then Zakharov suddenly looked up and asked what was planned for the afternoon.

St. James glanced at his watch. Three o'clock. He needed to spend time listening to the first of Lyndon Johnson's tapes to refresh his memory on what the former President had told President Nixon, Doctor Kissinger, and himself two months earlier in the Oval Office.

"Nothing more today, General. We'll meet at eight in the morning."

CHAPTER 8
WASHINGTON D. C.
MAY 9-10, 1972

"Your seven o'clock in the Oval Office has been cancelled," Stephen Merrill said to St. James. "Doctor Kissinger says the CIA had nothing new to report on the film, so he told the President a meeting would serve no useful purpose. Hold on a sec, , Justin just walked in, I'll put him on."

"Got something good for me on Zakharov?" St. James asked.

"Tons."

"I'll see you in half an hour."

☆   ☆   ☆

"Let's hear it," St. James said, placing his coffee mug on Justin's desk, then studied the man as he took a moment to scan his notes.

Justin sure likes expensive clothes, St. James thought, *but with that frame and serious look, he pulls it off without looking foppish.* He harkened back to the first time they had met, and how struck he had been by the blueness of the eyes. He immediately suspected contact lenses but learned later that was not the case. Unlike many of his flamboyant, hipster contemporaries, Justin's wavy brown hair was cut short. Stylish, but short, St. James mused, probably because it was a bureau dress code requirement, not unlike that other edict from on high demanding all agents wear white shirts.

Justin looked up, a signal he was ready. "First, the Canadians gave me a complete rundown on everything that happened after Zakharov banged on their door in Rome in the middle of the night. He told the deputy chief of mission he was a Soviet spy and wanted to defect. He said he was supposed to have been on the plane that had just crashed in Palermo." Justin paused to glance at his notes. "And here's where our Canadian neighbors really used their noggins. They got ahold of a passenger manifest from Alitalia and confirmed that a Frantz Webber was indeed on that flight. That alone convinced them Zakharov was telling the truth, so they went to work. First, they charred up his Frantz Webber passport, even going as far as using Italian jet fuel for the job. God only knows how they did that. Then they had one of their folk fly over to Palermo posing as an International Red Cross official and dumped it into the wreckage when no one was looking."

"Good thinking on their part," St. James acknowledged, "they really are the best."

Justin nodded and continued. "All the bodies and personal belongings were taken to a local high school which had been commandeered for use as a morgue. By late morning, the passenger list was published in all the major European newspapers, and relatives began flying in to claim next of kin. Remains which were easily identified were quickly turned over to their families—mostly Italians, from what I gather. Ditto for luggage and other personal effects. But that still left scores of badly burned bodies unidentified. By this time they had all been moved into refrigerated trucks which were parked on the school grounds."

Justin leaned closer. "Now comes the good part. Seems a Frau Webber from West Germany showed up, identified herself, and said she had come to take her husband's remains home. She made a big show of grief, tears flowing everywhere. Anyway, she could not identify Webber from among those remains that were relatively intact, which meant he had to be one of the really badly burned cadavers. The authorities handed over his passport, along with what was identified as his luggage. The grieving widow said she would make arrangements to reclaim the body as soon as it was identified. That was three days ago, and she's been neither seen nor heard from since. It's a fair assumption to say that Moscow thinks Webber got cooked on the hillside near Palermo."

St. James mulled that over for a few moments, then said in a voice reeking with skepticism, "Maybe." He was not about to write the Soviets off so easily. He moved on. "What did the Canadians do next?"

"My hat's off to them, Boss, they really handled this Zakharov guy well. They flew him to London using one of their own diplomatic passports and one of their own Air Canada planes. He had told them he wanted to defect, but only to the Americans. He said he had a ton of quality information with which to barter. The Canadians didn't squeeze him, and they didn't try and keep him for themselves. They handled everything quickly, quietly, and professionally. Their report was delivered this afternoon to the FBI director, and because he knows I'm an agent on loan to you, he had me personally come to his office to pick up a copy."

"Did Director Gray ask if you had anything you wanted to share about Zakharov?"

"Yeah, but I acted like I was just a messenger boy."

St James smiled.

"What do you really make of Zakharov, Boss?"

"That he is who he claims to be. But the really big news so far is that he also claims to have been the mastermind behind killing Kennedy."

That got Justin's attention. "You mean Bobby?"

"No, I mean Jack. Hell, maybe Bobby, too; I haven't gotten that far yet."

Justin's face showed his open surprise. "Could he be bluffing? Maybe for some reason you don't know about?"

St. James shook his head. "I doubt it. I reviewed some of President

Johnson's tapes before coming over, and what Zakharov said corroborates what the ex-President told us."

But Justin was not convinced. "Then what the hell is his motive?" He silently studied St. James for few moments then came to a decision. "Something's been gnawing at my gut ever since this "Ivan" popped up out of nowhere. Humor me for a moment and follow along, OK?"

"Fire away."

"What would make the KGB's number-two guy suddenly drop everything, and hightail it over to the White Hats? That only happens in bad spy movies. The whole thing seems too pat. Maybe the Kremlin is setting us up, and this guy's not even Zakharov. Maybe he's a throwaway, an expendable sent to divert our attention away from something big the Soviets are getting ready to pop."

"Like a diversion from what?"

Justin wore his frustration openly. He shook his head. "I don't know, but something major. Something like what British Intelligence did in 1944 when they dumped that body from a submarine into the ocean off Portugal. You know, he was supposedly an army courier carrying all of Ike's D-Day plans chained to a briefcase on his wrist. The Germans were skeptical at first—hell, who wouldn't be? The whole scene was too pat, too good to be true. Just like here. Nevertheless, they soon came to believe in their good fortune, and the German High Command decided that the Allied landing would be at Calais, and not Normandy. They came to believe it because they wanted to believe it."

St. James drained his mug before answering. "That's a pretty fair comparison, except for a couple of minor corrections. The year was 1943, and it was Spain, not Portugal. The Brits wanted to convince the Germans that Greece and not Sicily was where they would come ashore. Worked like a bloody charm, it did."

Justin reddened. "I would have sworn my recollection was correct . . ."

"Your reasoning was sound and that's what matters. Look, I'm also curious as to what made him defect. In fact, I asked him, but he just clamed up. Said he would tell me in his own sweet time, so I didn't press him. He knows we're going to check and re-check everything he tells me, but to answer your question: I don't think he's a plant."

St. James began to pace. He lit a cigarette, blew a cloud of smoke out the side of his mouth and said, "I need you to get me the CIA's file on Zakharov."

"I'm ahead of you, Boss. When I left the FBI, I drove over to Langley. There's very little on him; our boy's no publicity hound. The file photo is at least ten years old and fuzzy—if it's really him. Langley claims to have partial thumb and index fingerprints of his left hand but admits they're only a probable. I guess we can verify those prints anytime we want. As for the rest of the file, it's bigtime disappointing. You'll see for yourself."

"Figures," was St. James one word reply. He opened the Canadian report and speed-read the salient parts. He did the same with the CIA file, then looked up at Justin.

"What reason did you give the CIA for needing this?"

Justin's reply was to reach into his desk drawer and pull out two other folders. One was labeled: *Deputy Director of East German State Security (STASI)*, the other: *British Director*, M1-5. "I signed for them saying Kissinger wanted all three. I promised I'd have them back first thing in the morning. By requesting all three, no suspicions were raised. Those spooks saw it as another request from our eccentric doctor, and by then they had already forgotten about my earlier asking about Zakharov."

St. James laughed. "Now that's thinking on your feet. Good work."

Justin replied with a frown, and then a question. "Have you given any thought to what kind of a cover we're going to create for Zakharov? I mean, after we're finished pumping him dry?"

"Nope. I want you to come up with something that will pass muster. That shouldn't prove too much of a challenge, especially for a bright boy like you."

St. James woke with a start, entombed inside a tangled mess of sheets. And he was soaking wet. As he willed his breathing to slow and his heart to quit pounding, he tried to recall the dream. *Ten? What was significant about the number 10? Or was it 12?* Then he remembered. Ten days was the time he had left to discover the truth about the film. The pressure was taking a subconscious toll.

He showered, ate breakfast, and was waiting for Zakharov as the mantle clock in the living room chimed eight.

A haggard, ashen-faced Zakharov appeared in the doorway.

"You OK?" St. James asked. Illness was the last thing he needed. "I can have a doctor here within fifteen minutes," he added, thinking a thorough checkup was not such a bad idea.

Zakharov feebly waved a dismissive hand. He made his way to his chair and sat down heavily. "An upset stomach. It will pass."

St. James wasn't so sure. He mentally ran through his options, then asked, "Is it the same kind of upset stomach that made you get off the plane in Rome?"

Zakharov looked startled; it was as if he had not made the connection. Then, "Yes, it's the same kind of pain. I took some medication. An antacid. I'll feel better soon."

"The more I think about it, the idea of having a doctor examine you seems like good preventative medicine to me." He then asked in a low voice, but with genuine concern, "Is there something else bothering you, General?"

"First, if you insist I see a doctor, I will not argue." Zakharov paused, his face taking on a resigned look. "You're right, there is something bothering me. I spent the night turning a problem over in my mind and I do not like the answer I kept coming up with. So, before we go any further, Mr. St. James, I must have some reassurances."

"Reassurances? I've offered you asylum in America and a new identity. In return, all I ask from you is candor and honesty. What part of that deal don't you like? Do you think I might renege on our bargain after I've pumped you dry?"

"Something like that," Zakharov replied. "I realize now this film has taken on an importance greater than I ever imagined. In fact, I believe it has become the focal point of some major crisis within your government. I also have a sinking feeling that should it become expedient for President Nixon to go public with my defection, he will do so, and any deal you might have offered me be damned." Zakharov appeared to be calm, but the veins on both sides of his temple were throbbing wildly.

St. James subconsciously leaned in and looked Zakharov square in the eye. "I'm only going to say this once, so listen well. No matter what happens, you will not be exposed. That's a promise. My job is to get from you every iota of useful information I can. You will be spending months, possibly years, telling me and others whatever we need to know. About anything and everything. That's the deal we have." He shook his head in what he hoped came across as an open display of amazement. "General, you decided to defect; no one from my government put a gun to your head. You are not a prisoner, which means you're free to go any time you want. Just say the word, and I'll fly you back to Rome. But if you decide to stay, you will have to earn your keep. Maybe we Americans are naïve fools in your eyes. I'll even go so far as to suggest that if our positions were reversed, you would renege on a deal with me after you determined I had nothing more to give up. But I don't operate that way, so relax. You have my word, but more importantly, you have the word of President Nixon." After a couple of beats, he asked, "Any more questions?"

A huge smile creased Zakharov's face. "None, *Pegasus*. I'm feeling better already."

"So let's get to work." St. James fiddled with the recorder, then sat back and slipped into his persona of professional inquisitor. "General Zakharov," he began, "this morning I want you to tell me everything you know about the assassination of President Kennedy. I want to hear how *Romulus and Remus* were able to get to Dallas, and how they managed to slip away. But I especially want to hear what happened to the film of Vice President Johnson and Ambassador Dobrynin after it left your embassy."

Zakharov lit a cigarette. He coughed once, visibly winced as he struggled to find a comfortable position and ended by placing a protective hand over his abdomen. "I do appreciate how hard it must be for you to sit and listen to the man who masterminded the assassination of your President Kennedy. I will not sugarcoat events. I spent many, many days debriefing *Romulus* and *Remus* when they finally arrived home. But especially so with *Romulus*."

Zakharov stubbed out his cigarette and lit another. "First, I will recount what happened that day in Dallas, and then I will tell you what I did with the embassy film."

CHAPTER 9

DALLAS, TEXAS
NOVEMBER 22, 1963

"*MESDAMES ET MESSIEURS, votre attention s'il vous plait . . .*" "Ladies and gentlemen, your attention please. Air France announces the immediate loading and departure of Flight 56 to Montreal, Canada. Passengers holding tickets are asked to proceed to Boarding Gate 12 in the South Terminal."

In the Air France waiting lounge at Orly Field, south of Paris, dozens rose slowly and began making their way to the gate. The time was two-fifteen am on the morning of November 18, 1963, and Flight 56 had been delayed since six p.m. the previous evening. Most of the seventy-seven passengers were Canadians and Americans returning home from vacations or business trips in Europe.

Included in the group were two Roman Catholic priests, men claiming to have spent the entire month in Rome, Canadian clerics observing the Vatican II Conference. Although their passports showed they had left from Montreal, the two, in fact, had started their odyssey in Moscow. The older was code named *Romulus*; the younger, *Remus*.

Neither were strangers to the North American continent. However, they had not met each other until the previous June when they had been introduced by Colonel Zakharov.

★　　　★　　　★

Romulus had been stationed in the Soviet Embassy in Ankara, Turkey, awaiting new orders when he was unexpectedly summoned home. *Remus* was already at KGB headquarters. Neither had been given any particulars regarding their new assignment, they were only told it would rank high among the KGB's most ambitious undertakings.

Because both were already proficient in English, the entire month of June was devoted to a total immersion of all things American. To hone their skills, they were treated to hours of the latest Hollywood movies. They devoured American newspapers and magazines; they became fluent in the use of current slang, and within thirty days, their demanding instructors pronounced them ready for any assignment requiring assimilation into mainstream America. They suspected they would be going to either the U.N. Mission in New York or the consulate in San Francisco, both plum postings.

They soon learned differently. Zakharov said the assignment called for them to spend only a few days in America, and not the full, multi-year tour both had anticipated.

The first twelve days of July were spent at the Red Banner Institute's KGB Personal Firearms and Weapons Center ten miles north of Moscow. They received recurrent training in the use of a number of different handguns, ranging from small .22-caliber automatics to .44-magnums, and then to a variety of high-powered rifles with scopes. On the first day, they learned they would not be using any of these weapons during their upcoming mission. The practice was to sharpen their eye and reflexes. Both were thoroughly puzzled but said nothing.

The last half of July, and most of August, were devoted to learning their covers, and their entire lives were mapped out for them to memorize: Where they were born; the schools they had attended; the towns they had lived in; their parents' names and family histories; their brothers' and sisters' life histories; time spent in military service;

where they were stationed and when; the jobs and training they had received after the military; all was committed to memory. Both were soon unerring in their answers. A cursory background check by local law enforcement agencies would pass muster; a detailed check by the FBI would not. Zakharov weighed the laws of probability and deemed the risk to be acceptable.

Romulus and *Remus* next underwent a comprehensive course in photography. They learned about optics, photographic chemistry, and the art of splicing and editing raw film footage. They became proficient with motion picture cameras. By early September, it would have taken a true expert to uncover they were not what they appeared to be— freelance photo-technicians often employed by either the Canadian Broadcasting Company (CBC), or United Press International (UPI).

On September 7 they returned to the KGB range and were introduced to a completely modified Swiss Bolex 16mm motion picture camera. Outwardly, it appeared to be a stock production model capable of shooting at a speed of twenty-four frames a second. Because of its ease of handling and simplicity of design, this particular model was a worldwide favorite of newspaper and theatrical people alike. Loaded, it weighed under fourteen pounds and could be shoulder mounted for greater mobility.

They immediately realized this was to be their weapon. The instructor spent the next half-hour demonstrating and dry firing the camera's gun-mode, all the while explaining the mechanics and physics which made everything work in synch with its ability to record through special optics fitted inside the case. They practiced breakdown and re-assembly until they could do the task blindfolded.

Zakharov decided that *Romulus* would be the actual shooter, *Remus* his back-up. They took turns firing at silhouettes, stationary and moving; sometimes in the open and unobstructed, at other times, partially hidden from view. The actual gun had little recoil, minimal noise, no muzzle flash, and the bullets could destroy a target at five hundred meters. By September 10 both men were proficient in handling this unique weapon.

When Colonel Zakharov told them on September 21 who was to be their intended target, neither showed any emotion.

They spent hours with Zakharov weighing the pros and cons of killing the President either during a speech, or while riding in an open car. Finally, it was agreed a motorcade setting would be the preferred option because the noise of a crowd could be used to advantage.

By early November 1963, Dallas had been pinpointed as the city of choice. The decision was based on the simple fact that Governor Connally of Texas had publicly confirmed what was already widely known: the President's visit would be November 21 to 22, and a detailed map of the presidential motorcade route from the airport to downtown had appeared in all the major Dallas newspapers. A copy of *The Dallas Morning News* was flown to Moscow for the twins to study. Colonel Zakharov zeroed in on an area along the route which looked most promising: a spot called Dealey Plaza.

Their real break came when they learned President Kennedy had informed the Secret Service he wanted the top removed from the limousine for this trip—unless there was a torrential downpour, and not just a slight drizzle.

Romulus and *Remus* were told of a man Zakharov called *Gemstone* who would provide them with whatever assistance they might need. But *Gemstone* would be unaware of their actual mission. He thought they were simply a TV camera crew on assignment. Zakharov explained that *Gemstone* was a volatile, and oftentimes unstable character, who owned a seedy nightclub in Dallas, yet despite such baggage, the man had his uses. *Gemstone* had solid contacts within the police department, but was totally ignorant of the fact that he was employed and being paid by the KGB. He actually thought he was a paid informant for the Chicago Mob, and was proud of his reputation as one who could keep his mouth shut.

The last piece of the intricate assassination puzzle was added when Zakharov told *Romulus* and *Remus* a decoy had been hired to fire a rifle at the same time they would fire theirs. Zakharov then cautioned the duo: if *Gemstone* was known to be unstable, the decoy was ten times worse, and they should avoid him at all costs. He explained.

Out of nowhere, a character had shown up unannounced at the Soviet Embassy in Mexico City in late September, seeking help in getting permission to travel to Cuba. The resident KGB station chief—an agent Zakharov had partnered with in the past as assassins—didn't quite know how to handle the weird request, so he cabled Moscow for instructions.

The subject was a lifelong loser named Lee Harvey Oswald. Zakharov had never met the man, but after reading his file, accurately pegged him as a bankrupt, communist sympathizer who not only spoke Russian, but had actually married a woman from Molotovsk.

Zakharov saw the timing as nothing short of serendipitous. Only a few days earlier, on September 25, the White House had announced that a presidential trip to Texas was planned for late November and would include a motorcade in Dallas for the morning of November 22. The exact route had been published by the White House Press Office while Oswald was in Mexico City, and that's when Zakharov made his decision. *President Kennedy's assassination would take place in Lyndon Johnson's very own backyard!*

Here was a disgruntled American, a stooge he could plant at the scene. He wired encrypted instructions to the embassy station chief to make an arm's length offer to Oswald through a cutout masquerading as a Cuban national, for a ten thousand dollar very important assignment in Dallas sometime in late November. Two thousand to be paid immediately, the balance upon completion of the task, a fortune to the near-penniless Oswald. He was instructed by the "Cuban" to return to the U. S. and await further instructions.

Zakharov immediately put KGB operatives in Dallas to work, greasing palms and pulling strings, and in late October, an agent arranged for Oswald to be hired as a temporary worker in a book depository building alongside the presidential motorcade route. Oswald's instructions were explicit. As the parade of cars passed below, he was to fire three rounds in rapid succession into the air from a rifle he already owned, then drop it and run fast and far. Zakharov had openly scoffed at the idea of any marksman choosing a cheap, Italian Carcano rifle as an assassin's weapon, but it was perfect for this gullible individual and his assigned role. *Romulus* alone would kill President Kennedy. Zakharov's fervent hope was that Oswald would be killed while fleeing from scores of enraged Dallas police officers.

Zakharov wanted *Romulus* and *Remus* positioned in Texas two days early to familiarize themselves with the motorcade route and surrounding terrain in the plaza. They would depart the scene immediately after the shooting, return to Canada by way of Detroit and fly from there into separate European cities. *Gemstone* would arrange their transportation out of Dallas.

Romulus set aside his book. The plane's interior was dark, the majority of his fellow passengers either asleep, or wishing they were. He snapped off his reading lamp, tilted his seat back, and stared out at the nothingness beyond the oval Perspex window.

He realized he must have fallen asleep because the next thing he remembered was a stewardess nudging his shoulder and telling him they were starting their descent into Montreal. He shook *Remus* awake. Twenty minutes later they relinquished their passports to a yawning officer and declared they were bringing nothing back into the country. Entering the main terminal, he heard a loudspeaker announcement that a message for arriving passenger Father Thiebold was waiting for him at the Air France Information Counter.

"I'm Father Thiebold," *Romulus* said, proffering his passport for identification to a bored woman who gave it a careless glance, and wordlessly handed over an envelope. It bore the seal of the Chancellery of the Archbishop of Montreal.

Once registered in a nondescript hotel not far from the airport, *Romulus* tore open the letter signed by a Monsignor Henri Gauthier. The typed message in French thanked them for their interesting and informative dispatches from the Vatican Council and offered shelter should they be staying in the Montreal area for a few days before heading home to their motherhouse in Toronto.

Romulus reached for his well-worn breviary. "Let's see what we've really got," he said, as he began leafing rapidly through its pages. His search was not for the Word of God, but rather instructions from Colonel Zakharov. His prayer book was a codebook, the letter a message from the senior resident KGB agent in the Soviet Consulate General's Office in Montreal.

It took him twenty minutes to turn the innocuous letter into detailed instructions. When finished, he tossed the book down and intently studied the converted text which spelled out the where and the how they would get scrubbed passports, money, and American clothing packed in American suitcases.

"Our first stop will be at the last stall in the Greyhound bus station men's toilet room," he said, "but we can't make our appearance until eight-fifteen in the morning. I don't know about you, but I'm off to bed for a couple of hours sleep."

The bus station was swarming with early morning travelers. Following instructions, *Romulus* found the bathroom and locked himself in the last stall. He lifted the cover off the tank and felt around under the float. Yes! He pried loose a key wrapped in waterproof electrical tape, pocketed it, replaced the tank top, washed his hands, and rejoined *Remus* with a "mission completed" grin and a wink.

He ambled over to a wall lined with lockers stacked three-high and began pointing down the row until he found one with numbers 64T matching those on the small brass key. He pulled out a parking ticket for a car in the lot across the street.

Ten minutes later they were driving back to their hotel in a 1959 Chevrolet Biscayne, and forty minutes after that, lugging two suitcases from the trunk up to their room. Inside they found clothes, money, airline tickets, and more instructions in a letter from *Romulus's* non-existent cousin in Toronto. Revisiting the prayer book, they were instructed to drive to Ottawa, leave the car with valet parking at the airport, and catch Air Canada's seven-fifteen p.m. flight to Toronto. There they would pick up pre-paid tickets at the Eastern Airlines counter in the names of Joseph A. Thomas for *Romulus*, and Michael Stowe for *Remus*. They would then catch the one-thirty a.m. red-eye to Dallas, Texas.

At six-twenty a.m. on November 20, 1963, two tired, unshaven, free-lance TV camera operators contracted by United Press International (UPI), cleared customs at Love Field in Dallas, and took a taxi to the Downtowner Motel. By two-thirty p.m. that afternoon, having slept and eaten, they made their way to the nightclub owned by *Gemstone*. After exchanging recognition signals with the stocky, fifty-year-old, balding owner, *Romulus* and *Remus* were ushered into a small, untidy, second floor office in the rear of the rundown building that housed his Adults Only Club.

"Y'all have a good trip?" *Gemstone* asked, plopping down behind a decrepit wooden desk, his favorite dachshund settling in by his feet. "No problems?"

"No problems," *Romulus* replied, taking an instant dislike to the beady-eyed Texan. He didn't want to engage the man in small talk. "Has our equipment arrived?" The camera had been sent from Moscow to Washington in a diplomatic pouch, then forwarded to Dallas by special courier.

"Arrived yesterday," *Gemstone* said, pointing with the toe of a cowboy boot toward two wooden crates stacked beside his chair. "I haven't touched a thing. The bill of lading says they came from the UPI Washington office. You want to check 'em?"

"We do," said *Romulus*. He laid the crates side by side on the floor. Opening the first, he found the camera, wrapped in green felt and packed snuggly in Styrofoam. The other revealed three lenses, loaded film magazines, batteries, as well as sundry smaller parts, and a satchel of tools. For the next fifteen minutes the duo painstakingly examined each component for damage, then cross-checked the other's work until they had the camera assembled.

"Everything OK?" a curious *Gemstone* asked.

"Seems to be."

Gemstone pulled out a map from his desk. "Let's go over some facts about the Dallas area." He drew an X at the airport, then traced the main artery into the city. "This is the motorcade route. Now, things can change without warning, but I don't really expect them to. This here's a political trip for the President, and the whole idea is for him to be seen by the greatest number of people. That's why the open car. So any changes now will have to be kept to a minimum so as not to piss-off the good folks of Dallas. However, if there should be a change of plans, I have a radio tuned to the local police frequency, and we'd know of it at once. Tomorrow morning, I propose a dry run so you can get a feel for the layout. I've already noted the location where your decoy will be placed: it's a schoolbook depository building in Dealey Plaza. He's been working there since October."

"What can you tell us about this fellow?" *Remus* asked, with a feigned nonchalance, wanting to feel out just how much *Gemstone* really knew about Oswald.

"I've only met him a couple of times myself, but he's OK," *Gemstone* said, after an uncomfortable pause. His tone suggested otherwise. "You won't be meeting him; hell, he has no idea you guys are even here to film the parade for UPI. Like I said, he works at a book depository building on the motorcade route, right there," he said, pointing a stubby finger at a spot on Houston Street. "It's a seven-story brick affair that sits back some. It's also away from where the crowds will be gathered. He's been told to shoot off three shots into the air as the lead car in the motorcade passes beneath him, but not to fire at anyone or anything. Just pop off three shots and vamoose. But I'm sure he knows who will be in that car. He's definitely not the brightest, but I think he can follow instructions. If you have someone else in mind, I suppose we could dump him right now."

"What reason did you give this guy to fire three shots into the air?" *Romulus* asked, staring right through the Texan.

Gemstone shrugged. "Told him it's only a test. Said certain folks in high-up places wanted to see if he's good enough to handle other more important assignments. He's eager to show me he can follow orders."

"If you're OK with him, then so are we," *Romulus* said, and changed the subject. "What about our car? Was it delivered?"

"Yep, and registered to Joseph A. Thomas of Michigan. I was told you'll be driving nonstop to Detroit, so I put maps in the glove box of every state you'll be passing through. You shouldn't have any problems getting home in plenty of time for your next TV assignment."

Gemstone still had no idea of their true purpose for being in Dallas.

The following morning, *Gemstone* drove to the entrance of Love Field, turned his car around, and began down the presidential parade route into the city.

"OK, we're coming up on the site I propose for you guys," he said, swinging onto Elm Street and into Dealey Plaza. "That brick building over there is the book depository where the decoy will be. Now, look here just before the underpass, a little in front of it . . . see, over there . . . yeah, at that grass-covered slope." Both men followed the bead of his index finger. "That spot should give you the necessary height to see over the heads of the crowd. It's the perfect location for a camera crew. You should get some great footage."

Gemstone continued down to the Trade Mart where he made a quick turnaround and studied the route from Main Street traveling in the opposite direction. All agreed that close to the top of the grassy slope would be the best vantage point for them.

"Then it's settled," said an obviously pleased *Gemstone*. "Let me take you to your car." They rode in silence until he said, "It's the three-year-old blue Ford parked up ahead." He dipped into his shirt pocket and tossed a key ring to *Romulus*.

"I've already put your camera and other stuff in the trunk. The motorcade starts at the airport about noon, which means it should pass your position twenty to thirty minutes after that. I probably won't be seeing you again, so good luck."

Gemstone pulled over to the curb. His two passengers jumped out without a handshake, a word of thanks, or a backward glance.

Romulus shoved the marked-up Dallas map into his pants pocket and headed for the driver's side.

"Typical snooty TV camera crew assholes," *Gemstone* muttered under his breath then peeled rubber, causing his car to fishtail wildly as it rounded the corner and disappeared.

☆   ☆   ☆

On Friday, November 22, 1963, the weather in Dallas was warmer than had been forecast.

At eleven a.m., *Romulus* and *Remus* left the Downtowner Motel, and by noon were set up near the crest of the grassy knoll overlooking Dealey Plaza in downtown Dallas. The book depository was to their rear. *Romulus* was carrying the camera. A sizeable crowd had already formed along the street, and *Romulus* took note of the several police officers stationed on foot, on motorcycles, and a nearby overpass.

At twelve twenty-eight p.m. a murmur rose from the crowd. *Romulus* swung the camera to his shoulder and pressed his right eye into the viewfinder. The road jumped toward him. Seconds later the official motorcade came into focus led by several motorcycle officers. The first car in line was an open Lincoln limousine.

"I have him," *Romulus* said quietly, as the car rolled slowly past his position, the crosshairs now squarely on the back of the President's head.

The crowd began cheering, whistling and clapping.

A rifle shot rang out above the din. The head in *Romulus's* view-finder began moving to one side, and a moment later he fired his silent weapon.

"*That goddamn decoy has hit him!*" *Romulus* said aloud.

His own bullet penetrated the President's now-turned, but still moving head, a microsecond later. It exited, carrying in its wake, brain, bone shards, and hair.

A second shot rang out just as he fired his silenced weapon again. But the President's head had already disappeared from the center of the crosshairs. He immediately knew that bullet would miss.

Then came a third shot. The sounds of merriment from mere seconds earlier were now being replaced with screams, and many in the crowd began falling to the ground.

Pandemonium reigned.

Romulus held his breath and kept the viewfinder trained on the big convertible. He followed the Lincoln as it swung out of the motorcade, accelerated, and disappeared from view with a secret service agent crawling across the trunk.

Both men dropped to the grass. *Romulus* disengaged the magazine holding the film. "*Destroy it, now!*" he commanded *Remus*.

Romulus lifted his head in time to see dozens of uniformed police officers running helter-skelter, some with their revolvers out, all plainly confused. "Let's get the hell out of here."

Three minutes later they reached the car and tossed the battered remnants of the camera and film cannister into the trunk.

"You know that goddamn decoy hit President Kennedy, don't you?" *Romulus* exclaimed, as he steered the car onto the expressway.

"I thought so, but wasn't sure," *Remus* replied. "What do you think it means?"

"It means *Gemstone* is in a hell of a lot of trouble because his man didn't follow instructions. Wouldn't want to be in his shoes when Colonel Zakharov hears about this. But one thing's for sure, that stupid decoy is now as good as dead."

Late that night outside Springfield, Missouri, *Romulus* stopped long enough for *Remus* to heave the camera into the Sac River. They continued on to Detroit, stopping only for gas. After leaving their car in the airport long-term parking lot cleaned of all fingerprints they boarded a flight to Ottawa.

The next morning, *Romulus* flew to Paris, *Remus* to Rome. One week later they were reunited at KGB headquarters.

CHAPTER 10

WASHINGTON D.C. – 1963

IN THE INSTANT IT TOOK A BULLET to find its mark, Lyndon Baines Johnson became the 36th President of the United States. As he flew back to Washington aboard Air Force One, all he could think about was Dobrynin's warning, and the fact that he hadn't even had the opportunity to tell his wife about their meeting.

On Monday, November 25, 1963, President John Fitzgerald Kennedy was laid to rest at Arlington National Cemetery. Representatives from every nation on earth either came to the funeral or sent messages of condolence—all except one—the People's Republic of China. That fact was not lost on President Johnson.

Later, he met with various world leaders at the White House, including Charles de Gaulle and Soviet Foreign Minister Mikoyan. Ambassador Dobrynin also came to pay his respects. The two met in private for three minutes.

"Words cannot express how I feel, Mr. President," Dobrynin began. "What saddens me most is it happened before we had a chance to prevent it."

"And that's something I'll carry to my grave," Johnson replied.

"Mr. President, you must always remember that both Kennedys were warned, yet chose to ignore the warning. I'm sure terrible feelings of guilt now lie heavily on the heart of the attorney general." Dobrynin seemingly deliberately paused to let that sink in, then continued in a low voice. "If I may be presumptuous to offer you some small sliver of advice, it is this. Carefully weigh any counsel Robert Kennedy offers you. Even though he would mean well, his mind will be filled with grief, and he might want to blindly lash out, and suggest you tell the world of the Chinese plot. But what would be gained? Your countrymen would demand immediate retribution, and you would find yourself thrust into a war that could spell the end for mankind. I say this as a diplomat of many years of experience. You know my country's feelings toward China, excluding those of Secretary Khrushchev who will not be with the Presidium much longer. My advice is to bury the knowledge you and Mr. Robert Kennedy alone share. At least until a time when more rational thought will prevail. Think with this always," he said, pointing to his temple, "and never with this," pointing to his heart. "It is a hard lesson to learn, but one vital for a man with the awesome power that is now yours. The fate of us all is literally in your hands."

"Thank you, Ambassador, your advice is well taken." He escorted Dobrynin from the Oval Office, and upon return, made a public display of closing the door, a signal to the staff he wanted to be alone.

In the following months, President Johnson empaneled a commission under the leadership of Earle Warren, the Chief Justice of the United States, to determine exactly what had taken place in Dallas that November afternoon. They had no hard facts to go on, and the only man who could have told them anything of value was himself dead, namely one Lee Harvey Oswald, shot in front of a worldwide TV audience by a local cabaret owner. Because of the man's unstable background, and the fact so little was actually known about him, the commission found Oswald to be the lone assassin. Lyndon Johnson kept his silence. This would be his arena for retribution, and his alone.

He would bide his time to take the steps necessary to show the Chinese what a fateful error they had made.

In the spring of 1964, Lyndon Johnson declared himself an active candidate for election as President, come November. The announcement had long been awaited by three men in the Kremlin. It signaled them to put into action the next part of their plan.

CHAPTER 11
MOSCOW – 1963

Boris Rulev smelled worse than a corpse. He was in the backseat of a Soviet consulate limousine, chauffeuring him from LaGuardia Airport to Idlewild. He had the air in the car so unbearable that the driver was forced to open the window despite the near-freezing temperature outside.

Boris Rulev was impervious to his own smell, never giving much consideration to why people seemed to avoid him wherever possible. On those rare occasions when such thoughts crossed his mind, he told himself it was because they were scared. He would have been right. At 6' 6" and 270 pounds, Boris could aptly be described as Neanderthal. Small ears placed high on each side of his skull, no forehead to speak of, and a spatula of a nose that had been broken so many times even he couldn't remember the number. And hair. Hair which sprouted from beneath his collar, and marched across the top of his head, ending less than two inches above a single, shaggy eyebrow. His small, piglike eyes missed nothing.

Boris had been chosen for his life's work years earlier and had served his masters well. He was a courier. It was his job to ferry diplomatic pouches from the far corners of the earth back to the Kremlin, and he had been doing this since 1951.

In late October 1963, he had been dispatched by Zakharov to Washington to start escorting documents back to Moscow. This was his third trip in little more than a month, because Zakharov wanted Boris to be seen as a recognized regular on the route. New couriers are always noticed by the opposition, and if a courier is seen only once on a known route, that invariably means something important has just taken place. To eliminate any suspicion, Boris was worked overtime. It did not bother him in the least.

As soon as the limousine pulled up to the International Arrival Building at Idlewild, the driver jumped out and immediately began gulping huge breaths of cold, fresh air. Boris also got out, carrying a small overnight case in one huge hand and a larger, sturdier one in the other. This case was cuffed to his bough-sized wrist by a slim tempered steel chain. It had been locked by Anatoly Dobrynin and would be removed in Moscow by Colonel Zakharov.

The BOAC flight took him to Warsaw, where he was met by a Soviet Air Force captain and escorted to a waiting military plane. Two hours later it landed in Moscow, where a staff car whisked Boris to KGB headquarters.

The date was November 29, 1963, and the local time was six-thirty p.m.

Colonel Zakharov met Boris in his third floor office at KGB Headquarters, the building once home to the All-Russia Insurance Company in the days before the 1917 Revolution.

Zakharov motioned Boris to hold out his wrist. He opened the case, took out the lone package, locked it in a safe beside his desk, and turned back to Boris. "Here, let me remove that thing," he said, taking another key from his pocket. "As always, you've done an excellent job. Your devotion to duty is an inspiration to us all. I want you to make one more trip to Washington this month, then you will have a well-earned vacation."

"Thank you, Colonel, I do what I can."

As soon as Boris left, Zakharov picked up the phone and dialed a four digit number.

"Our package has arrived, sir," he said, "it's in my safe." He paused, listened, then added, "I'll do it right away."

He waited a few seconds and dialed a second number.

"This is Colonel Zakharov. I want Major Petropov." He suffered through an excuse-ridden delay, before yelling, "Then find him and send him to me at once." He slammed the phone down.

Twenty minutes later, a tall, thin man wearing the uniform of a Red Army major knocked sharply on his door and entered.

"You sent for me, Colonel?"

"I need your photo section to process a job for me right away." He re-opened the safe and extracted Boris' package, a film canister with a sealed envelope taped to the top. He pulled out a single sheet and began reading. A puzzled look formed on his face, and he handed the note to Petropov. "What do you make of it?"

The man scanned the message. "It's instructions for developing that film," he said, nodding at the canister. "Our people in Washington are telling us what chemistry to use. It's specially made by the American Eastman Kodak Company for processing their 16mm color film. I have some here. How soon do you need it, Colonel?"

"Tonight. I'll also need one duplicate copy."

Petropov returned at ten p.m. to find Zakharov waiting impatiently with a projector and screen already set up. He dismissed the major.

Five minutes later Zakharov watched as mannequin-like images of Lyndon Johnson and Anatoly Dobrynin sprang into life and began speaking. He followed the conversation in English with ease, and when the film came to an end, he rewound the spool and ran it again, this time wearing a victorious grin. Zakharov put both copies into his safe, then dialed the same four digit extension as earlier. The phone was answered on the first ring.

"It's better than we could have ever hoped for. I will leave it in my safe awaiting your further orders, Mr. Brezhnev."

CHAPTER 12
MOSCOW – APRIL 1964

LEONID BREZHNEV WAS NOW RECOGNIZED by the other members of the Politburo as the new architect of Soviet policy. This was the week of April 10-17, 1964, and Nikita Khrushchev was still de facto Party Secretary. However, since the memorable meeting the previous June when he had been overruled regarding his China policy, it was Brezhnev's opinion that carried the most clout. He was considered a "hardliner", and his strongest ally and supporter was now Alexei Kosygin. Among the moderates were Nikolai Podgorny, Anastas Mikoyan, the Soviet Foreign Minister, and Vladimir Semichastny, the KGB Chairman, a man of considerable influence in his own right. The very fact he had thrown his weight in support of Brezhnev made the moderates more careful in voicing differing opinions. Thus, of the twelve members, eight were strong supporters of Brezhnev's politics, while four—including Khrushchev and Podgorny—were considered more "revisionist" in outlook. In terms of Western Democratic politics, all twelve were hardliners; none were considered friendly.

Brezhnev waited for complete silence before he began to speak. "Mister Johnson has been President of the United States for five months now. The country has rallied behind him with a fervor that has frankly surprised me, but it is something that works in our favor."

His eyes swept the table from one man to the next, landing last on Nikita Khrushchev who quickly looked away.

"As of today, this is where we stand," he continued. "The removal of President Kennedy went better than we could have ever hoped for, thanks to Colonel Zakharov, seated there behind Comrade Kosygin. He deserves a round of applause for what we all know was a most difficult task. In hindsight, he made it look easy, then somehow managed to silence the American assassin within hours. So the possibility of any credible suspicion ever falling on the Soviet Union has been squashed. The only man we had to convince that Peking was responsible for killing the American President was his successor, Lyndon Johnson, and we know that is what he truly believes."

The room broke out in loud cheers, and an accompanying spontaneous clapping of hands. A beaming Leonid Brezhnev rose while continuing to clap, and within seconds the whole assemblage had followed suit.

A visibly embarrassed Colonel Zakharov finally stood, and waved his right hand in response. His mumbled "Thank you, gentlemen," was drowned out by the continued cheering and clapping. He could not remember another time when he was so overwhelmed.

A full minute passed until Brezhnev motioned all to sit. He again waited until the room was quiet before continuing. "We must never lose sight of the fact that ridding ourselves of President Kennedy was but the first step in a comprehensive plan to propel the Soviet Union to its rightful place as sole leader of the world's nations. Mister Kennedy was proving to be a very dangerous distraction, a cultlike figure mesmerizing gullible fools on a global scale. It was fitting he came to his end at the hands of our *Romulus* and *Remus*. The Soviet Union can now concentrate all its efforts in seeing Comrade Lenin's vision of a new world order finally becoming a reality. These next few years will prove critical to us in achieving our goals. And if we must sow chaos in many quarters, then so be it. The result will be the demise of America, and a turning of peoples everywhere to follow the best path forward which is found in the teachings of Karl Marx."

Around the table a dozen approving heads nodded in agreement, as too the functionaries seated behind the members of the Politburo. Leonid Brezhnev had given them their marching orders.

Later, in the afternoon meeting, all agreed that China had to be dealt with even more forcefully than the United States. The consensus was that China now presented the greatest immediate danger to the Soviet Union. Even Khrushchev cast his vote in support of Brezhnev's position, making it unanimous. Some of the more vocal members had raised the possibility of a preemptive nuclear strike against China, and Brezhnev did not rule out such an option.

China's annexation of Tibet in 1961 had been deeply troubling—not because the small Himalayan kingdom meant anything to him—but because he saw this as the first in a series of expansionistic moves. More recently, China had begun agitating on its border with India, while cozying up to the neighbor, Pakistan, all to the consternation of the Soviets.

On April 17, 1964, the Politburo adopted a formal four-point position on China.

Point One. It is the unanimous consensus of the Politburo that the People's Republic of China presents an immediate clear and present danger to the peace-loving citizens of the Soviet Union.

Point Two. Effective immediately, all aid to the People's Republic of China shall cease. All contracts between the Soviet Union and People's Republic of China for the purchase of military weapons by the latter are rescinded.

Point Three. In order to protect the citizens of the Soviet Union, borders in common with the People's Republic of China are hereby sealed. Any act of aggression on the part of the People's Republic of China shall be met with whatever force is considered appropriate by the government of the Soviet Union. Furthermore, the illegally held and occupied territory of Outer Mongolia by the People's Republic of China, shall be surrendered to its de jure and historical owners as a member of the Union of Soviet Socialist Republics. This shall be accomplished with all dispatch.

Point Four. As a sign of moderation and good faith, the Soviet Union will accept the retention of embassies, consulates, and legations of each country by the other. Recognizing the need for avenues of discourse to remain open, it is anticipated that the People's Republic of China will take those steps necessary to ensure that peaceful core operations and friendship can once more exist in a common struggle against imperialism.

The document was hand-delivered the following morning to the Chinese ambassador by Foreign Minister Mikoyan, accompanied by Colonel Zakharov. The ambassador read it, made no comment, and refused to be drawn into conversation on any subject.

A second topic of conversation during the same meeting concerned the upcoming general election in the United States. Though still six months away, candidates were beginning to make themselves heard. The KGB had supplied dossiers on all the contenders. Two had them concerned. The first, Attorney General Robert Kennedy; and second, the firebrand, fiercely anti-Soviet, senior senator from Arizona, Barry Goldwater. The Politburo's overwhelmingly favorite was the man presently in office, and his continuance was seen as a must. It was decided that should Barry Goldwater become the Republican nominee, then Soviet funds would quickly, but quietly, be channeled through legitimate organizations to totally discredit the man in the media. Goldwater must not become the next U. S. President.

On May 1, 1964, the world's news organizations covered the annual Moscow Victory May Day Parade. They were able to report that the twelve senior members of the Politburo were observed standing in their rightful places on the reviewing stand, a signal that all was well inside the Kremlin's walls. The parade was followed by a grandiose reception for the members of the diplomatic corps. All of those invited, attended—with the notable exception of the Chinese ambassador.

Two days later, Brezhnev and Kosygin retired for the weekend to the villa outside Moscow for relaxation and spring fishing. Colonel Zakharov was also invited.

By ten o'clock that Saturday morning, all three were dressed in rubber waders, their fishing poles at the ready as they gathered on the bank of a fast-moving stream. The water was ice-cold; the day crystal clear.

"Are you satisfied with the way events are shaping up?" Brezhnev asked Zakharov, as he cast his line into the roiling water.

"I am, but I'm also wary of the Chinese," Zakharov replied. "Their conduct has rightfully alarmed your comrades in the Politburo to the point that war may become the only option."

Brezhnev's brow momentarily furrowed. "That is a possibly, but I think not. The Chinese still respect our nuclear might, something very much in our favor. We have neither acted too hastily, nor too soon. And even if they manage to detonate a crude device, they still lack the ability to engineer a delivery system, so, for the foreseeable future we have the upper hand, and I intend to keep it that way. Within the next few months, we will make a show of posting at least thirty divisions on our border with China and hold that many more in reserve. No, Colonel, I am satisfied with the steps we have taken to date."

Kosygin weighed in. "Even Nikita has regained some semblance of sanity on the subject."

"I'm sure the fool suspects his days are numbered," Brezhnev answered, reeling in his line and rebaiting the hook. "We are as much to blame for his blunders because we allowed him free rein when we knew he was wrong. But, no matter now." He cast his line and continued. "Once we're sure President Johnson will be reelected, then we will make our move to oust Nikita, but I am worried by this Goldwater character. He's a loose cannon who could actually win, and that would torpedo all of our plans."

Kosygin was visibly aghast at the thought. He shook his head. "If we have to spend a fortune to paint Mr. Goldwater as a madman in the American press, then that's what we do. We must keep President Johnson right where he is and convince the Americans they need him too." His face softened. "Things will work out. We must be patient. Our labors will bear fruit."

"Agreed," said Brezhnev. "We have all worked too hard for what I have in mind, so yes, we shall do everything to make sure President Lyndon Johnson belongs to us."

CHAPTER 13
CHINA – 1964

By May 1, 1964, the nuclear research staff at Peking University and at Lop Nur, were on a round-the-clock schedule. Mao had informed them he wanted an atomic device exploded before the year was out. When told it would be impossible to detonate a bomb underground in so short a time, he informed the scientist he had no intention of detonating such a device underground: it was to be atmospheric. Mao wanted the world to know of China's entrance into the nuclear age.

The task was demanding. There was a constant back and forth of scientists between Peking and Lop Nur in the months that followed, and by the middle of August everything needed for the test at Lop Nur was ready; the tower on which to hang the bomb was ready; the block houses, and inspection stations were ready; everything was in place except the enriched uranium core. Sophisticated sensors and photographic equipment were installed, checked, and rechecked. Every day throughout September, dry runs were held, emergency procedures tested, so too, manual override systems in the event the electrical detonator failed. Decontamination scrubbers were inspected; nothing was left to chance.

On October 10, the enriched uranium core was delivered, and the target date was firmly set for the 16th, at five o'clock in the morning.

Mao gave the signal to go.

The American-trained physicist, Hsue-Shen Tsien, director of China's nuclear program, detonated the device from his bunker six miles from Ground Zero. For an instant, night turned into day. The ball of fire that followed was immense, whirling rapidly as it blossomed, soaring to a height of 40,000 feet. And through the periscope binoculars in the bunker, he saw the steel tower vaporize.

The maelstrom created by nature-gone-mad picked up boulders two miles from the blast site and tossed them through the air at velocities approaching the speed of sound. Then the shockwave hit. The bunker shook as a dog would worry a bone, but the massive steel springs on which it stood held the structure firmly intact, while those inside kept their eyes pressed to the periscopes. The winds slowly diminished, and the mushroom-shaped cloud began to dissipate, traveling ever eastward, ever higher.

China was now the fifth member of the prestigious nuclear club. She was a force to be recognized.

As premier, Chou En-lai had the task of directing various ministers in carrying out the will of the Chairman. Second only to the nuclear project, defense preparations for war were of prime importance, and he spent long hours in meetings with Defense Minister Marshal Lin Biao and the senior generals of the six military regions. China's internal security was being threatened on two fronts: the Soviets to the north and west; and the ever-increasing numbers of Americans to the south in Thailand, and Vietnam.

Reports from the borders adjoining the Soviet Union confirmed Chou's worst fears. Soviet military presence had intensified during the spring and summer months. Long-range Chinese reconnaissance flights brought back pictures of enemy mechanized units moving up to the border in large numbers, and the photographs revealed a feverish-paced construction of concrete fortifications and missile silos.

Radio monitors eavesdropping on the Soviet frequencies confirmed that the enemy was preparing for a protracted stay. Once they had a sizable force in the region, an attack across the border into China was considered a real possibility by the Chinese General Staff.

With August came more bad news. The Americans claimed two of their destroyers had been attacked by North Vietnamese motor torpedo boats in the Gulf of Tonkin in the early hours of August 2 and 4. The American Congress expressed outrage, and five days later a vote was passed giving President Johnson sweeping powers to deal with the attacks. Within hours, The Central People's Broadcasting Station told its listeners that a large force of American aircraft were spotted coming into the lower part of North Vietnam and attacking the port city of Vinh.

Even though China had no official access to the American diplomatic community, or vice-versa, for several years channels of communication were open on an unofficial basis for both countries in Warsaw. Messages had been passed by the Albanian government from one to the other, but in early 1963, President Kennedy had suddenly, and inexplicably, told the State Department to sever the contact. China was now totally adrift, and Mao had no way of knowing what official U. S. policy was to be in Asia.

CHAPTER 14
WASHINGTON D.C.
MARCH–NOVEMBER 1964

DURING THE MONTHS FOLLOWING President Kennedy's death, Johnson saw little of the attorney general, but knew Robert Kennedy was deeply depressed. The President never brought up China's culpability in his brother's assassination, and Kennedy never spoke of it either. Johnson realized that Robert Kennedy believed only he and his dead brother had been forewarned by Ambassador Dobrynin.

On June 11, 1964, Kennedy floored Johnson by requesting he be appointed ambassador to South Vietnam. He wrote that he saw this area of the world as representing the greatest problem to the United States and wanted to help in any way possible.

Dobrynin's words of a year earlier jumped to mind as he read the letter. *Carefully weigh any counsel Robert Kennedy offers you. Even though he would mean well, his mind will be filled with grief.*

What the hell is on his mind? Johnson asked himself. Saigon is little more than a stone's throw from Peking. *I've got to nix this idea and fast. I'll take care of the Chinese my way.*

On July 29, he turned down the request, and instead asked Kennedy to consider the UN ambassadorship. Kennedy declined, and a few days later announced he would seek New York senator Kenneth Keating's seat. A major crisis in-the-making had been narrowly averted.

Late in the evening of October 14, 1964, Radio Moscow announced to the world that Nikita S. Khrushchev had been replaced as First Secretary of the Communist Party by a man named Leonid Brezhnev. And someone named Aleksei Kosygin was now the Chairman of the Council of Ministers. Whether the deposed Khrushchev was dead or alive was anyone's guess.

When Johnson heard the news, his immediate thought was: *It's happening, just as Dobrynin had said it would.* And his next thought was: *I'm going to have to learn about this Brezhnev guy, and fast.*

CHAPTER 15

MOSCOW
1964-1967

ALMOST A YEAR HAD PASSED since President Kennedy's assassination, and Zakharov could feel the winds of change blowing in his face.

On October 8, 1964, while in conference with KGB Chairman Vladimir Semichastny, they were interrupted by a timid knock on the door. A lieutenant entered and handed Semichastny a note.

"Our troubles begin now in earnest," he said, passing the lone page to Zakharov. One of his most trusted agents was reporting that the Chinese had settled on a date to explode their first atomic bomb at Lop Nur. It was October 16, one week away.

Two hours later, Zakharov accompanied Semichastny while he gave the bad news to Brezhnev and Kosygin.

Brezhnev flew into a rage. "That's it!" he shouted, slamming both fists on the table.

"What's the date again?" asked a pale-faced Kosygin.

"The sixteenth, one week from today," Semichastny said.

"That's our new target date to do what we must, Leonid," said Kosygin.

"I don't understand . . . our new target date . . ." Semichastny's sentence trailed off.

Brezhnev answered. "Two days before that date arrives, Khrushchev will be gone, something that should not come as a surprise to you."

"Who else have you spoken to about this?" Semichastny asked Brezhnev, but his eyes were focused on Zakharov.

Zakharov read the look perfectly. *You are now fully involved in matters that could see you shot as a traitor if we fail.* Zakharov gave a slight nod, signally he understood.

"Other than Ambassador Dobrynin—and of course, Colonel Zakharov here, you are the first," Brezhnev answered. "Time now is of the essence. You know who in the Presidium cannot be forewarned, so they will learn the day Khrushchev goes, and not one moment sooner."

Semichastny cast his lot without hesitation. "You both can count on my full support. I have suspected for some months where events here and in Washington have been leading." It was his first reference to Kennedy's assassination. "Just tell me what you want of me, and I shall do it."

"Thank you, Vlad. There was never a doubt in our minds that we could not count on your support. We welcome your continued loyalty to the motherland."

"And you shall not regret your decision," Kosygin chimed in, then turned to Zakharov. "Colonel, what are your thoughts on all of this? Speak freely, you're among friends here."

"I'm worried about Foreign Minister Gromyko, and what his reaction will be."

Brezhnev waved a hand in the air as if shooing away a minor irritation. "I'll take care of Andrei. He understands the shifting fortunes of war; he will be with us." He swung back to Semichastny. "We plan to have three of us rule the Soviet Union as a *troika* going forward, so power will not be concentrated in one individual. Mr. Kosygin will become the new premier; I will function as Party Secretary; and Mr. Mikoyan will remain as head of state, which, as you know, is really only a ceremonial position."

"Will Secretary Khrushchev be shot?" Semichastny asked.

"*He will be disgraced,*" Brezhnev replied. "That senile old bastard poses no threat to us, whatsoever, so I see no need in wasting a bullet on him."

Brezhnev and Kosygin called for an emergency meeting of the Presidium. The time suggested was eight o'clock on the evening of the fourteenth. By then, nine members knew the purpose of the meeting; three did not. At two minutes to eight, an unsuspecting Nikita Khrushchev walked into a conference room on the first floor of the Kremlin and seated himself in his customary chair at the head of the oval table. He called the meeting to order.

"Comrades Brezhnev and Kosygin again have asked for this plenary meeting of the Presidium." He looked around. "I see we are all here, so let's begin."

Seated in a chair behind Brezhnev, Zakharov had an unobstructed view of Khrushchev and saw the wariness in his eyes. The Secretary was obviously still remembering their confrontation from a year earlier.

Brezhnev rose and faced Khrushchev. "We all know the Chinese intend to explode an atomic device at five a.m. two days from now. They are able to do so only because of the assistance given them by you over the objection of most of the members of the Presidium."

Khrushchev's face drained. A tic blossomed close to his left eye. He tried to speak, but no sound came out.

"You are no longer fit to govern," Brezhnev continued, "so, as of this moment, I am taking over the duties and responsibilities of First Secretary of the Party. Comrade Kosygin is to be the new Chairman of the Council of Ministers. As for you, you are no longer a member of the Presidium. In fact, you are nothing. You will return to your home under guard, and you will remain there. And if you so much as open your mouth, you will be shot." Brezhnev turned his back on the trembling figure, strode over to the heavy wooden doors and threw them open. "*OUT!*" he roared. "We have a long night ahead of us as we begin to repair the years of damage you have caused."

Khrushchev stumbled to his feet. He gave Brezhnev a wide berth as he staggered out of the room. Brezhnev slammed the doors on his departing back and returned to his seat.

"The first order of business is for Radio Moscow to announce to the world that a change of leadership has just taken place."

Zakharov immediately understood the reasoning behind Brezhnev's order. The sooner people knew of the change, the easier it would be to accept. And Khrushchev's supporters would be caught off guard, precisely what Brezhnev intended.

Gromyko was the first to comment. "Mr. Secretary," he began in his most formal voice, "permit me to introduce a line of discussion I see as being most urgent."

Brezhnev nodded his acknowledgment but said nothing.

"The imminent triumph by the Chinese is of such a magnitude that I'm sure Radio Peking will announce it within minutes. They can't keep it a secret because radioactive fallout will soon confirm what has happened."

"What are you proposing, Andrei? Please get to the point."

"What will be our response? Do we condemn; do we ignore?"

"Both," Brezhnev replied without hesitation. "We condemn them for spreading a poison that will last for thousands of years, and then we ignore them. We all know words mean nothing to the Chinese, but they do understand action. Well, action is what I propose we give them."

Eleven faces looked expectantly at the newly self-appointed first secretary.

"We will explode a nuclear device of our own—underground, of course because the Soviet Union always honors her treaty obligations," he added the last with a mirthless grin. "I'm thinking of an explosion of such a size that it will shake the very foundation of China. I want our message to be loud enough for Chairman Mao to heed its warning."

Brezhnev, Kosygin, and Semichastny continued to stare at the screen, each lost in his own thoughts. The day was January 5, 1967. Almost three years had passed since China had exploded its atomic bomb, and they were in Brezhnev's opulent Kremlin office.

The sound of film slapping against the freewheeling reel brought Zakharov to his senses. He shut off the machine and switched on the lights. "As you can see, gentlemen, the film is perfect. This is the only copy; the original is still locked in a vault. I would like to play it again for you, but this time I will stop and start the film and translate into Russian what both men are saying. It will give you a better feel for what actually took place in Washington a little over three years ago."

"We're ready," replied Brezhnev, lighting up a filtered Novost cigarette made from American tobacco delivered to him directly from Virginia.

The first image they saw was of two chairs on either side of a table holding a bottle of Remy Martin brandy, and two crystal snifters. An off-camera voice could be heard quite clearly. Zakharov stopped the projector, translated, then started it again. Two pairs of legs morphed into complete bodies: one belonging to Lyndon Johnson, the other to Anatoly Dobrynin.

For the next 20 minutes, Zakharov started and stopped the projector, translating everything, and even adding extra commentary where he deemed necessary. At the end, he rewound the reel, should they want to see it again.

Brezhnev brought both hands together in a loud clap. "Anatoly should be given an American Oscar! His performance was brilliant! And to think this masterpiece has been hidden in a vault for the past three years." He glanced out the window at a raging winter storm and laughed. "Nothing beats seeing a wonderful moving picture show on a snowy day."

Zakharov knew they all had reason to feel so elated. Things were going swimmingly. Everything they had spent so much time and effort implementing over the past thirty months was falling neatly into place.

"Gentlemen, let's be serious for a moment." Brezhnev said, looking at Zakharov. "How long will it take you to do what we know needs to be done to this film?"

"Mr. Secretary, this is one job I do not want to rush. I will have to gather together our most skillful technicians. In fact, I suggest we have Ambassador Dobrynin return home to help us. We are going to have to review this film frame-by-frame and cut out or rearrange those parts that are not to our liking. With Mr. Dobrynin here, we will be able to dub in replacement words as needed. I'm no expert, but I do know that the finished product must be perfect. It is essential that no one will ever be able to disprove its authenticity." Zakharov gave a quirky head bobble, then added, "I think I can have it done by the end of February."

"That's about eight weeks," mused Kosygin. "I shall have Ambassador Dobrynin here when the time comes because you are right: perfection is what we are looking for. Absolute, flawless, perfection," he said, his redundancy deliberate. "Use whatever people you need to get the job done right. Money will be no object."

"Of course, sir," Zakharov replied as he gathered up the reel and put it in its metal case. "If there is nothing further you need of me, gentlemen, I shall get started."

"Stop. There is one last piece of business, Colonel Zakharov," said Brezhnev, walking to his desk and picking up a small box. He turned to Zakharov and beckoned him over.

"My spies tell me that today is your birthday. They do tell the truth, da?"

"Unfortunately, yes. Birthdays are not what we like to be reminded of, especially those after forty."

"And which one is this, or is that a military secret?" Kosygin chimed in.

"Number forty-eight, Mr. Premier . . . I think," Zakharov added after a long pause and with an insincere look plastered all over his face.

The other three laughed.

"Maybe this will help brighten up such a gloomy day," said Brezhnev, placing the box in Zakharov's hands. "Open it, open it," he commanded with mock severity.

Peering inside, Zakharov did a double-take. Lying on a bed of red velvet were the shoulder board insignia of a KGB major general. He continued to stare.

"Could it be that birthdays are not so bad after all, eh?" Brezhnev asked. "With age comes recognition. A well-deserved recognition I might add, in your case, Alexei." He turned to Semichastny. "Chairman, please help your new First Deputy Chairman into his proper uniform."

"With pleasure." Semichastny removed the colonel's insignia from Zakharov's tunic and attached the new rank. He offered his hand. "Congratulations, *General,* and happy birthday."

Brezhnev and Kosygin followed suit, then Brezhnev said, "I don't know if you heard me or not a minute ago, or if it even sunk in, but you are now a new Deputy First Chairman of the KGB." He held up his hand. "No speech is necessary: you've earned it."

"Thank you." Zakharov solemnly saluted and left to let his wife know she was now married to a general.

That night, lying in bed and too restless to sleep, Zakharov's thoughts harkened back over the past three years.

Brezhnev had acted decisively on the foreign front. He personally supervised the military buildup on the Sino-Soviet border, reserving the right to have the final say as to what divisions would be deployed. He ordered an immediate expansion of the intercontinental missile program and began building hard silos to match those of the new American Minuteman missile.

And then there was Vietnam. The Soviet plan called for Vietnam to be the catalyst for America's downfall, and no effort would be spared to attain this goal. Brezhnev had rightly reasoned Johnson would commit to saving that nothing-of-a-nowhere-country from communist control regardless of cost, and his gamble was beginning to show promise. Much to Brezhnev's delight, there was no doubt Johnson saw the emergent struggle as being Chinese inspired. China was sending vast quantities of aid to its ally, and the strain on her nascent economy was showing. Peking was hard-pressed to maintain and equip a large army on her border with the Soviet Union, while at the same time helping Hanoi. But Brezhnev had no intention of being overshadowed by Chinese dominance in the region, so Soviet aid was also pouring into North Vietnam, especially with the new and deadly surface-to-air missiles. East European vessels clogged the harbor at Haiphong, offloading supplies around the clock. There were times when ships had to lie at anchor for two weeks before dock crews could empty their holds.

In early 1965, Brezhnev sent Kosygin to Hanoi to re-pledge support to Ho Chi Minh in his struggle against imperial aggression. The visit was meant to undermine Chinese influence. Ho Chi Minh told Kosygin that he would gratefully accept aid from any quarter, be it Soviet or Chinese, simply because his back was against the wall. The Soviet response was to send even more, in the hope of winning Ho Chi Minh firmly over to their camp. Brezhnev was pleased. America was now entrenched in a land war in Asia.

Another area of keen Soviet interest was America itself. Beginning in late 1964, the KGB's Department of Disinformation began earmarking substantial sums for Black American radicals. City after city was being torched by their followers, while on the college campuses, students were beginning to demonstrate against America's involvement in the war half a world away. By 1967, it was apparent that the first signs of collapse were beginning to show. The mighty American giant was beginning to falter. The end was in sight.

The last thing Zakharov remembered that early morning of January 6, 1967, was a distant clock striking four.

★　　★　　★

On March 10, 1967, Zakharov and several others, including Ambassador Dobrynin, were gathered in Brezhnev's office for the very first viewing of the now-altered embassy film.

Dobrynin shook his head in amazement at the finish. "If I hadn't been there, I would insist that what I've just seen is indeed what actually took place. It's absolutely incredible."

"Should the need arise, you will swear to the world that what you just saw did take place because the camera never lies, Anatoly," Kosygin said, in a rare display of humor.

"Oh, I will, I will!"

"And the experts," interrupted KGB Chairman Semichastny, looking directly at Zakharov, "do they feel it will pass muster, even under the most intense scrutiny?"

"They assure me it will, sir," replied a supremely confident Zakharov. "The entire conversation and the lip synchronization of both men is the very definition of perfection. The technicians employed a new American technique called voiceprinting. It tests voices spectrographically, looking for unique commonalities in a person's speaking characteristics and natural cadence. My experts insist this film will be accepted as authentic by even the most skeptical scientists."

"How many copies are there?" Brezhnev asked.

"The master, and this copy. Everything else was burned. The master is in a special vault. This one will be burned as soon as we're finished here."

"The people who worked on this project, you will vouch for their discretion?"

"They were handpicked by me," Zakharov replied.

Brezhnev heaved himself out of his chair. "Should the day ever come that I have to use this film, there's no question it will get everybody's attention."

CHAPTER 16
MOSCOW – 1967

THE SOVIETS NEVER UNDERESTIMATED the strategic value of the Middle East. For years they found it all but impossible to establish any significant presence in the area, but by the nineteen-sixties that all changed. President Nasser of Egypt opened the door by accepting Soviet help in the building of the Great Aswan High Dam. When completed, it would allow water, more precious than gold, to flow into the Nile Valley, and open up hundreds of thousands of parched acres to the plow. America had started the project, but as tensions between Egypt and the United States grew, it announced an end to the aid. But the Soviets, never ones to miss an opportunity, stepped in and filled the void. Technicians and engineers poured into the country and were soon followed by political cadres and the inevitable military advisors. By 1965, Egypt was for all intents and purposes a Soviet satellite despite Nasser's claim he was a fence-sitting neutral. The Soviets' next step was to ingratiate themselves to the surrounding Arab countries; their endgame: to eradicate all vestiges of U.S. influence in the area.

The ever-present thorn in the side of the Arab States was Israel. Their hatred of the Jews had already exploded into war in 1956, and the possibility of another was becoming very real. The Soviets initiated a skillfully orchestrated campaign to discredit Israel as nothing more than a puppet of the United States.

The plan was simple: arm the Arabs, continually harangue the leadership into a state of frenzy, then unleash them on the Zionists at the right moment. Zakharov was skeptical of this approach but said little because it was not within his area of interest.

Not so for Brezhnev or Kosygin. They were paying close attention for two important reasons: Oil and access to the Indian Ocean via the Suez Canal. The Soviets needed warm-water ports on the Mediterranean Sea for their capital ships. The United States Sixth Fleet headquartered at Naples, Italy, and operating in the Med and the Black Sea, was the undisputed master, but Brezhnev and Kosygin intended to challenge that dominance.

By early May 1967, the time to act had come. All the intelligence reports streaming back to the Kremlin from the "advisors" in the area confirmed this. For months, the Soviets had been spreading rumors that Israel was preparing a preemptive strike against Egypt and Syria, so much so, that the leaders of both countries were convinced it was true. On May 16, President Nasser of Egypt demanded all U.N. troops be removed from the Sinai. U-Thant, the Secretary-General of the United Nations, did Nasser's bidding, which frankly surprised the Soviets as much as anyone else. An emboldened Nasser raised the stakes even higher by declaring Israel would no longer have access to the Gulf of Aqaba. The fuse had been lit.

On the morning of June 3, Brezhnev, Kosygin, their military commanders, and Middle East experts, met in the Kremlin's War Room, the Soviet counterpart to the American Situation Room in the basement of the Pentagon. The walls were lined with largescale maps of the world, pinpointing the disposition of various Soviet troops, planes, and ships.

A vice admiral opened the meeting by detailing the location of the many ships of the American fleet in the Mediterranean. The number of U.S. Air Force bombers and fighters was also noted, as was the size of other NATO forces. He next showed the whereabouts of Soviet ships and explained that four wings of long-range Bear and Badger bombers were on alert at Soviet airfields only a few miles from the Turkish and Iranian borders.

He was followed at the lectern by an army general who briefed on the state of preparedness in Egypt, Syria, and other Arab countries in the immediate vicinity. He pointed out where the majority of the Soviet technicians were located, paying special attention to those in the Sinai Peninsula.

The next speaker was a civilian who gave an assessment of the strength of the Israeli army and air force. He ended on an upbeat note: Israel was hopelessly outnumbered.

"Well, there we have it, gentlemen," Brezhnev said. "The big question is this: What will America's reaction be once Israel is attacked?"

Defense Minister Marshal Grechko stood to reply. "Mr. Secretary, I confidently predict that before America has time to react, it will be over. Egypt and Syria together can smash all Jewish resistance in a matter of hours." His tone suggested that the very thought of any other outcome bordered on the absurd.

"I agree with the Marshal," said Kosygin. "It will be over before America can do anything. President Johnson is too preoccupied with one war in Asia to even think of joining another. No, the Americans will cry foul at the United Nations, but it will be for naught. The Jews do not exactly have many friends to call on for help." His face turned dark. "The sooner they are eliminated for once and for all, the better for everybody."

Brezhnev asked each man in turn for his appraisal of the situation. All agreed with Grechko and Kosygin.

"So be it," said Brezhnev. "The consensus is to strike, so the next question is, when?"

"This Saturday, the tenth," Defense Minister Grechko replied without hesitation. "Strike on their Sabbath. The Japanese taught the world the value of hitting on a holy day."

Nods of approval greeted his proposal.

Brezhnev looked at Grechko. "Give the necessary orders. I want this thing over fast. Also, we will all reconvene at midnight, Cairo time, on the ninth. And gentlemen, come prepared to enjoy a victory celebration luncheon at noon."

★   ★   ★

MAY 9, 1972

Zakharov stubbed out his cigarette. "But, as you know, Mr. St. James, events did not turn out as planned. Not by a longshot. The Israelis caught us all flatfooted with a preemptive air strike against Egypt and Syria in the early hours of June 5. They concentrated their attack on the wholesale annihilation of their enemies' air forces while their planes were still on the ground. Within hours, Israel controlled the skies over the entire Middle East. Then Israel moved its armor out from the confines of its borders, smashed into the Sinai and drove the Egyptian Army back to the Suez. And because they were taken so completely by surprise, thousands threw down their weapons and scurried to the safety of the west bank of the canal, leaving untold millions of dollars' worth of Soviet equipment in the desert. It was the same story on the Syrian Front. It took the Israelis only ninety-six hours to achieve total victory."

★   ★   ★

JUNE 1967

Brezhnev first heard the news from Kosygin who happened to be in the war room when the direct link to Cairo was activated by the senior Soviet adviser telling of the nightmare taking place. By chance, Zakharov was also there when the bad news came in.

"Leonid, come to the war room at once," Kosygin shouted into the mouthpiece. "All hell has broken out in Cairo!" He slammed the phone down before Brezhnev had a chance to say a word.

None could believe the reports coming in. The Israelis had destroyed the Arab air forces on the ground. *It was impossible! That just could not be happening!* But it was. There was no way for the Soviets to assess the situation, and it would take days to find out just how badly things had gone.

Brezhnev trembled with anger as Marshal Grechko started to speak.

"*Shut your mouth, you senile bastard,*" he screamed. "You say another word, and I'll have you shot on the spot." Brezhnev paced like a caged animal, running his hands through his hair, all the while trying to regain his composure. He stopped and wheeled to face Kosygin.

"Those brainless idiots have destroyed everything! The Jews should kill them all! They deserve it. Cowards, every last damn one of them. Alexei, we must cut our losses, and fast. Activate the hotline to President Johnson. Tell him that the United States must exert its influence to get the Jews to stop. Tell him we will bring equal pressure to bear on the Arabs. Ha," he laughed mercilessly, "we will try to stop more Arabs from getting their asses shot off as they run for home. Shit! We've got to find a way to salvage what we can from this mess."

The United States and the Soviets began working around the clock for a cease-fire. The Soviets demanded a complete withdrawal of Israeli forces to back inside its borders, but their demands fell on deaf ears. On June 10, the Israelis declared they had accomplished their objectives. A cease-fire was agreed to by all parties.

For days after the debacle in the desert, the Soviets were feverishly assessing the damage. The losses were staggering. Months, maybe years, would be needed to resupply the Arabs. The prestige lost in that part of the world was incalculable. Kosygin suggested he make an emergency visit to the United Nations in New York under the guise of trying to craft a permanent settlement for the still-highly explosive situation.

"I also think it is time for me to meet face-to-face with President Johnson," he told Brezhnev. "This will turn out far worse than the

Cuba fiasco, unless we get on top of it right away. Khrushchev must be laughing himself silly at the mess we've gotten ourselves into."

A glum faced Brezhnev nodded. "No doubt Mr. Johnson feels on top of the world at this moment. He might even be filled with a sense of false courage, which means you must take the initiative from the start."

Zakharov could see the wheels turning in Brezhnev's head, as he added, "Have Ambassador Dobrynin inform the President that you would be amicable to a meeting, but not in Washington. And under no circumstances must it appear that we are crawling on our bellies. Stay in New York; insist you meet on neutral ground."

"Neutral ground, yes, that's perfect. I'll have Anatoly tell him that. A meeting of two concerned leaders. It should work."

But Brezhnev wasn't finished. "This next part is the most important, so listen carefully, Alexei. You must insist on at least one private meeting alone; just the two of you, and your Russian interpreter. No American interpreter can be present. This is something you must insist on," he repeated. "Mr. Johnson is going to harangue you about our aid to North Vietnam. He's losing a lot of planes to our missiles, so he will definitely bring up the subject. He will shout that we are not helping find a solution to the problem. You will tell him we are trying our best to work towards a lasting peace in Southeast Asia, but like America, we too, have commitments to our allies. Make the President understand that as long as we control the flow of missiles to Hanoi, we can contain China. If we desert our ally, Peking will fill the void, and the war will escalate overnight. Make him believe that it is only because of our presence China is being kept in line."

"I could begin the meeting by telling him I have a peace offer from Ho Chi Minh. That would catch him off guard," said Kosygin.

"Possibly, but I would not count on it. He feels he can at least deal with us on an equal footing, but China is still the great unknown. Mr. Johnson is convinced China is the villain he must deal with, thanks to Anatoly. You could tell him our intelligence sources suspect Chinese subversion to be behind a lot of the trouble in the Black American cities. You know the line."

"But we must look at the other side, too," Kosygin countered. "He could well come to me with a feeling of self-righteousness. This debacle in the Middle East has obviously made the Americans reassess their attitude towards us. He could surprise me completely. He could even say he now believes China is not the cause of his troubles, but it's fifteen Soviet Republics that are his true nemeses. He could go so far as saying he no longer believes the Chinese killed Kennedy, but that it was all orchestrated by the Kremlin. What then?"

Brezhnev looked directly at Zakharov, who had been following the exchange but saying nothing, as no one had asked for his opinion. With eyes firmly glued to Zakharov's, he said, "If it comes to that, then all else has failed, and you bring up the film. Let him know that if he tries to make an issue out of our involvement in the Middle East, then we will release the film to the world. How will he look conspiring with Ambassador Dobrynin to kill President Kennedy so he can ascend to the throne? Then cutting a devil's deal with us to contain China and attack them together when the time is ripe? Anyone seeing such a film would believe it, simply because subsequent events proved it to be true. *President Kennedy was killed, and in Texas no less*! Johnson became President of The United States, and soon thereafter sent hundreds of thousands of Americans off to fight a war on China's doorstep, while we sent many divisions of troops to our border with China. No, my friend, Mr. Johnson would see himself boxed into a corner. The American Congress would most assuredly impeach him within hours, remove him from office, and then arrest him for treason. He could even be shot. No, Mr. Johnson will do our bidding."

Kosygin let out a long sigh. "I hope you're right, Leonid. All I need to do is describe the embassy room where he and Anatoly met, and he would know this is not an idle threat. No, you are right. That is how I will handle it if he leaves me no choice."

Ambassador Anatoly Dobrynin relayed a formal request to the State Department on June 17, asking for a meeting between the two leaders. The White House responded immediately. Yes, President Johnson would meet with the Premier. Washington was ruled out as a meeting site, as was New York. The tension of the past few weeks had made the city jumpy, and adequate security would be hard to provide. The small college town of South Glassboro, New Jersey, was suggested by the President and agreed to by the Premier. They would meet on June 23 and 24, and possibly into June 25 if the need for an extra day became necessary.

Moscow was prepared for any eventuality.

CHAPTER 17
CHINA – 1967

CHOU EN-LAI WAS THE FIRST to hint at the possibility China was the victim of a United States and Soviet conspiracy. He floated the idea during a meeting between Mao and various ministers of the government in September 1966, at the Imperial Palace in Peking.

"*There are none so blind as those who will not see,*" Chou began, catching his audience by surprise.

"What did you just say?" asked a quizzical Mao. "Who is blind?"

"Us," replied Chou.

"Blind?" parried Defense Minister Lin Biao, his face reddening in anger, taking the remark as a personal attack on his capabilities. "Who is so blind they cannot see the Soviets by the hundreds of thousands perched on our borders like so many vultures? Who is so blind they cannot see the Americans trying to establish another state for their union in South Vietnam? And even if we were blind, we would still smell them!"

"What I'm saying is we have not correlated the two events. We have not looked for the possibility there exists a common thread."

"Elaborate. What are you are driving at?" asked Mao.

"Our troubles with the Soviets began about the time the Americans began taking an active position in Vietnam. So I ask: Are these two events just coincidental, or did they occur with a purpose? What has happened? Well, I will tell you," he said, answering his own question. "China is surrounded by enemies: Soviet and American enemies. Each has found a reason for placing hundreds of thousands of troops on our doorstep, and we now find ourselves caught in the classic pincer with our backs to the sea." He rose and made his way over to a large, three-dimensional relief map hanging on the wall. He drew an imaginary circle around the outline of China with stiffened forefingers, then slowly brought his hands closer and closer together to form an ever-shrinking vise until his fingers were tightly entwined. A vivid picture of a crushed and battered China became visible to each man present. It was a sobering sight.

"You make it sound like we are already defeated," said Lin Biao. "Do you have any suggestions how we stop this?"

"Remember, Comrade, this is only a theory. I have no concrete evidence to back up what I've just said. I'm postulating, nothing more."

"It makes frightening good sense to me," said Foreign Minister Marshal Chen Yi, speaking up for the first time.

"It is a frightening prospect," agreed Chou, but before he could continue, Mao interrupted.

"That expresses my sentiment too. The signs are all there to support your hypothesis, so now we must prove it. Do you have any suggestions as to how we do that?"

"We need hard facts," said Chou, "and until we have facts, we cannot prepare for any eventuality. My suggestion is we make this a priority item for our intelligence agents around the world. We must ferret out hard evidence of an American and Soviet pact to destroy us. Our agents in America, and in the Soviet Union must be informed immediately, but so too must our agents elsewhere. What we are looking for could well be found in the most unlikely of places. The search must be thorough: China's continued well-being depends on it."

"Then we start today," said the Chairman, rising from his seat, a signal the meeting was over, "and you will take personal charge, my friend," he said to the Premier. "Report back every few days, even if you have nothing."

Later that day, Chou En-lai met with Kang Sheng, the head of China's Intelligence Ministry. He outlined the task, explaining what he was looking for: Hard proof that the Americans and Soviets were in a conspiracy to destroy China. Chou ended with a tongue-in-cheek, "I present you with a simple problem, yes?"

Kang exhaled slowly, the sound mimicking a whistle. "The problem is indeed a simple one, comrade; it's the solution that will prove most difficult because we don't have a clue what we're looking for. Maybe it will be found in a secondhand rumor, or a whisper here, or a different whisper there, perhaps? Yet, we somehow must have the ability to instantly recognize it, even though we have no idea in which haystack to search."

"Am I hearing a bugle sounding retreat before you even begin to charge?" Chou asked, suggesting to Kang he was not up to the task.

Kang's face broke out into a huge grin, and he brought both hands together in a resounding clap. "This is just the kind of challenge I've been itching for! If there is proof to be found of what you suspect, then I shall find it. Maybe it will take time, Comrade Premier, but you shall have the proof you need, I promise." It was a statement from a man supremely confident in his ability to meet any difficulty head on.

Three months later, in December, Kang's hopes were raised, then just as quickly, dashed. An agent in Honolulu had reported he was onto something. Kang immediately arranged to fly the man to Hong Kong where he would personally interview him. However, as fate would have it, the agent was killed en route to the airport by a drunken soldier on a motorcycle. "There was no suspicion of foul play, it was one of those things that happen at the most inopportune time," he told Chou En-lai. The Premier took the news in stride and encouraged his intelligence minister to keep to the task.

The new year came and still nothing. By early February, 1967, his spies had run down three leads that seemed to hold promise, but none bore fruit. Then, on the first day of April, a priority-coded cable came to Kang from the Chinese Embassy in Albania, the only European country that had remained a steadfast friend since the nineteen-fifties. And despite the difficulties with an ever-struggling economy at home, China had still found the means to annually send thousands of tons of grain, and other financial aid to Europe's poorest country. It was their only toehold on the continent, and from their embassy in the capital of Tirana, they funneled spies out to the other nations.

The message to Kang spoke of a film that was absolutely stunning in its content. Because the resident agent believed the footage to be priceless, he was sending it back to China by a diplomatic courier who would be accompanied by two guards. They would arrive in Peking within twenty-four hours.

Kang met the courier at the airport at two a.m. on the morning of April 3, 1967. Also present was Chou En-lai, whom he had informed immediately upon receipt of the cable. They already had a projector and screen ready in a meeting room in the airport terminal. Within minutes, the machine was threaded, and the film jumped to life on the small screen. Both Chou and Kang were reasonably fluent in Russian and English, and while they did not have need of the former, the latter was necessary to understand what they were seeing. The film lasted six minutes. They played it again. There was no mistake. This was the proof they had been seeking for more than half a year.

Chou's face was ashen when the projector was turned off. His theory was right. The Americans and Soviets had indeed entered into a covert pact to destroy China. What stunned him the most was the understanding had been reached over three years earlier. The film had just shown the then-Vice President of the United States, Lyndon Johnson, plotting with Soviet Ambassador Anatoly Dobrynin to kill President Kennedy so that Johnson would become President, while placing blame for the assassination squarely at China's doorstep. And once Johnson had indeed ascended to the Presidency, the two Superpowers would divide the world into separate spheres of influence, while at the same time collaborate to destroy their common archenemy, namely China.

The Premier finally found his voice. "This must be shown to the Chairman immediately. I told him of its possible existence and said I would view it upon its arrival in Peking." He shook his head as if to expunge the horror from his mind. "This is everything our agent in Albania told us it was. Now, the important questions are: how did we acquire this film; and second, is it legitimate? After we show it to the Chairman, can you run tests to see if it's a forgery?"

I'll get our experts on it right away, Premier. We should have an answer for you shortly. My personal feeling is it's genuine, but that's just a guess."

An hour and a half later, they had viewed the film three more times with the Chairman, and after several long minutes of silence, Mao addressed Kang. "I must know as soon as possible if this is legitimate. I cannot begin to make any decision until that question has been answered."

"I understand."

"Now, my mind is naturally suspicious," Mao continued. "Could we have been given a counterfeit by the Soviets, for some purpose we have not divined? But more importantly: I have to know exactly how we got our hands on this damning piece of evidence."

"That's a question I cannot answer, Comrade Chairman, but the same thought is uppermost in my mind. No report accompanied the film from Albania, but the agent who delivered it to our Embassy is still there. If it proves to be legitimate, security surrounding its very existence must have been intense, so, like you, I am curious as to how we obtained it. And if it is a copy, then how many others exist? There are many unanswered questions, Comrade Chairman, but I shall get you the right answers."

Mao stifled a yawn as he glanced at his watch. "It's almost four-thirty. I suggest we all retire and start fresh in the morning. You have lived up to my expectations of your capabilities, Comrade Kang. You will be well rewarded."

Several days later, Kang received two reports. The first was from the specialists who had analyzed the film. Their findings suggested it was a duplicate copy of an original, and they believed the footage had not been tampered with. There was no indication it had been spliced, edited, or altered. Their professional opinion was the six minute film was all it appeared to be.

The second summary was a detailed summary of how the film found its way into the hands of Chinese Intelligence.

Kang began to read. *On February 28, 1967, a Soviet film technician by the name of . . .*

CHAPTER 18
MOSCOW AND CHINA – 1967

Vasili Kerensky had just finished washing his hands which were wrinkled like prunes from the photographic hardening solution he had been working with for the past hour. He had been developing a series of 8 x 10 glossy prints his supervisor needed before five o'clock. He looked down at the pile collecting in the basket below the polished heating drum used to dry them. "Skinny, ugly witches," he said out loud, as he picked up the prints and began stacking them. They were personal pictures taken by his boss at a party last night to celebrate his wife's birthday. "I should show them to the major," he continued, "using government film, government paper, government employees to process this crap. I ought to turn you in," but knew he would not. Vasili picked up the stack, placed it in a large manila envelope, walked out of the lab and into the supervisor's office.

After spending a few minutes patiently listening to the old fool confide in him how important these pictures were, and how pleased the ladies would be to each get a photo, blah, blah, blah, he was relieved when the supervisor changed the subject.

"Vasili, I've been told there's an important project coming soon for us to handle, and General Zakharov wants only the top people working on it. All I know for now is it involves some 16mm color

■ *131* ■

film footage of a meeting that took place in America, something very important and top secret, so I'll want you to do the developing and any copying. How does your workload look for the next few days?"

"Nothing important. I've been making copies of some of our "educational" films to be sent abroad. You know, the usual dreck."

The educational films were propaganda pieces the Department of Disinformation continually exported to trade fairs, the foreign press, and the likes, showcasing how wonderful life was in the Soviet Union. Scenes of wheat harvests in Ukraine; stories of factory workers happily producing quantities of consumer goods, such as television sets and washing machines; footage of Soviet scientists making breakthrough discoveries in the field of medicine. The supply was endless.

"Yes, well, I'll need you for this special project. Now go home, you've done a good job."

Vasili left. A few minutes later, while on a tram moving slowly in a light snowfall, he remembered he was supposed to meet his friend Admir at the Red October Bar around the corner from his apartment. Admir had said six o'clock, but looking at his watch, he knew he'd be late. Admir would wait.

He had first met Admir a little over a year ago, and they had continued to meet off and on since. Admir had listened to Vasili on too many occasions telling how life was passing him by, how he should be a movie director and not just a menial lab technician. He was an artist, and his talents were being ignored by his superiors. Time and again, he had requested to be sent to special schools to improve himself, but they kept telling him to be patient, not to push things. Shit! He was thirty years old; time was running out. If he did not do something soon, he would die an old man in that photo lab.

Admir sympathized with his plight, and promised to intercede, but was quick to point out that such things took time. He said he worked in a local *Tass News Agency* office and knew some pretty influential people who could help when the time was right. Well, he was getting tired of Admir's promises, and his not delivering.

He thought back to the meeting with Admir when everything changed.

One evening, Admir asked him for quality photos of St. Basile's Cathedral in the Kremlin. "I need them for a story I'm doing, and the pictures we have in our files are pathetic. I need some sharp color prints. It's important to me, Vasili, I'll even pay you fifty rubles for them."

Vasili had laughed at the proposition. "St. Basil's Cathedral?" he scoffed. "You can get good pictures anywhere for nothing. Don't waste your money."

"You won't do it?"

"I'm just saying you don't need me to steal copies from our lab files for you."

"Very well," said Admir, sounding hurt. "I ask a small favor from a friend, and he won't help." He shook his head slowly in disbelief.

"Look, if it means so much to you, I'll get them. But you'd better not tell where you got them if you're asked. That's all I'm saying."

A week later he gave Admir the prints, and he got his fifty rubles in return. It was like stealing sweets from a baby. The next time they met, Admir was full of thanks. His story had been accepted by some magazine or another, and the pictures were to be printed, too. He would surely get a raise and promotion if he continued his good work.

Over the next few months he had supplied Admir with other photos. Once, it had been several shots of a prototype tractor and other farm equipment, and later, a set of black and white glossy photos of the May Day Parade. Then, two months ago, he asked for a single picture of a new surface-to-air missile, and Vasili refused. But when Admir promised him five hundred rubles, he convinced himself it was really no big deal. The missile had been shown at last year's parade, had it not? Yes, it had been hidden under a tarpaulin, but still, it had been shown in public. It took Vasili a nervous two weeks to get the picture, and true to his word, Admir gave him the money. It was then Admir mentioned there was a very good chance he could help Vasili soon get a transfer from the lab into a specialized moviemaking unit.

"I know what it means to you," Admir said. "I'm going to help, to show my thanks for what you've done for me. I mean it, Vasili, I really do. Maybe you will have to leave Moscow to realize your full potential. Maybe school first, and then move to Poland."

Now, they were to meet, have a couple of drinks, and see what Admir had been doing for him.

When Vasili entered the bar, he was hit by a blast of hot, stale air. The place was dingy and packed with college students. Three bartenders were in constant motion, filling orders and making them-selves heard over the babble of voices and laughter. Pushing and shoving, he spotted Admir.

Finished with his second vodka and after telling Admir of the crap he'd been doing all afternoon including about a special project he was going to have to work on in addition to his regular work, he stood and looked around for a waitress.

Admir's antennae went up. "What kind of special project?"

Vasili looked down. "Hell, I don't know. My illustrious supervisor said we had some important film coming from America that needed to be processed, and duplicates made." He sat, unable to catch the eye of a server.

"Well find out," said Admir, his tone harsh, immediately realizing his mistake and regretting it. "I didn't mean that," he added with a smile. He leaned close. "Look, I'm excited. I've been talking to a friend who approves internal passports for people to study in other Soviet countries, and I told him how you want to study film directing in Poland. I know, I know," he said, holding up his hand, "you never really said anything about Poland, but it's a chance to learn what you need to know. Believe me, if anyone can do it, this guy can, and I've convinced him you should be selected. Plus, he owes me a favor or two. I'll be able to tell you a date soon, then all you have to do is submit your application, and it will be approved. That's my promise to you, my friend."

Vasili was stunned. It was going to happen. The break he had been waiting so long for. It was fantastic!

"Well, there you have it," said Admir "I told you I had influential friends— eh?"

Vasili caught the attention of a waitress and signaled for two more. His face was flushed with alcohol and excitement.

"Now, Vasili, I want you to do me a favor," Admir was saying. "This film from America, find out what it's about. It's important to me."

Vasili shrugged, his mind filled with thoughts of Poland and school. "Sure, I'll find out," he said absently.

"Listen carefully, my good friend. I must know as soon as possible. I will come here every night at six and stay until seven. When you know what it is, tell me. The sooner the better. Will you do that for me?"

"Sure. Of course I will."

Two days later, he met Admir at the bar.

"It's a pretty important film, from what I'm hearing," he began, as he finished downing his drink and ordering a second. "It's something about a meeting with the American President, and our ambassador. I overheard the General talking to the supervisor about it."

Admir could barely contain his excitement, but he kept his voice calm, betraying nothing.

"Hmm," he said, as if to himself. "I wonder if there's a story there?" He was silent for several seconds, then, "Vasili, what would be the chance of getting a copy of that film?"

Vasili jerked upright, as if shot from a cannon. "Are you mad, or just drunk? That footage will be so closely guarded nobody could steal a copy. Whenever we work on special projects, we are searched thoroughly before going home every night. Extra precautions are taken to destroy work-copy filmstrips, cuttings, prints, and whatever garbage we produce is incinerated immediately. There's no way of me walking out of there with a copy of the film, so don't even ask."

"Meet me here tomorrow at the same time," said Admir, and before Vasili could refuse, Admir got up and left, leaving some rubles on the table to pay for the drinks.

☆　　☆　　☆

An hour later, Admir met with another man in a grubby apartment three miles away. Both were agents of the Red Chinese government, and they spent the better part of the night working out a plan to get a copy of the still-unknown film from the KGB photographic lab inside the Kremlin. Just before dawn they found their answer.

That night, Admir again met Vasili at the bar.

"Tell me, what will you be doing with this film?" He began.

"I'll make copies of it," Vasili replied. "If they tell me to make two copies, I'll make two copies."

"Then I want you to make three."

"Oh sure, and I'll just carry it out under my hat, right? Shit, I'd be shot."

"No, no, listen. You've told me you make tons of copies of educational films that get shipped off to all sorts of different places, right?"

"Yeah, right."

"Trade fairs, foreign governments, universities, and the like?"

"Yes, I've said so a thousand times."

"Can you give me a list of the ones you are working on now and where they are going?

"I guess so," replied Vasili, somewhat cautiously.

"Here's what I want you to do. Tell me when you'll be working on the American film. If it's not for another week, or even two weeks, don't meet me until you're sure of the exact day you will be making the copies. Also, tell me what other films you're working on, and where they're going. Can you do that? I will still be here every night at this time, but you only come when you know the day you'll be reproducing the film."

Vasili nodded, but it was painfully obvious he did not like the idea. His was the face of a man knowing he was getting into something way over his head.

"Listen, my good friend," said Admir, sounding paternalistic, "there is no cause for alarm, you have my word. Now, I have some good news for you. Very soon, you will submit your application for school. It's as good as done. Well, almost. But it will be before the end of next month." He slapped Vasili on the shoulder and grinned.

☆   ☆   ☆

On March 3 Vasili returned to the bar and a waiting Admir.

"I will be working on the American film first thing in the morning," he said. "And probably making just one copy," he added, almost as an afterthought.

"And what other films are you working on?" Admir asked.

"I'm finishing up duplicating films for Ukraine, Albania, and Poland about how to properly use fertilizer. They'll be packaged for the Ministries of Information, stamped with the correct addresses, shipping date, and mailed."

"Does anyone else check the copies after you make them?"

Vasili laughed. "Check film about fertilizer? Are you kidding me? Hell no, we send stuff like this by the ton every day. It's garbage propaganda, no one ever checks it. Shit, I'll even wager no one ever looks at it at the other end either. It's junk, but we just keep cranking it out day after day, year after year."

"Great. Now here's what I want you to do. Make a second copy of the American film, then put it in the canister of fertilizer film for Albania. If it's short, splice it into the middle. If it is long, well, just put it into the canister by itself, seal everything up, slap on the label, and forget about it."

"But it'll go to Albania," Vasili said, in a troubled voice. "You'll never get it then."

"Don't worry about that. Just make absolutely sure it goes in the fertilizer film can for Albania, and that it gets shipped tomorrow. That's all I ask."

Vasili swallowed visibly.

"Don't let me down, I'm working hard to help you," said Admir, his tone hard.

"I'll do it, don't worry, I'll do it," Vasili replied.

The next morning, Vasili was given the 16mm American film, and told to follow the instructions taped to the cannister. "Handle this as though your life depends on it. Because if you mess it up, I suggest you kill yourself. Now, I want one perfect copy made from this original. Here is your chance to show what good work you can do."

Vasili locked himself in the darkroom and studied the footage. It was not a long piece. His experienced eye under the low wattage red lights told him it was about six, maybe seven minutes playing time. He set up his duplicating equipment and went to work. The moment the first copy came out of the dryer, he spliced it into the Albania fertilizer film, not even stopping to check the quality of his work. He sealed the container and labeled and dated it. *The sooner done, the better*, was his only thought as he placed it in the middle of a large batch of other cartons for bulk mailing with the lowest delivery priority.

Vasili took the original footage and the second copy to the supervisor. Late that afternoon as he was ready to leave for the day, he was congratulated on a job well done. Vasili mumbled a thanks and hurriedly left.

Less than a month later, the fertilizer film was intercepted by a Chinese agent in Albania and taken directly to the Chinese Embassy. Twenty-four hours after that, the inserted American footage was in Peking being viewed by the Chairman.

Kang put down the report. Halfway through the summary, he had already made up his mind. The Soviet photo technician, Vasili Kerensky, had to be eliminated. Should this man one day decide to inform the KGB of his actions, his Chinese intelligence network inside the Soviet Union and Europe would be irreparably damaged. But the real clincher for his decision was Admir could not deliver on his promise to intercede on Vasili's behalf to help him gain entry into film school in Poland. It would only be a matter of weeks before Vasili would come to realize he had been duped and used. Before that day would come, Vasili would have to be silenced. Kang took immediate steps to solve this problem, informing the Premier what he intended to do.

On Monday, April 10, 1967, at eleven forty-five p.m. Moscow time, the coroner's office received a badly mangled body. An autopsy performed that same night determined that one Vasili Kerensky had died after having fallen from the platform and under the wheels of an oncoming subway train. Witnesses, when questioned by the police, stated that as far as they could recall no one seemed to have pushed the unfortunate man. The autopsy also revealed Vasili Kerensky had enough alcohol in his system to power a rocket to the moon.

Throughout that spring, the Chairman and Premier, along with a handful of other ministers, met several times to discuss what China should do in light of the evidence revealed by the intercepted Soviet film. Hour after hour, they argued back and forth as to what approach to take, but no solution was forthcoming.

They also followed the deteriorating situation in the Middle East. The Soviet-supported Arabs were calling for war against Israel. From China's vantage point, it appeared the two superpowers were being drawn into an unwanted showdown, and because of the incriminating film they now had in their possession, the Chinese were closely monitoring the state of affairs. Chairman Mao was not so naïve as to think that America and the Soviets were in a pact that somehow made them agreeable on all issues. He knew that in their mutual distaste for China, the two would be in accord, but as to their relationships with Third World and nonaligned countries, each would continue to try to outmaneuver the other.

This was the state of world affairs during the first week of June 1967.

News of a preemptive Israeli strike against the Egyptian and Syrian forces took Chinese intelligence agents in the region by surprise. Before they could get accurate information back to Peking, the conflict was over, leaving the Arab World in shambles. Within days, Mao received a second round of shocking news. The President of the United States would be meeting with the Soviet Premier in America. It would be the first time the two would get-together, the hope was to find a permanent cease-fire solution for the Middle East. Chou En-lai did not think so. He believed the two leaders were meeting only to affirm their prior agreements in the wake of the potentially damaging war. He felt each needed to assure the other that political circumstances had forced them to support their prodigies, and this clash was not to be seen as a US—Soviet confrontation.

Mao agreed. The Chairman had been incessant in his hounding of the physicists at Lop Nor to detonate a hydrogen bomb and demanded they do so before the first day of summer. Mao knew Johnson and Kosygin were to meet on June 23, but he wanted to serve a warning to both men that China would not be attacked with impunity by either, whether alone, or in concert.

On June 17, 1967, less than one week before the two leaders were to meet, China exploded her first hydrogen bomb, less than three years after detonating their first atomic bomb at Lop Nor. She had bought herself more time.

CHAPTER 19

CHINA – 1967

THE INTIMATE OBSERVER can always tell when Chairman Mao is engrossed in thought and not to be interrupted. He has a peculiar habit of drumming lightly on his head with the index and second finger of each hand, while cradling it with the thumbs at the temples, elbows resting on a table or desk. He can spend an hour like this, trancelike, oblivious to everything around him. Edgar Snow had often witnessed such a scene.

This is how Mao's wife, Chiang Ching, found her husband one morning in late June 1967. She knew not to disturb him. Mao had a large book open on the desk before him, but his mind was obviously elsewhere. Chiang later told Edgar Snow she suspected he was ruminating over the ongoing Cultural Revolution. Chiang was a powerful woman in her own right and, as a result, made a formidable foe. She was Mao's fourth wife. For some unknown reason—possibly jealousy—her archenemy was Premier Chou En-lai, and she did nothing to hide her contempt. However, she had long ago ceased to try to remold her husband's opinion of his old friend, so she simply avoided all contact with the Premier.

At eleven, the Chairman pushed himself away from his desk for a light snack, then slept for two hours. Early afternoon found him back at his desk, again lost in thought. His fingers continued their light tapping, and the eyes were unfocused. Shortly after two o'clock, a smile crossed his face. He rubbed his eyes and stood. Mao had obviously reached a decision of some kind. He seemed pleased with himself.

It was not the Cultural Revolution that had held his attention for so long, but rather the Soviet film of their ambassador to Washington, and the then-American Vice President. He was sure he had at last found the right solution to what he had deemed an insurmountable problem. He phoned the Premier and called for a meeting that evening. Mao needed Chou's opinion before proceeding further.

"Ever since we received that Soviet film," Mao began, "I've been obsessed with the thought of finding an answer. I kept asking myself: Who can we trust? Who can we share this terrible secret with? China is a pariah nation to all but a handful of Third World countries. When we sealed our borders in 1949, we thought we were protecting our people from the evils of a degenerate world, but unfortunately, soon discovered that we must exist, or rather coexist, with that world. I still think time will prove us right, but at this moment, our self-imposed solitude has created a problem of near unsurmountable proportions."

Chou nodded his agreement. "I also have not found an answer."

"Well, I think I have, and that's why I've asked you here. I want to know your feelings, and if you agree, then we must act fast."

"Please continue, Comrade."

"Who would believe such a film? Who can we share our troubles with? Who is the one leader not aligned with either Moscow or Washington? A major figure in a major country with a strong voice in world affairs? A man not aligned with China, either politically, economically, or culturally?"

"There is no such leader," Chou said.

"*But there is! General de Gaulle of France. He's our man!*" Mao shouted in his excitement. "The general fills all of the requirements, and it's as if he has known something's been very wrong these past few years." Mao raised a questioning eyebrow, a silent signal asking Chou for a response.

Chou slowly nodded. "General de Gaulle is indeed the only one. At least he will listen, but whether he believes us or not is another question entirely. So how do we approach him? We cannot just call in the French ambassador and tell him about the film. Neither can we show it, and then have him tell the General what he saw. The ambassador would think it a trick, especially now that we are embroiled in an internal purge that makes no sense to the foreign diplomatic corps."

"You're right," said Mao. "But I have also given much thought to that part of the problem, and think I have the answer there too. The General must be approached by someone he will know by reputation as being a person I trust implicitly. There is only one such man: Our good friend, Edgar Snow."

"An excellent choice, but my immediate question back is: Will Edgar do it?"

"I think so." Mao, a notorious chain-smoker, lit another cigarette, then continued. "Edgar is our only hope. General de Gaulle must know of Edgar because he's a world-famous author and a universally recognized friend of mine. He's an extremely patriotic American, which is also a well-recognized fact. Edgar must be persuaded to inform the General of the film's existence and its legitimacy. Someone in a position of power in the West must be told of the dastardly collusion between the Americans and the Soviets. It's a secret we cannot keep to ourselves any longer; it's simply too big. Edgar must be shown the film, and then he must tell General de Gaulle."

"You're right. Our friend will be leaving for America soon on his way home to Switzerland. Do I ask him to come here tomorrow?"

"I see no other solution, so yes." Mao sat back and murmured as if for his ears alone, "Everything will then be in the hands of our dear American friend."

The streets had been noisy for hours, but now, shortly before one o'clock in the morning, the city was finally settling down to rest. Even on the upper floors of the Peking Hotel, the noise and summer heat had penetrated the walls, making sleep next to impossible. Edgar Snow was in a fourth-floor room and finding himself in a losing battle. He was winding up a six-week visit to China, and the plan was to catch a train to Canton in the morning. From there, another would take him into the British Crown Colony of Hong Kong. However, train schedules were no longer reliable, and he knew he could well spend a couple more days in Peking just trying to make his exodus. China was in a state of turmoil, reminiscent of the days following the overthrow of Generalissimo Chiang Kai-shek in 1949. He actually felt uneasy for the first time just being in the country. In the past, he had traveled extensively throughout China and had been treated with respect wherever he went. Not so this trip. The people were openly hostile towards him, and once or twice his Chinese bodyguards had to whisk him away from crowds that had become alarmingly dangerous. The present mood of the country in the summer of 1967 upset him, and he had so told the Chairman.

Snow had last seen Mao four days earlier, when they had dined in his home. Mao had explained the purpose of the Cultural Revolution, saying how China was undergoing a necessary purging, and promised she would emerge all the stronger for having done so. Snow countered by suggesting that maybe the cure was more severe than the ailment, but the Chairman had said, no, that possibly no Westerner could fully understand what was taking place, not even an old China hand like himself. They were completely at ease with each other in expressing their opinions, an ease which had been nurtured over a period of thirty years.

Now, as he lay in bed trying to fall asleep with a determination bordering on desperation, a hesitant knocking on the door startled him. The sound became more confident, striking a note of urgency. He opened the door to find a soldier with an envelope in his outstretched hand. It was a message of only three lines from the Premier requesting they meet at the entrance to the hotel at eight a.m. to then go to the Chairman's residence. Snow realized this was not a request but a demand, and told the soldier to convey his reply that he would indeed be ready at eight o'clock. The soldier nodded and left. Snow returned to bed; his mind now filled with curiosity. Sleep eluded him until shortly before dawn, and when he woke at seven-thirty, Snow felt not the slightest bit refreshed.

At a few minutes past eight he was ushered into the back of a small car, and along with the Premier was driven in near silence to the Chairman's residence.

"Thank you for coming on such short notice, my friend," said Mao, pulling himself up unsteadily from his favorite chair. "You will understand the urgency shortly, but first, we eat." Fifteen minutes later, Mao lit a cigarette and faced Snow.

"Edgar," he began, "the Premier and I had a meeting last night to thrash over a problem we've been trying to solve for months. It involves some Russian-made film. I finally came to the conclusion you are the only person in a position to help us."

Chou tinkered with a movie projector; a reel of film already threaded. He lowered a screen.

"We want you to look at this, Edgar, it speaks for itself. We received it back in April, and less than six people in all of China are aware of its existence. How many Soviets know of it, I cannot say, but I can tell you this: the Soviets have no idea we have this copy. Anyway, view it, then give me your honest opinion."

Six minutes later, Snow asked to see it again. When the screen went blank for a second time, he turned to Mao, visibly shaken, and whispered, "It's a fake. It has to be."

Mao was pained to see his friend so upset. "That was our assumption also. However, our technical experts say as far as they can determine, it is a genuine copy of an original. I can appreciate your feelings as an American, and I'm sorry that circumstances have forced me to show it to you. It would appear Mr. Johnson has joined the Soviets in a diabolical plot that will not only destroy China, but possibly the rest of the world as well. To say nothing of their obvious collusion regarding the killing of President Kennedy."

Mao continued. "I feel that a responsible leader in the West must be made aware of this film's existence. And I further feel that the only man who can be told is the President of France. He has no axe to grind and is the one leader we trust."

"*And you want me to tell him?*"

"*Yes,*" replied Chou, somewhat abruptly, and before the Chairman could intercede, he asked, "Have you ever met the General?"

"Yes, but there's no reason for him to remember me. It was at a reception in Paris for the press . . . oh . . . some three—or maybe it was four—years ago. There were many of us. No, he definitely would not remember me."

"But you are a world-famous author," Chou insisted. "A recognized authority on China. Edgar, I'm sure he knows of your work. Anyway, we want you to inform the French general of what you've seen here today."

"And what do you want him to do?"

"We leave that up to the General," said Mao. "This is not the sort of information one would act rashly upon hearing. Indeed, what can any one nation do? Or any group of nations, for that matter? Because if the leaders of the two most powerful countries were immersed in a sinister plot, as we truly believe is the case here, then I confess, I have no ready answer. But you will have the more difficult task of making the French General aware of this film, and also to believe what you tell him."

"Then why not just give me a copy? Let me show it to de Gaulle. Let me also show it to people in Washington."

"And who in Washington would that be? Who can you say for certain might not also be a participant in this conspiracy? No, we have thought this through and have decided to follow the course just outlined. We cannot allow a copy of this film to leave China. At least not yet."

"Edgar, we really do not expect General de Gaulle to do anything," added Chou, "and we want you to make that clear. Our only purpose for informing him is that should certain events take place sometime in the future between Washington and Moscow which would appear to make no sense on the surface, at least Monsieur de Gaulle will have an understanding of the motivation behind such happenings. We in China have our hands full just protecting ourselves. We are a weak nation, surrounded by those same powerful Soviets and Americans. We believe that they can, and will, launch an attack in unison against us, using any senseless argument to justify their actions."

Snow shook his head. "As an American, I can say for certain you have nothing to fear from us. It's not our way, and it never has been. Sure, I can understand you fearing the Soviets, but not us."

"We know the American people are basically good," replied the Chairman, "and we have no fear of them. It is your government, headed by Mister Johnson, and controlled by a few warmongering fanatics whom we fear. And justifiably so. Vietnam proves our fear is not groundless."

Snow exhaled loudly, but said nothing. He knew the Chinese mind as well as any Westerner could ever hope to, and he had to admit, from the Chairman's vantage point, his interpretation of events was a logical one. After a full minute, he spoke.

"I'm sure you both are aware General de Gaulle is going to Canada in a few days. I will try to see him there. If not, I will stop off in Paris on the way to my home in Switzerland. One way or another, I will get this information to him. I will say that I have seen the film, and as much as I would like to deny its authenticity, I will tell him exactly what it shows. God, this is a hell of a mess! The hardest part is that de Gaulle has never liked Johnson, but he loved President Kennedy. They had their differences to be sure, but they were real friends, and they trusted each other. Remember, it was Charles de Gaulle who was the first head of state to announce his coming to Washington for Kennedy's funeral. I don't know how the General is going to take this; I just don't know."

"I have written a short letter to the French President," said Chou. "It explains why we have asked you to deliver this message, and not his

French ambassador. You are the only Westerner Comrade Mao and I trust with our lives. You are one of us."

"There is no higher compliment you could pay me. I will do it, and as quickly as possible. What the results will be, I cannot speculate. And as with all our other conversations, I will tell no one of what I have seen and heard, unless you instruct me otherwise. I pray this will soon pass, and that somewhere there's a plausible answer."

Mao spoke up. "You have my permission to divulge anything we have spoken about here this morning. I leave it up to you as to the who, the when, the where; and how much you choose to tell."

"Thank you," Snow said, taking the envelope from Chou. He couldn't help but notice it was sealed with wax, something he had not seen in years. It was a throwback to a gentler, more civilized time.

"I have a small plane ready to take you to Canton this afternoon. From there the train into Hong Kong leaves at eight o'clock tonight, and I guarantee it will leave on time." Mao rose and clasped his friend's hand. "Come back and see me soon, Edgar. I always look forward to your visits. China will be a more peaceful place when you return, I promise. Maybe someday you can divulge the contents of your private diaries to the whole world. We shall see. Until then, all I can say is thank you. I'm sorry that I had to ask you for help, but you are the only man I can turn to. Goodbye, and I wish you a safe voyage."

Chou En-lai and Edgar Snow stood silently as Mao shuffled slowly out of the room.

CHAPTER 20

THE U.S. AND CANADA – 1967

AT TWENTY MINUTES PAST MIDNIGHT, Snow was awakened by a porter telling him he was in the station at Kowloon. Once off the train, he took the Star Ferry across the Bay to the Kowloon side of the colony, and checked into the Peninsular Hotel. At noon the next day he reserved a seat on a Pan Am flight to Los Angeles, and from there, one to Kansas City, his birthplace, and the home of a close relative. He killed time by taking the Star Ferry to the Hong Kong side and going up to Victoria Peak on the Peak Tram and sitting on a bench overlooking the city, the harbor stretched out far below. His mind was filled with many thoughts, and he could never remember feeling more depressed and emotionally drained in all his life.

Late that night, he boarded the Pan Am jet and settled down for the long journey back to America, via Japan and the Arctic Circle Route. Thirteen hours and fifteen time zones later, he arrived in Los Angeles. After clearing customs, he had a two hour wait until he was once more airborne on the last leg of his journey back to Kansas City.

He had been abroad just over ten weeks. It was a lifetime.

A week later, Snow had still not reached a decision as to how he would contact the French President. The newspapers had printed his itinerary, and stated de Gaulle was expected to be in Canada for a week. This was not to be a "full-fledged" state visit because de Gaulle had specifically asked the Canadian Government to keep pomp and circumstance to a minimum, and Prime Minister Pearson had graciously agreed.

Snow decided on the straightforward approach. He entered the French Consulate in St. Louis, Missouri, on the morning of July 8, 1967, having secured an appointment the day before.

"Mr. Snow, I'm honored to meet you," said the consul, shaking hands warmly. "Your books have done so much to educate us all on China. Now, how can the French Consul be of service?"

"I have a problem I hope you can help solve," he began. "I have recently returned from a long visit to China, and the day I left, Chairman Mao and Premier Chou En-lai asked me to personally deliver a letter to the French President. But, more than that, they asked me to convey an oral message of extreme importance to the General as well. I understand the request is highly unorthodox and that is why I'm here. I would like to speak to the General for about ten minutes while he is in Canada."

The Consul looked at Snow in wonderment. "To say this is a highly unusual request would be an understatement." The man looked truly flustered. "I'm afraid such an audience is quite out of the question. The General's itinerary has been planned down to the smallest detail. I just don't think it's possible. I am truly sorry, Mr. Snow."

Edgar Snow was not about to be dissuaded. "Sir, I am trying to tell you this is not a social call I plan on making. I have been asked to convey a message in person from the Chairman of the People's Republic of China to the President of France. The request was not made lightly by Chairman Mao, and I am astounded that it would be treated in such a cavalier manner by a French consul." He deliberately sounded angry. The tone was not lost on the man.

The Frenchman wiped his hands nervously on the pristine linen handkerchief he had dug out of his pocket, not knowing quite how to handle the situation, and hoping that whatever decision he made would be the right one. He kept silent, obviously trying to solve the problem. Finally he spoke.

"This is highly unusual, sir, highly unusual. However, due to the nature of your request, I will do this. I will send a message directly to Paris on our telex. I will outline your request and state that an answer is imperative as soon as possible. That is the best I can do, Mr. Snow. Could you please give me your home telephone number? As soon as I hear from Paris, I will call you. If the General agrees to a meeting, I will tell you the time and place. Is that suitable, sir?"

"Very much so. Thank you for your help. You have been most generous with your time. Here is my number in Kansas City. I shall be back there by seven o'clock tonight. Good day." They shook hands.

Just as Snow was finishing breakfast the next morning, the phone rang. It was the consul.

"Mr. Snow, the President has agreed to meet with you. He asks you be in Montreal on the evening of July 23 at nine p.m. sharp, at the Ritz-Carlton Hotel. Is that suitable?"

"Please inform the General I will be there," Snow replied. *Well, that's the first hurdle crossed*, he thought, *but my news is not going to please the General, and that's a fact.*

Security was very much in evidence as Snow alighted from the taxi outside the hotel in Montreal on the evening of July 23. As he approached the entrance, a uniformed Mounted Police officer stepped up to him.

"Are you staying at the hotel, sir?" he asked politely.

"No, no, I'm not. I have an appointment with General de Gaulle at nine p.m. My name is Edgar Snow."

"Very good, sir. Would you please follow me?" They entered the lobby and spent the next ten minutes waiting while Snow was verified by security. Five minutes after that, a young man came up to him and introduced himself as de Gaulle's *aide-de-camp*. Yes, the General was expecting him. They entered an elevator and rode up to the penthouse, neither speaking. On the top floor, they passed more guards, uniformed Mounties and French plainclothes officers, and entered the Presidential Suite. A moment later, Snow was ushered into a formal sitting room.

"*Bonjour, Monsieur Snow,*" said the President of France walking towards Snow, the voice cold, the small eyes betraying nothing. "*C'est un plaisir de vous recontrer.*" "It is my pleasure to meet you." One step to de Gaulle's left, a translator turned the words to English in a distinct Oxford accent.

"Good evening, Mr. President. I thank you for your indulgence," Snow replied in flawless French. De Gaulle smiled slightly. It was definitely a mark in his favor. It broke the ice.

"I have read your works over the years on China, Mr. Snow, and I found them to be invaluable as a reference. Your relationship with the Chairman is unique among Occidentals. It's a pleasure to meet you," he repeated.

"Thank you, Mr. President. As you are aware, I have just recently returned from China, and the Chairman and Premier asked that I do all in my power to speak to you alone on a matter of the greatest importance. But first, I have a personal letter to deliver from Premier Chou En-lai." Snow handed over the envelope and watched as de Gaulle broke the seal. He reached into his breast pocket, took out a pair of glasses, and read the letter while standing in the middle of the room. It was in French.

M. Charles de Gaulle   30 June 1967
President of France
Your Excellency:

    The fact you're reading this letter means you are with
Mr. Edgar Snow. That you have graciously agreed to see him
is deeply appreciated by the Chairman and me. Chairman

Mao has implicit faith and trust in Mr. Snow, and when you hear what he has to tell you, you'll realize why the usual and established diplomatic channels were not utilized to convey the information M. Snow brings. He is authorized to speak without reservation on behalf of the Chairman. His agreement to relay this information to you at considerable personal inconvenience is appreciated beyond measure by the Chairman and me.

Thank you for your kind consideration.

Sincerely,
Chou En-lai.
Premier, The People's Republic of China

Snow studied the General as he read. He had not seen the man in slightly over three years, but standing beside him now, it seemed like yesterday. He had not changed. The face was a caricaturist's dream. The whole visage gave one the impression it had been constructed from spare parts. The ears were elephantine, as was the nose, while the eyes were small, and set close together. The head was long, angular, and thin; the mouth small and drawn. There was no denying the General was not a good looking man, yet there was definitely something intangible that made him attractive and awe-inspiring. He was someone you would never forget.

Finishing the letter, the General looked directly at Snow. He seemed to peer down that long Gallic nose, almost haughtily, but there was no animosity in his eyes. Snow could well appreciate the discomfort of those unfortunates who suffered the withering stare and displeasure of this man.

"Please be seated, Mr. Snow," the General said, sweeping his left arm in the direction of the sofa. "Could I offer you any refreshment?"

"No, thank you," Snow replied, as he sat stiffly on the edge of his seat.

"Now, what is it that you have to tell me?"

Snow said nothing, but stared at the interpreter who was now behind the seated President. De Gaulle had forgotten the other man's presence. He understood the silence immediately.

"*Vous pouvez attendre* à *l'extérieur*." "You may wait outside."

Once the door was closed and they were alone, Snow recounted his meeting with the Chairman and Premier on his last morning in China. He told of the film he had seen, and explained why both Chinese leaders wanted the information passed on to de Gaulle. At no time during his monologue did the General interrupt. Indeed, he remained so passive, that for a moment Snow felt an inner panic that maybe his command of French had deteriorated to such a point that he could barely be understood. When Snow was finished, de Gaulle continued to stare with those cold, porcine eyes that betrayed nothing. Finally, he pursed his lips for a second, then spoke.

"What was your personal opinion of the film you viewed, monsieur? Do you think it was untampered? Or maybe many films spliced together to make one new film?"

"No, Mr. President, I do not think so. Much as I would like to think that, I'm afraid it must be accepted for all it appears to be. Also, events that have taken place since that film was made shortly before Mr. Kennedy's death strongly supports the visual evidence. I wish with all my heart I could stand before you and say otherwise."

"I see. Now, can you tell me what actions the Chairman is planning to take in light of this information?"

"Quite frankly, he is not going to take any action at the moment. As you know, General, China is having her own difficulties at home. There is much unrest among the people. Also, the Soviet presence in such large numbers on their northern border, and the sizable American military force in Southeast Asia leave the Chinese with the uncomfortable feeling of being surrounded by enemies. The Chairman is quite alarmed, but at the same time, he sees caution and inactivity as the prudent course to follow. This might change should outside events change, but for the moment, China will do nothing."

"And what do they expect of France?"

The subtlety of the General's phrasing was not lost on Snow. De Gaulle truly believed that he and France were one and the same. He was the embodiment of the whole nation, so when he asked what the Chinese expected France to do, he really meant, *What did they expect de Gaulle to do?*

"Chairman Mao did not speculate or even suggest. He simply wants you to be aware of what has transpired. There is no other leader in the world he feels he can trust. Whatever you decide to do, the Chairman will support that decision. He understands France might well do nothing, yet he wants you to be in the position of knowing what might be the catalyst behind some future, unexpected events. Theirs was a decision that was not made lightly."

"Mr. Snow, if the American government and the Soviet government have entered into some evil conspiracy, then maybe it is too late for us all. However, I can tell you this: France will not act like a fool in light of what you have told me. France controls her own destiny, and will continue to do so. And France is everyone who is French or has a French heritage. That includes Americans who have taken the time and trouble to learn our language." This last he said with the barest hint of a smile.

"Will you tell others what you have learned in China, Mr. Snow? Obviously, as an American, you are deeply troubled. What are your plans?"

"Mr. President, those are questions I have asked myself for weeks. Where would I turn with such information? America is in a bleak period of her history. For the first time ever, the people are becoming more disenchanted with much that America presently stands for. Our cities and universities are on the brink of collapse, all because of our foreign policy. We can no longer count on many of our old friends abroad to support us. I am not a diplomat, Mr. President, and I don't know what to do. Maybe there will be proof found somewhere which will vindicate Mr. Johnson. I hope so. But for the moment, I will remain silent." Snow shrugged, unable to say more.

"Thank you for your candor. Now, I must excuse myself and work a while longer on the speech I am to deliver tomorrow. Thank you for coming, Mr. Snow." The President escorted him into the hallway, firmly shook hands, and returned to his suite.

Snow took a taxi to the Hôtel Saint Laurent about a mile away, where he had made reservations a week before. Because his flight back to the States was not until late the following evening, he decided on the spur of the moment to attend the French President's speech.

Twenty hours later President de Gaulle made headlines around the world. His early evening speech made from the balcony of Montreal's City Hall was before a large crowd of French Canadians, many who favored the separatist movement that called for Quebec to leave the Dominion and form an independent state allied to France. The audience had interrupted his speech more than a dozen times with their applause and cheering, and now, the French President looked down on the crowd as would a king upon his subjects. He held up his large hands for silence. Slowly the crowd obeyed, a sea of upturned faces gazing at this man who was already a legend.

"*Vive Le Quebec libre!*" He boomed into the microphone. "*Long live independent Quebec!*" A few faces took on a startled look as they heard the words, then all pandemonium broke loose. The majority roared their approval.

Members of the Canadian government, mingled among the throng, were stunned, all refusing to acknowledge what they had heard. The French President had just declared his support for a Free Quebec. It was tantamount to calling for a civil war. And he was a guest in the country. It was incredible. Within hours, Ottawa responded by angrily denouncing the French President's speech, heralding it as unprecedented among civilized nations. De Gaulle reacted to the rebuke by cutting short his visit to Canada, and flying back to Paris on a French Air Force jet.

Snow wondered whether somehow the speech had been the result of his meeting with de Gaulle the night before. He remembered the

President had said something about all French-speaking people being French, but he had not been able to discern the real meaning behind the President's actions. *What will he do when he returns to France?* Snow pondered. *He had said that France would not act foolishly, but in light of what had just taken place, I'm not so sure about that.*

CHAPTER 21

WASHINGTON D.C. – 1967

"OK, Bob, thanks for the heads up." President Johnson placed the receiver back on its cradle and turned to George Christian, his press secretary. "That was McNamara over at the Pentagon saying the Chinese have detonated an H-bomb. We've been expecting it, but it's a shock, nonetheless. That piece of hardware is soon going to be owned by every two-bit nation that can't even afford toilet paper."

Christian shrugged. What could he say?

"Well, this is something else I'll have to cover with the Premier. Everything set for the meeting?"

"Yes, Mr. President. Our folks are going over the area and installing the necessary communications gear as we speak. Security will be ironclad, but I know the Secret Service is having fits. It would have made life a lot easier if the Premier had agreed to meet us at McGuire Air Force Base."

But Kosygin had refused. He would not meet on any United States military installation: the setting was too warlike. Johnson then countered with the college town of Glassboro, New Jersey, and the Soviet premier agreed. At this moment, preparations were underway to immortalize the small, sleepy borough.

The summit would take place in Hollybush Mansion, the residence of the president of Glassboro State College. All the participants would spend their nights on the campus.

★　　★　　★

On June 23, 1967, and after a few minutes for picture-taking and answering questions from the press, President Johnson and Premier Kosygin retired to the second-floor study with only their interpreters.

The pressing topic as far as Kosygin was concerned was the Middle East, and he wasted no time getting started.

"No other matter can be discussed until we settle this most dangerous situation that the Israelis have brought to the Middle East," he began. "Their blatant aggression against their neighbors could only have come about because of the United States and her blind support. Soviet resistance is the only thing that has kept the situation from getting totally out of hand. So our demands are simple, Mr. President. The Israelis must withdraw their forces to back inside their prewar borders, and they must bring their case for access to the Gulf of Aqaba to the International Court. If this does not happen, then we will be forced to enter the fray as our Egyptian allies are asking us to do. Should that happen, well, the consequences will be most grave."

Johnson had sat stone faced as he heard the Soviet out, then leaned in to fully occupy the space dividing the two. He pointed an index finger close to Kosygin's face. "Mr. Premier, I want peace in the area as much as you do," he began in his familiar Texas drawl, "but you Soviets have not exactly been the innocents you now claim to be. For more than two years, you've flooded Egypt with guns and military folk, and you have done all in your power to stir an already boiling pot. You goaded Nasser and his pals to shout for all the world to hear how the Arabs were going to destroy Israel for once and for all. The Jews reacted as expected. They took the threat seriously. Not saying I condone their attack, but I sure as hell understand it. And the damage that's been caused by misguided Soviet influence in that sensitive area will take years to rectify. I sure hope we can start that rebuilding process today." Johnson sat back and listened to the interpreter translate rapidly into Russian.

The meeting lasted two hours. They touched on other matters but stuck mainly to the subject of the Middle East, then adjourned to attend a general conference that included both staffs for the remainder of the afternoon.

On Saturday, in their second private meeting, Johnson raised the question of arms and missile limitations, but Kosygin wanted to skirt the issue, so Johnson brought up Vietnam, reminding him that for months the Americans had been asking the Kremlin for help in convincing the North Vietnamese the time had come to negotiate a settlement. The Soviets had done nothing. In fact, they had been more a hindrance than a help, and their massive influx of missiles and materiel into North Vietnam led Johnson to believe they wanted the war to continue indefinitely.

Kosygin replied that the Soviets had treaty obligations with the North just as America had with the South. Then he sarcastically pointed out they had not seen fit to send half a million men into North Vietnam.

As they had done the day before, the two met in a public session where President Johnson suggested that in the future, Soviet and American leaders should meet at least once a year, as the world had become such a complex place. Kosygin agreed to give the suggestion serious consideration.

That evening, Johnson joined Secretary of State Dean Rusk and others to review the past forty-eight hours and assess how the meetings had gone. He recounted Kosygin's attitude in their private meetings and told how the Premier appeared to be bargaining from a position of weakness. The recent debacle in the Middle East had dealt his government a serious blow to its prestige around the world, and President Johnson believed the Premier needed to bring a solid commitment to end hostilities back to the Kremlin.

Rusk shook his head. "I suggest we offer them nothing," he said. "They have only developed a conscience in the last few days, and the Premier wants to win your trust by flaunting good intentions that do not exist. You have him cornered, Mr. President. He is in no position to barter. When you see him tomorrow in your final private meeting, let him know that you expect concrete steps to be taken by the Kremlin in tamping down tensions in the Middle East. Tell them a good start would be to stop arming the Arabs and put them back on a short leash."

They had scheduled a meeting for ten a.m. in the second-floor study, but Kosygin surprised the President by calling his room at eight and proposed a joint walk before breakfast. Johnson agreed. The Premier further suggested that because it was such an impulsive idea, they share only his interpreter so as not to scramble both staffs at such an early hour. Johnson said yes, thinking nothing of it.

Ten minutes later the two leaders were walking slowly through the garden, one on each side of the lone Soviet interpreter, while both security details kept their respectful distances. Johnson readily saw the Premier was in a somber mood.

"Mr. Premier, I think we have accomplished a lot this weekend," Johnson began, choosing his words thoughtfully. "The world has had a nasty scare, and I do not want to see a repeat because next time we could find ourselves drawn into a conflict we can't extricate ourselves from. Then, we'll really have a problem. Now, in light of what's happened and to avoid any possible repetition, the United States must insist …"

"*Tuxo!*" "*Quiet!*" The single Russian word sounded like a rifle shot. Kosygin looked directly at Johnson, his eyes mere slits. His whole demeanor had changed, and he began speaking rapidly.

The interpreter nodded many times as Kosygin droned on, and when finished, the man cleared his throat, and looked warily at the American President.

"Mr. President," he began, "the Premier has instructed me to be most careful with my translation. He says there must be no misunderstanding of his words, and if anything I say is not clear, he wants you to make your confusion known right away."

"I'm glad we're finally getting down to facts."

"Mr. President, for the past two days I've been unable to make you understand the position of my government vis-à-vis the situation in the Middle East," Kosygin began, "so I will tell you in unvarnished detail what it is, and what I expect of you. Simply put, you will use your considerable influence to disassociate America from her position of unconditional commitment to Israel. Without the United States' blind support, that rogue country will cease to exist; indeed, it should never have been created at all."

Johnson's face turned red with anger as he looked squarely at the interpreter. "You get this straight, feller," he said in a deliberate voice. "This is a two-way street, and I want your boss to understand exactly what I'm about to say. Got it?" The interpreter translated quickly into Russian, his voice calm, not echoing the anger he was hearing.

"In all my years of dealing with foreign ministers and diplomats, I have never heard anything more preposterous than the words you've just spoken. No one, but no one, could even hint that I would become a party to such an act of betrayal, least of all Brezhnev's lackey here, who just happens at the moment to be a guest in my country."

Kosygin stopped in his tracks and looked Johnson in the eye. "You will do exactly as I say because you have no other choice. That is the reality, and nothing can change that fact. Israel must be completely and irrevocably abandoned by the United States, and you are the man who will do it. We Soviets knew four years ago it was inevitable that this day would surely come."

"You translating properly?" Johnson asked the interpreter with a look of naked bewilderment. "This damn conversation is not making any sense at all!"

"There is no error in the translation," said Kosygin, stunning Johnson with his command of English. The Premier continued, his accent strong, his words halting, but fully understandable. "Four years ago, you met with Ambassador Dobrynin in the Soviet Embassy in Washington. At that time you discussed many things, including the upcoming assassination of Mr. Kennedy. We have a film of the meeting."

"So what?" Johnson replied, his face now fully diffused with anger. "You photographed a meeting where Dobrynin warned me of an attempt by China to be made against President Kennedy's life, a warning I must remind you which proved accurate."

"Wrong, Mr. President," the interpreter replied. "We photographed a meeting where *you* and Ambassador Dobrynin plotted to kill Mr. Kennedy in Texas so *you* could become President. That same film also shows how *you* agreed to help contain China, while making sure they would to be scapegoated as responsible for the assassination. And you consented to many other things as well. It is all on the film, I assure you."

Johnson's face drained of color and his breathing turned to short gasps as he slowly realized the enormity of what he was hearing.

"You lying bastard! No one would believe such a distorted, doctored piece of crap. It would be immediately recognized as the phony garbage it is by anyone seeing it."

"Quite the contrary. It is a masterpiece. Mr. Kennedy is indeed dead, killed in Texas as you prophesized. And all those other events you and Dobrynin plotted together that day in Washington have indeed come to pass. No, the film will be believed by everyone around the world." Kosygin let loose a small, humorless laugh. "You are already in enough political trouble at home. Your own people are disenchanted with you and are becoming more vocal with each passing day in their opposition to your policies. You could not defend yourself by saying the film is a fake. People only remember what they see. I dare say you would be removed from office after a trial in your Senate, and then tried for the crime of treason."

Johnson shook his head as if to physically banish the stinging words from his ears. *Treason. Murder. Impeachment. Prison. This cannot be happening!* He actually closed his eyes for a second, then reopened them. The Soviet Premier was still there.

"But none of this ever need come about," said Kosygin, his voice now soothing and non-confrontational. "You simply announce Israel will no longer be supported by the United States in light of the dastardly, sneak attack on its neighbors. Once you've done that, there will never again be any talk using the film, I assure you."

President Johnson knew in that instant who and what he was dealing with. "You're the lowest form of life there is, and that's a black-mailer. I'll be damned before I ever agree to something like that. No one will believe your lying film, and you know it."

"There is no need to be so emphatic at this moment. I will give you several months to make up your mind. I am prepared to wait until the last day of March in 1968 before making the film public. Should you declare on or before that date that America will no longer support Israel, then we will immediately destroy the film."

"This is insanity," Johnson said, as if to himself. He looked at Kosygin. "The Congress would never go for such a thing, and I wouldn't do it anyway. You're really quite mad!"

Kosygin remained unruffled. "I have nothing more to say on the subject. We await your reply before the end of March." He turned and headed back to the mansion.

Johnson told no one of the true purpose of that fateful, early morning garden walk. His whole world had come crashing down, yet he could not bring himself to share the grief and fear he felt.

That night, back in the White House, he tried to sleep, but sleep was elusive. At two-thirty a.m. he rose, and went to his study in the family quarters on the second floor.

What in the hell has happened? he thought, trying to put the events of the past three days in perspective. *I went to Glassboro with such high expectations, and now, I have no idea what in God's name to do next.*

CHAPTER TWENTY-TWO
WASHINGTON D.C.
JANUARY 1968–JANUARY 1969

THE TWENTIETH AMENDMENT to the Constitution of the United States is specific as to the time and date of Presidential succession. So, on this January 20, 1969, at precisely twelve o'clock noon, Lyndon Baines Johnson watched as Richard Milhous Nixon was sworn in as the 37th President of the United States. As he sat on the rostrum listening to the new President's inaugural address, his mind wandered back over the events of the past several months.

It was a deeply depressed President Johnson who left Glassboro. He had gone with such high expectations, only to see his ambitions for peace so dashed. He understood that no matter how much he protested his innocence should the Soviets release the film, he would be found guilty in the court of public opinion. Support for his administration was waning by the day, and he had counted on Glassboro to bring needed concessions from the humbled Soviets. And with a newfound pressure from the Kremlin on an intransigent Ho Chi Minh, he had hoped to bring peace to Vietnam, and the rest of southeast Asia.

For a few days following the meeting, Johnson gave serious consideration to resigning, reasoning that once he was gone there could be no pressure the Soviets could bring to bear on the United States. He quickly rejected that thought. To a majority of Americans such an action would appear as an act of cowardice or worse. Outright defeatism. And not knowing the true reason for his departure, they would accuse him of dragging the country into a quagmire only to abandon his post, leaving America's cities held captive in the hands of anarchists, and her army beleaguered half a world away. The country could not withstand such treatment, so he swore to himself: *I'll damn well die first.*

Between July and the following January, Soviet Ambassador Dobrynin made two discreet inquiries as to whether Johnson had made up his mind regarding Israel, and twice President Johnson ignored the query.

Kosygin had given him until the end of March 1968, and here it was now January, and still no word. A pressure squeeze from Moscow was what he was expecting, and Johnson found himself waiting for something untoward to happen.

At two twenty-four a.m. on the morning of January 23, 1968, he was awakened by the duty officer calling from the Situation Room in the bowels of the White House.

"Mr. President, one of our naval vessels has been seized by the North Koreans and is being taken into Wonsan Harbor by force."

"What ship?"

"The USS *Pueblo*, Mr. President."

Johnson was silent for a long moment. "Name's not familiar. What is she, a destroyer?"

"No, sir, an intelligence gathering vessel."

"*Shit!*"

The duty officer then gave him a rundown of the *Pueblo's* mission and ended by stating the Navy was positive she had been captured on the high seas.

While the Cabinet and the nation puzzled over North Korea's action, Johnson instinctively knew the Soviets had a hand in the affair and that there was a clear message in it for him.

Eight days later he was confronted with a second crisis when the North Vietnamese launched a massive offensive on the first day of Tet, the Vietnamese New Year Holiday. The ferocity of their attack had taken the American Command in Saigon completely by surprise, and it was not until late March that the situation was brought back under control. General Westmoreland had suffered tremendous casualties, and the public's confidence in Johnson's Presidency and his administration, was now near nonexistent. It was the final straw. There could be no further delay. He had to act.

On March 31, President Johnson addressed the nation and told a stunned audience: "*I will not seek, and I will not accept the nomination of my party for another term as your President.*" At the same time, he announced that air and naval bombardment of North Vietnam would cease and asked the leaders in Hanoi to accept this as a sign of good faith, and in turn agree to come to the Peace Table.

But things got no better. In early April, Martin Luther King, the black civil rights leader, was shot and killed in Memphis, Tennessee. The black communities throughout the nation exploded in a new round of burnings. City after city was wracked with the convulsions of anarchy. The most popular and charismatic leader of the nonviolent civil rights movement was dead; his followers filled with despair. Sixty days later, tragedy struck again. Robert F. Kennedy, running for election to the Office of President, was shot to death in a Los Angeles hotel kitchen on the night of June 5. He had just won the all-important California primary, and it looked like a very real possibility he would be the next occupant of the White House.

Johnson speculated in silence that both those assassinations had been Soviet-inspired, despite the evidence pointing to two solitary madmen operating alone.

The Warren Commission had found in 1964 that Lee Harvey Oswald had acted by himself, and a majority of Americans accepted that as fact. And Johnson had believed Ambassador Dobrynin when he spoke most convincingly of how the Soviets had uncovered a Chinese plot to assassinate President Kennedy, only to have the truth flung in his face by Kosygin four years later during the Glassboro Summit. He had been thoroughly duped by the Soviets. They had murdered President Kennedy.

As Lyndon Johnson now listened to President Nixon bring his Inaugural Address to a close, he looked out to the crowd in front of the dais and thought: *As of this moment, that film should not be worth a potful of spit.* Immediately another filled his mind. *Maybe they'll use it to blackmail Nixon; or worse, maybe they already have a doctored film of him they will hold over his head hoping to gain the same results. Maybe this nightmare isn't over. Maybe it never will. How in God's name do honest men fight such unadulterated evil?*

Lyndon Baines Johnson, 36th President of The United States had no answer.

CHAPTER 23
MOSCOW – 1969

THE PRESIDIUM HELD its second meeting of 1969 late in September, and, like the first, it was to assess the new President of The United States and also set Soviet policy vis-à-vis his administration.

President Nixon had been in office less than a month when the initial gathering had taken place during the last week of February. The KGB had been kept busy preparing dossiers on the new players since the preceding November's presidential election, and now the Soviet hierarchy was called together to study their opposite numbers. There were a lot of unknowns. In addition to the dossiers, the KGB gave numerous slide presentations, and answered all questions as completely as possible. The process took two full working days. On Friday, February 28, Brezhnev chaired the working session. Zakharov was present.

Brezhnev opened by saying, "Mr. Nixon is not exactly an unknown, but we cannot say the same for his close advisers, cabinet members, and other functionaries. What influence they can exert remains to be seen, but we should see a pattern evolving within six to eight months. In the meantime, we make use of what we have and plan accordingly." He paused, looked around to make sure he had everyone's undivided attention. He did.

"Now, we all know Mr. Nixon claims to have a secret plan to end the war in Vietnam. To end it with honor, no less, to paraphrase him. Well, we must bide our time to see what this great plan is. The Americans and North Vietnamese have been in Paris for some months trying to craft an armistice agreement, yet it seems that they cannot even agree on the shape of the table they plan to gather around."

There were smiles as Brezhnev said this, even outright laughter from some. He continued. "We have been approached by Mister Rogers, the new Secretary of State, through Ambassador Dobrynin's office, to use our influence to persuade the North Vietnamese government to cease stalling and get down to serious negotiations. I have no interest in making life easy for Mr. Nixon, so we shall commit to nothing. We have our own problems, most of them still in the Middle East, but others on the Chinese border. I am most interested in what Mr. Nixon's policy will be regarding the Middle East, so maybe we did not lose much by having Mr. Johnson resign. Yes, his withdrawal upset our plans momentarily, but I feel we just might come out well ahead with Mr. Nixon at the helm. We know he's not loved by the Jewish communities in America, so possibly his support for the Zionists will not be as fervent. We can afford to keep a wait and see attitude for a while. Time will tell." He shuffled through a sizeable pile of papers before finally extracting one.

"Now, this nugget interests me. We know Mr. Nixon has chosen a university professor to be his foreign affairs adviser. I'm speaking of the German-born Doctor Henry Kissinger. He apparently worked in the past for both Mr. Kennedy and Mr. Johnson on special projects, but now he's going to work for Mr. Nixon in the White House fulltime. The man has impressive credentials, which means we must take him seriously. Mr. Nixon needs a man of superior intelligence to implement a sound foreign policy strategy, and I do not think the new Secretary of State is such a man. He's window dressing, which means Mr. Kissinger will bear watching."

☆   ☆   ☆

On September 26, the Politburo met for the express purpose of updating their view on the nascent Nixon government. This time, Brezhnev was in a businesslike mood, but to some he seemed tense and agitated. There was no light banter. Again, Zakharov attended on Brezhnev's orders.

The Chinese-Soviet Border confrontation had escalated into armed clashes during the month, resulting in casualties on both sides. The Kremlin had met the crisis by ordering fifteen additional divisions into the region. There was the growing feeling that a wider conflict was now inevitable, and the possibility of having to use nuclear weapons against the Chinese hordes was being given serious consideration.

The second event causing concern was the unexpected death of Ho Chi Minh of North Vietnam on September 2. True, he had been in failing health for some time, but his death had come as a heavy blow, nonetheless. Moscow did not feel as well-entrenched with other North Vietnamese party leaders as they had with Ho, and now worried the new leadership could easily swing the country firmly into China's camp. Plans had been hastily approved to have top Soviet officials rushed to Hanoi to reaffirm mutual pacts. Mao sent a Chinese delegation to attend the state funeral, but also to impress upon the new leadership that Chinese assistance would continue unabated.

Premier Kosygin followed Brezhnev with a review of the American President's actions in Southeast Asia over the past few months. He recounted how in May President Nixon had spelled out an eight point peace plan which called for a mutual withdrawal of all foreign forces over a twelve month period. The President followed up one month later with an additional announcement stating that America would show her good faith by immediately withdrawing 25,000 soldiers from the combat zone. Four weeks after that, Nixon flew into South Vietnam for a conference with top U.S and South Vietnamese officials. He returned to Washington after publicly announcing the allies would make no further concessions until the

North Vietnamese showed their good faith by beginning substantive talks in Paris.

"One area we've been keeping a close watch on is the American bombing campaign against the infiltration routes used by our allies in Cambodia," Kosygin said. "We know news of these raids have been kept secret and that the American public is unaware of this activity, which is telling me Mr. Nixon is now showing all the signs of floundering like his predecessor. The peace plan he spoke so glowingly of during his campaign appears to be only so much hot air. America firmly identifies this war as Nixon's war, and he's coming under heavy attack from his critics in the Congress. I think we can summarize by agreeing America is in a mess, and that's exactly where we want her to stay. Our friends in North Vietnam will continue their struggle with an even greater fervor, and very soon, the Americans will drag themselves from the area in disgrace, shattering the myth it's an invincible giant. All in all, I see things as being near-perfect from our point of view."

When the meeting adjourned at nine p.m. the Politburo had been in session ten hours.

CHAPTER 24
CHINA – 1970

"No, I PROTEST!" Chinese Defense Minister Marshal Lin Biao shouted at the Chairman, leaving the other ministers present speechless. No one had ever reacted like this to a demand from Chairman Mao. The date was January 6, 1970.

Mao looked steadily at the marshal and replied, "You may protest all you want, but it will be to no avail. My mind is made up. You swayed my judgment a year ago on this matter, and that represents one lost year. I say the time has now come to renew our informal talks with the Americans in Warsaw." He turned to Foreign Minister Marshal Chen Yi and directed him to make the necessary contacts.

Those unofficial meetings had stopped when China acquired a copy of the Soviet film, but with Nixon replacing Johnson, Mao had decided to reopen the Warsaw pipeline to see if he could determine what the Americans were really up to. He announced his decision a few days later to Lin Biao, but the man persuaded the Chairman to rescind his order, holding fast to the opinion Nixon was in league with Johnson, and that nothing had changed.

Lin Biao's star had risen dramatically during the Cultural Revolution to the point he was now being touted as Mao's heir apparent. For some unexplained reason, Mao accepted the Defense Minister's argument and rescinded the order to meet with the Americans in the Polish capital. The word reached Poland six hours before the first scheduled meeting, leaving the Nixon delegation totally baffled.

His purpose now was to feel out the American President and determine if he in any way was involved in the conspiracy between Johnson and the Soviets. He realized this would take time, but events were forcing his hand. The situation on the border with Russia had so intensified, that by late summer and into early fall of 1969, he had been convinced there would be war. Mao ordered nuclear fallout shelters built in the cities, and construction began immediately. Skirmishes were becoming more frequent, and the news from the front was bleak. He had dispatched Lin Biao to assess the situation, and the Marshal confirmed the reports: War must now be considered inevitable.

However, the new year came, war was averted, and Mao turned his full attention to a study of the American President and his foreign policy. It appeared Mr. Nixon was earnest in his attempts to extricate his country from the war in Southeast Asia, but it also seemed he would not leave on terms other than those he considered honorable. Reports from Warsaw confirmed he would not abandon his South Vietnamese ally without concessions from Hanoi.

Over the course of the next few months, events moved swiftly, but quietly. De Gaulle had been deposed in April 1969 and was now a private citizen, but his influence in France and around the world, was still powerful.

In September, the ex-President and Henry Kissinger met for lunch at the General's home in *Colombey-les-deux-Églises* just outside of Paris. The General had been aware of Kissinger's visits to Paris on behalf of President Nixon, a go-between shuttling peace proposals to the North Vietnamese delegation. The meetings were secret, known to only a handful of men on both sides of the Atlantic, but Nixon had decided from the outset that de Gaulle be kept apprised of the progress of the talks.

The two spent three hours together, and after the meeting, de Gaulle began writing the first of many drafts of a letter addressed to Chairman Mao and Premier Chou En-lai saying he thought the time had come to explore the possibility of a face-to-face meeting between President Nixon and the Chinese leadership. He closed by mentioning he would write to President Nixon suggesting the same and would arrange for the letters to be delivered to Washington and Peking through the offices of the French ambassador in each capital.

Charles de Gaulle's letter arrived in Peking through diplomatic channels and was delivered to the Premier on November 8, 1970.

The letter was in French, and Chou translated for his friend.

2 November 1970.
Chairman Mao Tse-tung
Premier Chou En-lai.

Excellencies:
May this letter find you both in good health. Some
time has passed since your message was relayed to me by the
American author, Edgar Snow. What he divulged has been in
my thoughts constantly, and although I'm no longer guiding
France's destiny, I still have obligations to my people and to
friends of France around the world.

The trying days of 1967 are no less today. The only
difference is in the cast of characters; the play, though, remains
the same. One such change has been with the Presidency of
The United States. After following his actions for the better
part of a year, and indeed, conferring with him privately on
two occasions, it is my firm belief that President Nixon has no
ties to his predecessor.

Because of this, I have reached the decision to inform
the President that I strongly consider it in his best interests to

normalize relations between the People's Republic of China and the United States of America. There is a bridge to be built that must span a gap of twenty years, and it is my belief the time has come for both nations to start building that bridge.

It is not my intention to divulge to the American President that which Mr. Snow spoke to me about. What I am willing to do though, is to relate to the American President, on your behalf, the idea China would not be opposed to a rapprochement with the United States. The time is right for such a move.

If this is acceptable to China, please transmit your reply to French Ambassador Étienne Manach. I trust your responses will be in the affirmative.

Sincerely,
Charles de Gaulle.

Mao spoke up immediately. "We accept. This is exactly what's been needed for some time. I had been giving serious thought to having Edgar approach the American President with just such an offer. As you know, he's due to arrive here in early December for a visit. I will ask him to deliver a similar message to Mr. Nixon. The President cannot ignore the request if it comes from two independent sources almost simultaneously." Mao pointed an index finger at the letter from de Gaulle. "The General has been most timely with his offer. Can you draw up a response to be delivered to the French ambassador?"

"Of course," replied Chou, "but a thought just crossed my mind. This will obviously come as a surprise to the American President, and he might become suspicious. Mr. Nixon has never been a friend of China's, and we honestly don't know what his relationship is with the Kremlin. So, to allay any feelings of misgiving and to further give visible proof of our good intentions, I will obliquely point to our "unexpected" releasing back in July of that American bishop we had in jail." Chou En-lai was referring to Bishop James Walsh of Cumberland, Maryland, who had been a prisoner of the Chinese for twelve years, sentenced to life imprisonment as a spy for the American Central Intelligence Agency. Walsh was now old, in poor health, and any useful purpose in holding him had long ago been served. He had been suddenly freed on July 10, 1970, without forewarning, and had walked slowly, but unaided, across a footbridge to freedom in Hong Kong.

"Excellent. We shall now infer it was humanitarian grounds that precipitated our actions, but the true meaning will not be lost on the President." Mao paused, his face forming a frown. "I can foresee opposition to all of this from Lin Biao. He's becoming obsessed with power, so much so, he is now a danger to China. The man will not support us; in fact, I suspect he might overtly try to obstruct us, which means we must be prepared to act swiftly and without reservation against him, should the need arise."

Twenty-four hours later, Charles de Gaulle of France was dead.

On December 10, 1970, Mao hosted his old friend, Edgar Snow at his residence in Peking. The Chairman was in an effusive mood, and it was contagious. Chou En-lai was present, and the three talked for hours.

"Things are much quieter since I was last here in 1967," Snow said. "I must confess that I did not understand the Cultural Revolution then, and still don't, but I admit the people I have spoken to on this trip seem happier than I can ever remember. So I suppose your revolution has worked. Anyway, I'm glad to see it over."

Mao beamed. "I told you three years ago no Westerner could understand the revolution, not even an old China hand such as yourself. Do you remember?"

"I'll never forget."

"And I also gave you a message for General de Gaulle. You did me a great service, and I will always be in your debt."

"That message has greatly troubled me. So has the film."

"My dear friend, I now want to relieve you of that burden," Mao said. "It is our feeling the time has come to share our secret. The internal situation in America grows worse by the day, and the war in Vietnam has much to do with fanning the flames of defensiveness, but I also feel the Soviets have had a heavy hand in aggravating the situation. Although Mr. Johnson is no longer President, it is entirely possible he is still working with the Soviets. In fact, other members of the American government could be involved. It's impossible to say. However, I'm sure Mr. Nixon has no idea what has transpired, which means he cannot combat that which he does not know. What I am taking so long to say is this: Mr. Nixon must be informed of the meeting between Mr. Johnson and Mr. Dobrynin."

"At last, thank God!" Snow was overwhelmed with a sense of relief on hearing those words. It was as if an invisible weight had been removed from his shoulders. "You don't know how long I've prayed for the day I would hear those words."

"There will be no immediate overnight change," Chou cautioned. "International diplomacy is not known for swiftness of action. What the Chairman means is the wheels will be put into motion."

"No, the wheels are already in motion," corrected Mao, then he told Snow how de Gaulle had written a letter to President Nixon suggesting that the leaders of both countries make arrangements for an historic in-person meeting in China.

"Now, we ask you once again to carry a message for us, Edgar. We would like you to personally inform Mr. Nixon of our agreeing to the proposal General de Gaulle has put to the American President. Hearing a similar suggestion coming from two disparate sources can only enhance the chances for success."

"This is one message I will gladly deliver," Snow replied. "Just how much do you want me to tell?"

"That China is desirous of more normalized relations with the United States, and how we would not be opposed to a face-to-face meeting with Mr. Nixon. You can mention the film in passing, just don't speak of it in any detail, Edgar. The timing for that is not quite right. Tell him we see the film as being of great importance to the continued well-being of the United States, and that I promise to show it when he comes to China. That should be enough."

"I wonder?" Snow said, sounding skeptical.

"Edgar, in matters political, please trust us."

As soon as Snow returned to Kansas City en route to Switzerland on the morning of December 15, he wrote to the President requesting a meeting. The letter was short and polite, yet clearly stated he was making the request on behalf of the Chairman of the People's Republic. He sent the letter via special delivery, and it was duly signed for at the White House less than 24 hours later.

CHAPTER 25
CHINA
SEPTEMBER–DECEMBER 1971

IT WAS NOT UNTIL LATE 1971 that Snow returned to China for a short visit. The Chairman spent hours bringing him up to date as to what had transpired since his last meeting.

Even while the Chairman and the Premier were busy preparing for the unprecedented visit of the American President, they had also kept a close eye on Defense Minister Lin Biao. By September, both realized their vigilance had been worth the effort.

For his part, Lin Biao saw his dreams of power crumbling before his eyes. Deep down, he realized he had gambled and lost. It would only be a matter of time until Mao would give the order for his arrest, as well as his close supporters. His brief moment of glory in the sun had been intoxicating. He had almost succeeded in having absolute power over all of China. His had been the fight well-fought, but he was not yet ready to give up entirely. He faced the reality of his situation and decided that retreat was the prudent course to follow at the moment. Even the Chairman had counseled in his writings that the intelligent general knew when to withdraw and regroup. Lin decided to execute his own disengagement plans immediately, and when the time was right, he would attack again and succeed.

In early September 1971, the Defense Minister implemented his scheme. Back in June, he had decided his best chance for survival lay with the Soviets, and for the past three months, he had secretly gathered a small group of no more than a dozen intimates into his fold. Included were his wife, his daughter, and his son, an air force commander. The remainder were all trusted military advisers.

Lin had developed a casual, but friendly relationship with the Hungarian ambassador in Peking, one of the few white men he did not openly loathe. On one occasion, during the throes of the Cultural Revolution, he had literally saved the man's life. It was time to be repaid.

Lin Biao knew that once committed, there could be no turning back. To be caught by the government in what he was about to do meant instantaneous death for himself, his family, and coterie, but Lin was confident he would triumph.

He had a trusted aide carry a letter to the Hungarian Embassy on September third, with instructions it be delivered to the ambassador personally. The diplomat read it and immediately realized he was caught squarely in the middle of the power play.

Lin Biao had instructed him to inform the Soviet leadership he was willing to defect to the Soviet Union, bringing with him vital information, only asking in return Soviet guarantees he would be welcomed along with his family and a few close advisers. He stressed the information he possessed was of vital interest to the USSR, while also assuring the Soviet government he would not require any overt help on their part in making good his defection. He outlined his plan.

He would leave Peking on the night of September 12, in a British-made Trident jet owned by the Chinese national carrier, CAAC Airlines. Once across the borders of China and Mongolia, it would land in Irkutsk in the Soviet Union. The Soviets could dispose of the airliner as they saw fit. He asked that a reply of acceptability be made through the Hungarian Embassy no later than September 6. Nowhere in the letter did he plead, instead, his request sounded more like a demand. He was gambling for his life.

Within twenty-four hours Brezhnev had decided to accept the defection of the Chinese Defense Minister, seeing it as ranking high among history-worthy political defections of the Twentieth Century. Word was passed back to the Hungarian Embassy in Peking, giving Lin his affirmative answer well before the deadline date.

Lin Biao had relied on a speedy execution of his plan as being the best guarantor of success. What he did not know was he had a spy in his midst, one who had been continuously passing information directly to Chang Kang, the director of Chinese Intelligence. Both Chairman Mao and Premier Chou En-lai were being fully apprised as to what the marshal was planning. The turncoat was none other than Lin's own daughter, Lin Liheng, known by her nickname, DouDou, a senior staff member of the influential newspaper, *Liberation Daily*, and an adoring follower of Chairman Mao.

"So that jackal has finally made his move," Mao said to the Premier and Chang Kang, as the three met on the afternoon of September seventh to finalize their strategy. "In my wildest dreams I never expected this. It only reconfirms my notion that you can know a man for fifty years and really not know him at all. Well, he's forced our hand. He cannot be allowed to leave China alive, so we must decide how to best handle our problem." It was not until the next day that the three agreed on a course of action to follow.

At six p.m. on September 12, all civilian aircraft throughout China were grounded without warning. They knew from Lin's daughter that her father's scheme called for him to depart from Shanhaiguan Military Airport at approximately ten p.m. that night and make for the Soviet frontier under cover of darkness. They would track the rogue plane on radar, and once it crossed into Mongolia, it would be intercepted by a flight of Chinese fighters and shot down. Should there be any repercussions, China would innocently claim the Soviets had shot down an unarmed Chinese civilian aircraft. The fighter squadron stationed at the air base near Erhlien was placed on alert for the mission. There could be no mistaking the plane; it would be the only civilian aircraft airborne in all of China during the night in question.

Lin had instructed his group to assemble at the airstrip in the small resort town just east of Shanhaiguan no later than nine forty-five p.m. At ten p.m. the aircraft would leave, regardless of who was, or was not, there to go with it.

At ten-fifteen p.m. the order was given to the pilot to depart, having waited fifteen extra minutes for Lin Biao's daughter who had not arrived. It was apparent to Lin she must have been picked up by the police on orders from the Chairman or the Premier, and he decided not to wait any longer.

The plane climbed to 25,000 feet and set a course to Irkutsk. The navigator had estimated a flight of a little over two hours. Lin Biao mentioned in passing he wished the weather could have been worse. The moon was almost full; clouds were scattered at the 10,000 foot level, but up at their cruising altitude, visibility was unlimited.

At ten minutes to midnight the plane crossed the Mongolian border, and all occupants began breathing easier.

At exactly midnight, a flight of four MiG 19s, equipped with heatseeking air-to-air missiles, broke ground at the air base near Erhlien, and was vectored to a position behind the civilian aircraft by a radar controller on the ground. At twelve-twelve a.m. they locked onto their target, and fired two missiles apiece at the plane less than two miles away. It's very possible all nine passengers on the Trident never knew what happened. The aircraft was obliterated. The fighters had memorialized the event on their gun cameras, and the film was shown to Chairman Mao the following morning. After reviewing it, Mao left without saying a word to Chou or the Air Force general who had accompanied the Premier to the Chairman's home.

"Do your pilots know who was in the plane they shot down?" Chou asked, as he accompanied the general back to the airport.

"No, Comrade. They just followed orders."

"I need not remind you, General, that you say nothing of this to anyone," said Chou, his eyes fixed on a point somewhere outside the window.

CHAPTER 26
WASHINGTON D.C.
MAY 12-13, 1972

AT TEN O'CLOCK THE FOLLOWING MORNING, St James was in the presidential "hideaway" office situated in the Executive Office Building across the street from the White House. He was with President Nixon, Henry Kissinger, and Justin Scott. They had been meeting since eight-thirty, with St. James doing most of the talking. He was now winding up the summary of what he had learned so far from the Soviet defector. He had interspersed his commentary with excerpts from President Johnson's March 11 recording in the Oval office, and snippets from Edgar Snow's China diary. He sat back and waited for the questions he knew would be coming.

Nixon was the first to break the silence. "So, Mr. Johnson was telling us the truth?"

"There's no doubt in my mind, Mr. President," St. James replied. "Zakharov has told me independently of any other source, the how, why, when, and where of this whole sordid affair. It would appear the Soviets are totally unaware that we even know of the film's existence."

"What time did you say Director Helms is coming over?" the President asked Kissinger.

"At ten-thirty, sir, but I must caution you, he will probably end by telling us that disproving the authenticity of the Soviet Embassy film is still a work in progress."

"Damn! Why is it so hard to find the proof I need to show Brezhnev that I'm wise to him, and the rest of his thugs in the Kremlin? Zakharov tells us the film is a phony; Johnson says the same thing; *but my CIA is telling me they can't prove it.* We're running out of time gentlemen. I need to hear some good ideas and fast." The President was angry.

Kissinger replied. "Of course, Director Helms understands the importance of the CIA uncovering the proof you need before you head out for Moscow, Mr. President, but at the same time, he must do it without exposing the fact General Zakharov has defected and talked."

President Nixon turned to face St. James as he leaned far back in his swivel chair. A frown creased his forehead. "What do you really make of the film, *Pegasus*?" By using St. James's code name, he was subconsciously asking for his unvarnished thoughts. "Is it really so good the best intelligence service in the world is finding it impossible to prove it's nothing but a complete fabrication?"

"It's good, Mr. President. On second thought, I'd say it's superb. I've gone over it on two separate occasions with the photographic experts at Langley, and it holds together. Even a blind man could see the Soviets have spent a lot of time on this one, and for once, it appears they've gotten it right. But then again, the stakes were high enough to motivate them to strive for perfection. Justin was with me on both occasions," added, glancing at his underling.

"And your opinion is . . . ?" asked the President directing his gaze at Justin.

"I concur with *Pegasus,* sir. The film's a masterpiece."

"You guys are making sure my day is already a total disaster, and it's not even ten-thirty yet. So what you're really saying is that I'd better not plan on taking up the subject of the film in Moscow." Nixon bolted upright. "Well, I'm not buying that defeatist attitude. I'm damn well going to have my proof, and I'm damn well going to ram it down Brezhnev's throat one week from today in Moscow. Is that perfectly clear, gentlemen?"

Three heads nodded in silent unison.

"And while we're on the subject, *Pegasus*, has anyone told you you're coming to Moscow with me?"

That news took St. James by surprise. He had accompanied Kissinger on both of his trips to China and had been with the President on his historic journey to Peking, but no one had said anything about going to Moscow.

"You speak fluent Russian, don't you?"

"I do, Mr. President."

"Well, you'll be coming ostensibly as one of my interpreters because when I confront Brezhnev with this counterfeit film crap, I want you right there beside me, and not some State Department wuss who knows bupkis about this whole mess. You've been on top of things from the moment President de Gaulle and Edgar Snow dropped it into our laps, but more importantly, you're the one who's been working with that Soviet defector. And I'm also thinking you'll know right away if Brezhnev is trying to bullshit me. Any objections?"

Who objects to an order from the President? St James thought. "No, sir, I see no problem at all. *Orion* can continue debriefing Zakharov when I'm gone. My plan was to start getting information from him about current KGB operations both here and in Canada. It's going to take months, maybe years, to squeeze all the juice out of him that we and our allies can use."

"And this is the guy responsible for President Kennedy's assassination?" the President said in an awe-filled voice.

"On Khrushchev's and Brezhnev's orders, yes, sir. He planned the whole affair from beginning to end. In fact, he was once an active Soviet assassin himself, so he understood the need for discipline and thoroughness. And I venture to say he has no equal anywhere at doing what he does, Mr. President."

"Jeez, that's an understatement. So why did he defect all of a sudden? What's motivating the man?" Nixon placed an empty pipe between his teeth and began chewing on the stem. Rarely did he smoke the thing, but he liked to have it close at all times.

"He's promised to tell me, but in his own good time, Mr. President, and I've decided not to push him. All the information he's given us so far tracks one hundred percent with what President Johnson and Mr. Snow have told us. He's not holding anything back or trying to hoodwink us. I suggest we give him the space he needs for that information to come out. I'm betting it'll be worth the wait."

"Whatever you say, *Pegasus*, you're the expert."

There was a discreet knock on the door, and a moment later, CIA Director Helms entered. It was exactly ten-thirty.

"Good morning, Mr. President," said Helms, approaching the desk. He glanced towards the others and nodded a greeting.

"Seven days from now I'll be in Moscow, Mr. Helms," Nixon began, in his most formal voice, "and the success of my talks rests squarely on the proof your agency will provide me regarding that piece of film. So, my question is simple. Do you have the evidence I need? Evidence any man on the street would understand?"

"I would have to say no, but with qualifications," a glum faced Helms replied. "We've determined beyond all doubt the film is a fake, but it's not the sort of proof that would be understood by a layman. It's technical, it's complicated, but we're positive it's a ringer."

"Well, that's just not good enough," replied a testy President Nixon. "How about explaining to me in detail exactly what the CIA has done with this film since it was handed over to you. You see, I need to wrap my arms around understanding just what the problem is."

An uncomfortable Director Helms squirmed in his chair while marshaling his thoughts. "The morning I received the film, Mr. President, we began work immediately. By the end of the week, I had put together a team of eight photographic specialists for this project. You'll remember, I came over here with all of their dossiers, and you approved each man personally for the assignment." The President nodded and again placed the empty pipe between his teeth.

"The first thing I had the team do was make a working copy of the film. The next step was a viewing by the team. We played it at least a dozen times, then each man spent a full day alone writing a report on what he had seen, noting specifically, if anything seemed odd, peculiar, or out of place. Those reports were thoroughly studied for a commonality of ideas. Nothing earthshattering was uncovered.

"Then the task began in earnest. The original film was put through a series of deterioration tests which told us it was approximately four years old, give or take a couple of months. Lab analysis also confirmed the film base was of Eastman Kodak origin, and that the chemistry used in this processing by the Soviets was also Eastman Kodak. It was noted the film had been extremely well-cared for and showed minimal wear. Remember, this is a duplicate copy, so we have to assume the original is still either in the Kremlin or in the KGB photographic laboratory.

"Once this information was established about the film, we returned it to Mr. St. James at the White House and started work on our own home-reproduced copy. The first thing we did was to voiceprint the entire footage, comparing Johnson's and Dobrynin's voices with voiceprints we had on file. As expected, they matched up perfectly. After that, we meticulously started to break it down frame by frame, looking for the obvious: things like overt evidence of dubbing—such as the adding of voices after the fact. Each frame was scrutinized, and the voice track analyzed, plotted on an oscilloscope, and graphed. The resultant graph mimics an electrocardiogram, but our technicians were now in an excellent position to determine if it had been tampered with. The graph was expected to show in detail what areas of the soundtrack fell out of pattern. For example, it would pinpoint a sudden, unexplainable excitedness or a suspicious silence in the middle of a sentence. All unusual flows of ink from the needle were flagged and analyzed minutely. Within a month we proved beyond a doubt to ourselves that dubbing had indeed taken place, as well as some very professional editing and splicing. But it's the kind of proof that would only be accepted by a scientific panel of photo and electronic experts, and then, only after several months of arduous work.

"We have run about every test we can think of, but nothing becomes evident, other than what we already know. We're trying our damnedest, Mr. President, but I have to warn you, it doesn't look promising."

Nixon was having none of it. He rose from his chair and stood behind his desk, looking down at the director. "I refuse to buy that crap. You can't convince me the Soviets are capable of cobbling together a piece of phony film, but somehow the most sophisticated spy agency in the world can't prove it's a damn fake. And I don't care what a panel of scientists would say. I want the average Joe on the street to understand it's a frigging piece of crap! Got that?"

"We'll continue working on it, Mr. President," the director replied lamely as he left.

"What do you think, Henry?"

"That we prepare for the worst. We can confront Brezhnev with the knowledge we know all about the film, and what Kosygin threatened to do with it at Glassboro. You tell him we know it's an amateurish, sloppy piece of work, and that Johnson had told us everything years ago. He might buy into your bluff, but should he call your hand and demand to see the proof, well, that's when we would be in trouble."

The President turned to St. James. "Is there anything more our Soviet guest can tell you about this film? Something we're all missing?" he added, grasping at straws.

St. James rubbed his cheek as he tried to find a suitable response. The President's frustration was palpable. He felt it himself. "I don't think so, Mr. President," he finally said. "But I do agree with you on one important point, and it's that the answer is sitting right there before us. I'm convinced of it. We just have to find it."

Nixon ran his hands through his hair. "Great," he muttered, then sighed. "OK. When you find it, let me know immediately, day or night." After a long moment, he added, "Be prepared for a rough tussle with Mr. Brezhnev. I'll be depending on you, so don't let me down."

★   ★   ★

St. James and Justin bought sandwiches in the White House canteen and ate them in the office. They thrashed over the problems while eating, but reached no conclusion. Finally, in desperation, St. James had a thought. "What have you got planned for later tonight?"

Justin shook his head, implying nothing.

"Then let's go over to Langley and study that film again. The answer is there, I just know it is. I have a feeling deep down in my gut we're overlooking the obvious."

"Fine with me," Justin replied. "I sure hope you're right, Boss."

"Yeah," St. James said, his mind moving to Zakharov. "Justin, a couple of things. When you get the medical report from the agency about Zakharov's condition, let me know. Also, I want you to get back to the Canadians and inform them that we have not forgotten their request. Tell Ottawa we expect to be dealing with information that is relevant to their security as well as ours. Let them know Zakharov appears to be the big fish they suspected him to be, but don't even hint at his true identity."

Justin just nodded.

St. James continued, "When I leave for Moscow, you'll take over the debriefing. Set a pace that Zakharov can comfortably live with. Hopefully, the medical reports will guide us as to what that should be. And lastly, keep working on a suitable new identity for him. When we're finished, I want someone the Soviets would never find in a million years."

"Will do. Anything else?"

"Can't think of any." St. James rose. "I've got to get back to the house and maybe squeeze in a session with Zakharov. The big job for me at the moment is to read the last part of Edgar Snow's diary. I'll call you later about our going over to the agency to review the film.

Just stay loose for the next few days. I might play hell with your free time, but it can't be helped. See you later."

When he was halfway between the safehouse in Virginia and the White House, it began to pour. The wind picked up, and within minutes St. James was caught in the middle of a full-fledged storm. Traffic slowed to a crawl, then a complete standstill. It would have been suicide to continue. He inched his way over to the curb, turned off the motor, cracked the window and lit a cigarette. It was almost one o'clock. His mind turned to Edgar Snow's China diary. Its content had him enthralled.

Snow had been as close to Chairman Mao as any man. St. James found himself in awe of the information Snow had been privy to over the years, yet it was obvious the Chairman had seen the necessity of developing such a friendship, going as far back as the 1930s. And now Edgar Snow was dead, at the very moment he should have been savoring his greatest triumph. It was a depressing thought, so he turned his mind to other things. He reminded himself to call his sons before leaving for Moscow and promise them a special visit when he got back. He felt a deep twinge of guilt having to cancel their weekend. What a job!

Two cigarettes later, the rain had eased enough to allow him to continue, and fifteen minutes after that, he pulled into the garage and locked the door. Entering the kitchen, he saw Zakharov drinking tea and playing checkers with Tibbitts. The general was crucifying him.

"The guy's unreal, Andrew," Tibbitt's said feebly. "This is the third game in less than ten minutes, and look at the mess I'm already in." As he spoke, a second agent, George Hoppenhower, came into the kitchen and laughed as he sized up the punishment his partner was taking.

"Don't you laugh, smartass! Let the general get ahold of you, and we'll see how great you are. I'm just glad I never learned chess."

Hoppenhower looked at his watch. "Andrew, I'm supposed to split this shift and come back at midnight. Is it OK if I leave before the rain starts again?"

"Sure," St. James replied, then walked him to the door. In reflection, he never knew what made him decide to watch as his friend zigzagged around the puddles, but he did. Just as Hoppenhower placed his key into the door lock, the sky lit up with a giant streak of lightning. Hoppenhower never stood a chance. The bolt hit the car's aerial, then arced over to land on the top of his head. The sheer force of the electrical charge lifted Hoppenhower completely off the ground and slammed him violently against the door. The whole car shook as Hoppenhower collapsed onto the street, visible smoke arising from his scalp. St. James found himself living a nightmare in real-time.

"NOOOOO!" St. James roared. Tibbitts came charging out of the kitchen reaching for his shoulder holster, Zakharov fast on his heels.

"George has been hit by lightning," St. James yelled. "Stay with the general, I'm going to get him."

He took off across the street, reaching Hoppenhower in a matter of seconds. Too late. His friend was dead. A jagged hole in the skull had exposed the brain, and horrific burns had melted the left side of his head and face, and disappeared under the collar. His pants showed a burn hole exit on the left leg, the shoe still smoldering. The sickening sweet smell of burned flesh was everywhere. St. James picked up Hoppenhower's radio, slung it over his shoulder, then gathered up the corpse and carried it back into the house. He lay the body down reverently in the foyer. It was hard for him to believe this good man was gone forever. His eyes welled as he checked the radio, then pressed the transmit button.

"*Orion*, this is *Pegasus*; I have a code red. Do you read?"

"I read you five by five *Pegasus*," came Justin's reply a moment later.

"I need an ambulance. *Helios* is down," he said, identifying Hoppenhower by his code name. "Use a State Department asset and tell them we want the body taken to Fort Belvoir Hospital." St. James let up on the transmit button, thought for a moment, then spoke again. "Get a replacement over here right away. I'm going over to *Helios's* home and break the news to his wife. If need be, you can reach me there, or on the car radio. Any questions?"

"Negative, *Pegasus*, I'll get on it right away," then a pause, "I sure am sorry. He was a helluva troop."

"That he was. *Pegasus* out." St. James looked at Zakharov, who was standing a few feet away staring at the body.

"General, I'm going to be busy for a while, but I do want to have a short session this evening. Please be prepared."

"Yes, of course. And please accept my condolences; he was a fine young man."

St. James stared at the Soviet for a long moment, then nodded an acceptance. "Remain with the body until the ambulance comes," he said to Tibbitt. "I'm going to get cleaned up and go to the widow. And stay close to the general until I come back."

"Yes, sir." Tibbitts was badly shaken. He, too, had lost a friend.

St. James changed clothes and headed out to Hoppenhower's home to break the news to the wife and three daughters. It ranked amongst the darkest days of his life.

It was seven o'clock by the time he returned to the safehouse. Because he was running late, he had canceled the planned trip to CIA headquarters with Justin, saying they would do it tomorrow instead. The thought of dinner had no appeal, but a scotch and water did. However, after only two sips, he poured the remainder down the kitchen sink, thinking: *What a waste, but duty calls, and I need to have my wits about me.*

He rang Zakharov, asking him to come downstairs for a session at eight. He needed to get his mind off of his dead friend.

"The next thing he remembered was Zakharov gently shaking his shoulder. He woke with a start.

"I hope it was a good sleep, Mr. St. James, you needed it."

"Not long enough, but good. Before we begin, General, I need to ask you a question."

"Please do."

St. James lit a cigarette. "I'm going to Moscow next week with the President for an official state meeting with Mr. Brezhnev. I'm going ostensibly as an interpreter for the President which could present us with a problem. Here's what I need to know: Is my real identity and occupation known to the KGB? You've mentioned that only a couple of non-government people *might* have known of my true identity beside yourself, so my question takes on a far greater importance now. Think carefully, General: Would anyone in the Kremlin know me as *Pegasus*?"

Zakharov thought about it for several long seconds, then slowly shook his head. "No, I'm sure not. *Pegasus* was my secret, and I shared it with no one. I will tell you one day how I came to know of you and of your true identity, but to answer your question: You will be safe." He paused, then asked, "Does your going with the President have anything to do with the film and my debriefing?"

"It does. However, the Soviets will not know of your defection. Mr. Brezhnev will be confronted by President Nixon about the film, and I will be there posing as the official American interpreter. I'm expecting it to be quite the party, General. Now, let's get down to work, and see what more there is you can tell me about the film."

"There's really is not much more I can tell you. I've covered everything I know and how Mr. Johnson caught us all flatfooted when he announced to the whole world in March 1968 that he would not run again for the Presidency. We really believed he would capitulate and do our bidding regarding Israel."

"And Richard Nixon was elected. What happened then? What was the attitude in the Kremlin at the time? And what is it today?" St. James posited the questions rapid-fire.

"There is not much to tell on that score, but I will do my best." Zakharov began talking and continued for an hour. St. James sat and listened, never interrupting, but smoking more cigarettes than he knew were good for him.

After Zakharov finished and had said goodnight, St. James retreated to the coffin with the recording and exchanged it for the last reel of Johnson's taped Oval Office meeting.

CHAPTER 27
WASHINGTON D.C.
MAY 13-14, 1972.

St. James opened his eyes and blinked once before realizing something was wrong. Then it dawned on him. The light. He looked at his watch and groaned. Two minutes to nine. A glance at the alarm clock confirmed his worst fears. He had forgotten to set it last night and had overslept by two hours.

Fifteen minutes later he made his way to the kitchen for coffee. The day was clear and bright, with no sign of yesterday's storm. Justin was there, sipping coffee and reading the paper.

"Good afternoon, sir," he deadpanned.

"You're a regular wit," St. James replied sheepishly, pouring a cup and sitting down to enjoy it with a cigarette. "What you got there?" he said, pointing to a manila folder.

"Came this morning," Justin said, and handed St. James the folder.

It was Zakharov's medical report. He flipped through the pages rapidly, not understanding one-tenth of what he was reading. But the last page was written with the nonmedical reader in mind. It spoke of a prior heart attack; blood pressure that was elevated and in need of watching, and signs of a rundown individual. The stomach trouble was diagnosed as being a result of the overall condition, but stated there was no evidence of ulcerated tissue at this time. However, this was not to rule out the possibility of ulcers forming in the near future unless the patient changed his ways. An immediate regimen of therapy was recommended. The report was signed by a Leland Wainwright, M.D.

St. James made a mental note to contact the man right away and have him do whatever was necessary for Zakharov. Primarily, St. James wanted to know what his pace for continuing the debriefing should be in light of what he had just read. "Where's the general now?" he asked.

"Upstairs. He ate breakfast, but complained of feeling tired, so he went back to his room."

"You've read the report?

"Yeah. Did he ever mention to you a prior history of heart trouble?"

"Not a word," St. James replied. "Why he didn't is beyond me unless he doesn't even know it himself. That is a possibility," he added, doubtfully. "Anyway, I'm going to get that doctor over here today to prescribe for Zakharov whatever is necessary to make him comfortable. He can also tell us what kind of schedule we should follow. If need be, we can leave him alone for a couple of weeks and let him rest. I've squeezed everything out of him regarding the film, and that's the main thing for now."

"OK. And for the rest of today, what have you got planned?"

"You and I going over to the CIA to look at that film again. I'm going downstairs to call the doctor and have him stop by here at four o'clock," St. James said, studying his watch. "That'll give us about five hours over at Langley."

St. James went down to the coffin and spoke with the CIA deputy director for covert operations. He asked if he could come over within the hour to review the film with an assistant, and was it possible to have a technician available to help them? He was assured someone would meet them in the reception area.

Because it was Saturday, traffic was light, and they arrived in twenty minutes. Their credentials were studied by the guard at the entrance to the parking area, and they were given a visitor's pass to display on the dashboard while in the VIP lot.

Ten minutes later, they entered the spacious lobby, were identified, cleared, issued visitor's badges, and instructed to remain in place until an associate arrived.

The man was huge. St. James guessed at least six-five, and 240 pounds. He appeared to be in his early thirties, and strode across the marble and glass lobby exuding an air of confidence. He was wearing a white lab coat, starched and creased to perfection, and while still approaching, held out his hand in greeting.

"Mr. St. James?" He asked, shaking hands with Justin, who was the closest.

"Do I really look that old? No, I'm Justin Scott."

"How do you do? Mr. Scott," the giant queried in a well-modulated Boston accent. "I'm Elliot McCandless." He turned to St. James, again held out his hand, repeated the greeting, and added, "It's a pleasure to meet you, sir." He sounded as if he meant it.

"Please, the name is Andrew," St. James replied, taking an instant liking to the man.

"Thank you, sir . . . I mean, Andrew. And I'm Elliot. The deputy director has briefed me on what you will require, sir. He confirmed you both have top secret, special access clearances, with a 'need to know' identifier. So please follow me, gentlemen, and we can get right down to work."

They trailed him to a bank of elevators and took the first car up to the third floor. They passed through two checkpoints until finally entering a windowless room somewhere in the middle of the building. McCandless switched on the lights and locked the door. He went to a screen, straightened it, checked a reel already loaded on a projector, and looked up at St. James. "Anytime you're ready," he said.

"Do you know what it is we're up to?"

"Yes, sir. You're hoping to find any clues that will prove this is nothing more than a slick piece of Russian disinformation." McCandless sort of tutted as he said this, but not in a condescending way. "Believe me, we've been studying it for a beaucoup number of days, and keep drawing a blank. Our electronic graph readouts tell us there's solid confirmation pointing to quite a bit of editing, dubbing, and splicing, but any layman viewing that evidence would be highly skeptical of our findings. In the vernacular, he'd say we were full of shit and call it a day."

St. James let loose a short laugh. "Yeah, I'd say you're right, Elliot, but we've still got to try. So let's run through it from beginning to end with no interruptions, and we'll take it from there." He sat back, forced his mind into a relaxed state and said, "Roll 'em." The projector started, and the overhead lights shut off automatically.

The scene came alive to reveal two empty chairs separated by a small table holding a bottle of *Remy-Martin* and two brandy sniffers. A camera, secreted behind the fireplace's mirrored walls was already memorializing every movement, every sound.

"Thank you, Mr. Vice President," an unseen voice said off camera. "I shall be as brief as possible. Please join me here and make yourself comfortable." A blur followed, two pairs of legs appeared, then morphed into the bodies of United States Vice President Lyndon Johnson, and Soviet Ambassador Anatoly Dobrynin. St. James involuntarily stiffened, though he had seen the footage a countless number of times before.

Once both men were seated, the ambassador poured a dollop of brandy into the snifters, and each raised their glass and took a small sip. "Please bear with me for a moment," Dobrynin began, "so that I can give you an up-to-date background report on the elimination of President Kennedy and how we plan to make China look responsible.

"For some time now, Secretary Khrushchev has granted vast sums of aid, along with technical assistance, to the Chinese government. This was strenuously opposed by the majority in the Presidium. However, the most vocal objection was raised regarding our nuclear assistance, but the Secretary turned a deaf ear to everything he had been told about the Chinese. The final straw came last June when matters came to a head and Mr. Khrushchev's policies were reversed by the other Presidium members. As a consequence, our military and economic aid has now been drastically reduced, and our technical staffs at the Chinese nuclear facility, and at the University of Peking have been withdrawn completely. Unfortunately, we believe the damage has been done, and the Chinese will soon have a crude, but effective nuclear capability. The very thought, frankly, worries all reasonable men, as I'm sure you will agree."

Dobrynin continued. "Of course, the Chinese did not take this lying down. They believed they'd lost face, and that's where we stepped in. It took a lot of hard work, but our Intelligence Services have now deliberately left a trail purportedly showing that the Chinese naturally concluded our action was the result of a secret agreement between Washington and Moscow to limit its ability to wage war. So, beginning this past September, we undertook a false flag operation against our own government, and as of today, three of our diplomats have been murdered by assassins from the KGB Thirteenth Department. And by sending coded message traffic to all of our embassies through a known compromised code group of ours called *sigma*, we've convinced your American CIA, and Britain's MI6 that the Chinese are the culprits. We followed that up by again using *sigma* to warn our embassies how we've uncovered a further Chinese plot to implement a two pronged terror campaign: one against Moscow, the other against Washington. And to springboard their attack against the Americans, we will make it look like China was behind the recent killing of the President of South Vietnam, under the guise of making it look like a terrorist assassination by some junior South Vietnamese army officers working in concert with senior military leaders there."

"Yes, I know all this," Johnson replied, while reaching to take a sip of brandy. "Tell me something I don't know."

Ignoring the interruption, Dobrynin continued. "The Chinese have always been fearful of America's influence in the Pacific, particularly with Okinawa, Japan, and South Korea. Now, by adding Vietnam to the list, they definitely see themselves blocked in by enemies, the United States to the east, the Soviet Union to the west. For the grand finale, fingers will point squarely to Peking when we assassinate President Kennedy."

Johnson wore a dour look. "It's no secret there's been bad blood between me and President Kennedy for some time, but when I'm President, my administration will differ from his in every way possible when it comes to our relations with the Soviet Bloc. A brand-new President means brand new ideas, Mr. Dobrynin, and I never agreed with Kennedy's foreign policy to begin with, especially when it came to dealing with Cuba and the Soviet Union. Your Warsaw Pact alliance will have nothing to fear from a President Johnson. *"East is east, and west is west . . . ."* That is my clearest possible statement on the subject, and I sure hope you will convey that to the leadership back in the Kremlin."

"I understand perfectly, Mr. Vice President," said a smiling Dobrynin. "You will have your sphere of influence, and we will have ours. And as you and I have agreed to during past meetings, what takes place inside our borders is strictly our affair. And likewise, that which takes place in the West is of no concern to us, and we will never interfere."

"Who else knows about Khrushchev?" Johnson asked, changing the subject. "I mean specifically regarding his possible ouster?"

"A few trusted members of the Presidium," replied Dobrynin. "When the time is right, Mr. Khrushchev will be replaced before his damaging ways become completely irreparable. His blind commitment to the Chinese, as well as countless other blunders, makes us now question his very capacity to govern. My promise is that you will not have to deal with that senile old fool much longer."

The two continued in similar vein until Johnson began to fidget. He tugged on his ear, and peeked at his watch before saying, "Mr. Ambassador, I've been here about eight minutes, and that's long enough. Thank you for the information. President Kennedy will be in Texas this coming week. That's when the deed must be done. So I'm counting on you and your operatives in the Kremlin to make sure that when I leave Texas to return to Washington, I do so as President of the United States."

"You will, Mr. Vice President, that you will."

Both men disappeared, and the screen went blank.

CHAPTER 28

WASHINGTON D.C.
MAY 13-14, 1972

"It's good," St. James finally said, "I'd almost forgotten just how good. If they ever decided to release this gem President Johnson would be a doomed man. Easy to see how the KGB is proud of this one."

"So what's next, Andrew?" Justin asked. "You want to just free-wheel it for a while, stopping and starting to see if we notice anything? We can jot down frame numbers that look interesting," he suggested, referencing that each frame was numbered in the upper right-hand corner. When the film was run at normal speed, the numbers were not visible, but appeared as a white dot. But as a frame was frozen, the number became clear.

"OK by me," St. James said. "If anyone sees anything, sing out, and we'll all take a closer look. That work for you, Elliot?"

"Yes sir, that's fine. I know you're both aware we've done this a ton of times before, plus doing a deep dive study of each frame separately under a magnifier."

"Yeah, I know, but we've got to do it again. Maybe we'll be lucky and spot something."

After two hours St. James called it quits, and they broke to grab sandwiches in a cafeteria that was only open for breakfast and lunch. Although it was a Saturday, the place was crowded.

"I hope you're not too dejected," St. James said to McCandless as they ate.

"Uh, uh," McCandless replied with a grin and a full mouth. After a few moments and a sip of coke, he continued. "Hell no, I'm not dejected, because I believe the answer is in there too. We've just got to find it."

St. James raised his eyebrows in silent agreement. He swallowed some coffee then asked McCandless how long he'd been with the "company" as the CIA is euphemistically referred to by its employees.

"Three years next month," he replied, "and I've enjoyed every minute. I had some misgivings at first, but not anymore. It's a great place to work."

"What's your specialty?" Justin asked.

"Strictly photographic sciences. I got my basic degree at Rochester Institute, then a master's and doctorate at MIT. I was recruited on campus by the CIA and went directly from there to here. And like I just said, no regrets."

St. James had to admit his credentials were impressive. He knew the folks here had to pull their weight, and those few who didn't soon found themselves out of a job.

They returned to the projection room and worked until three-thirty, when it was time to head back to the safehouse to meet Dr. Wainwright about Zakharov's condition.

"Can we impose on you to meet us again at eight for another go?" St. James asked, as Justin and he were readying to leave.

"Yes, of course sir," McCandless replied immediately. "No inconvenience at all."

"Thanks. We'll meet in the lobby at eight."

Dr. Wainwright was seated in the living room watching a stockcar race when both agents entered, along with Zakharov who was looking like an errant schoolboy waiting for what he knew was to be a bad report card.

"Doctor, please tell your patient what you found, and what you recommend."

Wainwright nodded, and speaking slowly, gave a clear, concise summary of his findings, using words they all could understand. When he came to the electrocardiogram results, he asked Zakharov if he was aware of having had a heart attack in the past.

"Yes, Doctor," Zakharov admitted in a quiet voice. "In 1970, I had an attack. It was not too severe, but it scared me nevertheless."

"I'll bet it did," Wainwright replied, then continued with his findings. After he was finished, he asked Zakharov if he had any questions. The general shook his head.

"I don't know exactly what stress you are under, but I gather it's significant," he said, looking first at St. James, then back to Zakharov. "But I can tell you this. You're working in overdrive trying to get an ulcer, to say nothing of another heart attack." He turned again to St. James. "My immediate recommendation is rest for at least three weeks, but preferably a month. Is that possible?"

"Whatever you say, Doctor." St. James studied Zakharov's face, and added a few seconds later, "So that's it then; no more work for a full month."

"I don't have to stay in bed, do I?" Zakharov asked in a pleading voice.

"That won't be necessary," replied Wainwright. "However, I will strongly suggest sleeping late in the morning and going to bed early at night."

"Your orders will be followed," St. James assured the doctor, rising to his feet. "When do you want to see your patient again?"

"If everything goes normally, I should see him in about three weeks. In an emergency, I can be here in no time."

"Thank you for your help, Doctor," said Zakharov, rising to shake hands. "My apologies for putting you to so much trouble."

★   ★   ★

McCandless met them in the lobby and led the way to the screening room.

"I'm sorry about ruining your day," St. James said. "I hope your wife understands." Then after few moments, "You are married?"

"Yes, sir," he replied, not bothering to look up as he worked. "But no problem. My wife's in Europe for a month with her folks. Her dad is a vice president with IBM in Brussels."

Moments later, the projector went on and the lights went off, and the three stared at the screen through four more showings of the six minute film.

St. James found himself getting restless, a restlessness not brought about by boredom, but because the subconscious area of his brain had spotted something and was trying to get a message across to the consciousness side.

Ever since they had started viewing the footage again at twenty minutes past eight, St. James had felt overwhelmed just knowing they were running out of time. Time was his enemy now, and he had conjured up a mental picture of a giant clock with its second hand sweeping inexorably toward the dreaded twelve at the top of the dial.

It was during the fourth viewing that the message was finally received and understood by his cerebral cortex. It occurred at the exact moment he saw Lyndon Johnson reach over to the small table with his left hand, and pick up his brandy sniffer.

"*Stop the film!*" St. James shouted, jumping up and striding toward the screen.

McCandless obeyed.

"OK, now back it up," St. James said, eyes glued to the frozen image. Then a second later, "*freeze it right there!*"

The other two studied the screen, seeing only Johnson in the act of reaching out his left hand. Both frowned in unison.

"All right, now go forward, but in slow motion."

McCandless started the projector and ran the footage until told to stop again.

"You see anything?" St. James asked.

Both shook their heads.

"Run it back to where I asked you to stop. Frame 218A was our starting point." St. James lit another cigarette as McCandless reversed the film. "OK, now be ready to freeze it when I say." Moments later he called, "freeze!" St. James pointed to Johnson's watchband and a partially hidden image of the watch face peeking out from under his French cuff.

"I can't make out the time if that's what you're getting at," said Justin.

"That's exactly what I'm getting at," St. James replied, engrossed in studying the screen. "Make a note of these frames; 218A to 234A inclusive." All three wrote the numbers in their notepads. "OK, let's continue. Here's what we're looking for. There are several other frames where President Johnson is seen moving his left hand around. I want to isolate those frames in slow motion, and see if we can maybe get a better look at his watch."

Justin spotted it first. "*Stop!*" he commanded, and McCandless froze the image. "All right, let's go," he said, and the projector was started again. They followed along as Johnson's left arm came up to tug once, then again, at his earlobe. "*Stop!*" Justin repeated. "That was frames 450C to 461C. We can see the watch band for an instant, but again, the watch face is not quite turned towards the camera."

A minute later, St. James gave the signal to start again. They stopped the film two more times for false alarms, and as they were coming close to the end, he called "*stop!*" They all studied the screen. Here Johnson was clearly seen eyeing his watch while being heard on the soundtrack saying that it was time for him to leave because he had already been there for eight minutes.

"Make a note these are frames 1214D to 1227D," St. James said.

McCandless shut off the projector.

"What's your theory, Andrew?" Justin asked.

"We've been worried about looking for evidence of splicing, dubbing, lip sync anomalies, and God knows what else, but we've been overlooking the obvious."

"Which is?" said McCandless standing by the projector, his arms folded.

"Which is about the proper sequence of time," St. James replied in an excited voice. "I want us to do a McCandless-style deep-dive study of those frames under a Veriscan Viewer. I need to see if we can read that watch face." St. James was referring to a machine that could take a photographic image and blow it up to a magnification of two hundred times the original, depending on the quality of the film being studied.

"Our team went over each frame of the film several times," replied McCandless in a quiet voice, "but I don't think the idea of studying what you're now suggesting occurred to anyone. If it had, I would've heard about it."

"Hell, this might not pan out," St. James said, "but we've got to give it a shot."

Two hours later they all sat back, tired, and thoroughly dejected. They had scrutinized each of their flagged numbered frames inch by inch, but were unable to capture a clear image of Johnson's watch face, and the position of its hands. The angle was always wrong. It was back to square one again.

"*Damn, damn, damn!*" Justin repeated, rubbing bloodshot eyes. The room was blue with smoke as St. James and Justin had chain-smoked for hours, while McCandless the non-smoker, had suffered in silence.

"Any suggestions?" St. James asked after a minute of silence. Both men shook their heads.

McCandless removed the film from the Veriscan and put the reel into its canister. As he was securing the lid, he stopped, a quizzical look crossing his face. He seemed lost in thought. St. James stared at the man, but said nothing. After what seemed like an eternity, he looked up and caught St. James's eye.

"Have either of you ever seen or heard of a machine called the Converter?"

Both agents looked puzzled. St. James shook his head, and the look on Justin's face confirmed that he hadn't either.

"What's a Converter?" St. James asked.

"There's only one, and it's at the Jet Propulsion Laboratory (JPL) in Pasadena," McCandless replied. "It's used primarily by NASA to enhance the clarity of our spy satellites' photographic imagery. I mean like by a magnitude of ten. Among its first challenges back in 1969 was to help create an incredibly detailed 3D mockup of the landing site for Apollo 11 in the Sea of Tranquility. Good thing it did, too. Neil Armstrong spent hours studying that mockup, and because of it he was able to take control of the Lunar Module (LM) at the last minute, avoid crashing into several large boulders, and manually fly it to a picture-perfect touch down. He averted what would have been an unmitigated disaster. There's also a bunch of other sensitive stuff I'm not in the loop to know about. Heck, I've even heard whispers of it actually converting radio signals and deep space infrared light waves into some of the sharpest photographs of the Cosmos known to man. So until NASA finds a way to build and launch a next-generation telescope into the heavens, the Converter will remain lightyears ahead of anything else. But this rascal also has one very important feature that truly makes it unique."

"And that is?" asked Justin.

"And that is the Converter has the capability of actually twisting and bending a photographic image while enhancing it at the same time. It can make visible certain images on the electromagnetic spectrum which remain hidden to all other known photographic retrieval systems. One has to see for himself what this thing is capable of to fully appreciate its value. Of course, peons like us would never be allowed access to it." He chuckled before adding wistfully, "It was only a thought." He shrugged. "Maybe it could have done something for our piece of film."

"Is that your professional opinion?" St James asked.

He looked at St. James's face and saw the intense look in his eyes. "Yes, sir, it is."

"Have you actually seen this Converter?" Justin pressed.

"Nope, but I have studied some of its pictures. It's everything I've said, and then some."

St. James looked at Justin. "We've got to try it." He glanced at his watch. It was almost one o'clock in the morning. "I would normally use our scrambler phone to the White House, but at this time of night I'm sure the President will be asleep, so I'd have to call on his domestic line . . . unless . . . . "He was referring to the scrambled phone line in the President's bedroom, and not the one in the Oval Office, or at the Executive Office Building across the street from the White House. Then he asked McCandless, "Is the only CIA scrambler phone still located in the director's office?"

McCandless let loose a nervous laugh. "Man, we'd all lose our heads if we ever activated that baby." He snickered again, then abruptly stopped. "You're serious, aren't you?"

"Yes, Mr. McCandless, I'm serious," St. James replied. "Please call the duty officer and have him open the director's office for me."

McCandless shook his head. "I'm sorry sir, no can do. I was told to help you work on this piece of film, and I'm more than happy to do so. But I cannot let you into the director's office to call the President on the scrambler phone. Neither can the duty officer."

Without another word, St James walked over to the extension phone hanging on the wall, picked up the receiver, dialed nine for an outside line, then dialed an unlisted number he had committed to memory. After three rings, the phone on the other end was answered with a sleepy, "Hello."

"This is *Pegasus*," he said to the just-awakened Director of the CIA. "I'm at your company headquarters building and I need to scramble immediately to *Top Drawer*." St. James continued to talk, using the President's special code name known to less than a dozen people. "Please instruct your Mr. McCandless, who is with me right now, to have the duty officer open your office." He motioned McCandless over to the phone.

McCandless listened for about fifteen seconds, said "yes sir," twice rapidly, then hung up. He turned to St. James shaking his head ever so slightly, a look of awe in his eyes. "I guess I don't know who you really are, Mr. St. James, but the director just told me to follow any instructions you give, and that's good enough for me."

Five minutes later St. James was sitting in the director's chair listening to the phone ringing in the President's bedroom. "Yes, what is it?"

"This is *Pegasus*. Are you scrambled, *Top Drawer*?" There was a clicking sound, and a moment later, "Go ahead, *Pegasus*, we're scrambled."

"I apologize for the late hour, Mr. President," St. James began, "but I think I'm onto something with the Russian film that could be a gamechanger." He gave the President a succinct rundown on what he wanted to accomplish out at the Jet Propulsion Lab. Securing Nixon's permission was a must, in that he had specifically commanded that only a select few CIA experts were to work on this project, and no other outside agency was to be involved. President Nixon immediately saw the validity of the request.

"Can you get out there, do what you have to do, and get back here with enough time to spare?" the President asked, referring to his upcoming trip to Moscow.

"Yes, sir."

"All right, *Pegasus*, do it. Come directly to the White House when you land. Also, you may take that CIA fellow with you. You said his name is *Candles*. Is that a code name?"

"No, Mr. President," St. James replied with a hint of smile. "His full surname is McCandless," he clarified, emphasizing the first syllable.

"Oh, OK. I'll have Colonel Albertazzie, the Andrews Air Force Base Wing Commander, personally assign Air Force Two as your mission aircraft, and I'll make sure the clearance you'll need to use the JPL facilities will be processed by the time you land in California. I sure hope this is the answer, *Pegasus* because it sounds like everything's now riding on it."

"Yes, sir, that's my thinking too."

Moments later, St James was instructing Justin and McCandless to be ready to leave for Pasadena at four o'clock. This would give them time to rush home, pack, and go to Andrews. He instructed them to have an agency driver take them home, then out to the base, and for them to come back armed. He then called Andrews and told Flight Operations to have the jet ready for a four o'clock takeoff to Hollywood Burbank Airport, the closest one to Pasadena. March Air Force Base was sixty miles and two hours farther away trafficwise, and St. James did not have that time to waste.

Their plane was a C-135, the Air Force equivalent of the civilian Boeing 707. However, the public knew this particular plane as Air Force Two in the Presidential Fleet. It was capable of making the journey to the West Coast nonstop.

CHAPTER 29

PASADENA, CALIFORNIA
MAY 14–15, 1972

THEY LANDED IN PASADENA at twenty minutes to seven in the morning, local time. The trio had slept a little over three hours on the long journey, but were awakened in the last thirty minutes for breakfast by the steward.

McCandless had the film secured in a briefcase, which in turn was chained to his wrist. As an added precaution, all three were armed and would shoot to kill should anyone try to separate them from the package.

After engine shutdown, St. James briefed the aircraft commander that he expected to be in Pasadena for as long as twenty-four hours, but that as soon as the job was completed at the Jet Propulsion Lab, he would be returning to Washington immediately, regardless of the hour.

His first surprise upon deplaning was spotting a colonel at the bottom of the ramp. St. James was first down the stairway, followed by McCandless, who in turn was followed by Justin. As St. James reached the last step, the officer saluted and introduced himself as the deputy wing commander at March Air Force Base. St. James could see it was bothering the officer that he did not recognize any of them, but the fact they were traveling on Air Force Two seemed to assure him they were important. He escorted them to a waiting civilian limousine while explaining how the Military Liaison Office in the White House had made all the arrangements while their plane was en route.

St. James knew the Jet Propulsion Laboratory as a world-renowned, one hundred and sixty-eight acre campus, serving the scientific and space community with a reputation well-justified and well-earned. Some of the best minds in the world were in residence, and the accomplishments taking place behind its doors oftentimes read like fiction. Few knew the full scope of the facility's achievements, and St. James readily admitted to himself that he was not among them.

"Mr. St. James?" asked a civilian gate guard, peering into the back of the car at all of them.

"I'm St. James."

He opened the door and climbed into one of the two jump seats facing St. James. "I'm Robert Burns, my mother loved his poetry," he added with a shrug, by way of explanation. "We will be going to the Annex; that's where the equipment you'll be needing is located." He instructed the driver to turn left and follow the marked route for about a quarter mile. He then went on to explain how the Annex was used for special projects, thus its more stringent security requirements.

He dug into his pocket and extracted three plastic identification cards. St. James studied his, noticing it contained a thumb print, four colored squares of blue, red, green, and yellow, and along the bottom, his name in embossed letters. Burns explained that their right thumb prints had been wired from Washington, along with verification that all had top secret clearances and were to be provided access to the whole facility, as well as having the freedom to call on the entire staff for assistance, if needed. His instructions had come from the Oval Office. Burns was impressed and said as much.

When they arrived at the Annex, an oversized golf cart was waiting for them at the security checkpoint. St. James instructed the limo driver to be back at six, and said if he was not yet ready to return to the airport, he would leave further instructions at the gate.

As they set off, Burns instructed them to clip their ID cards to their lapels, and make sure they remained visible at all times. "You'll notice each card has four colored blocks on it. That means you can go anywhere in the complex. Even though you guys are cleared for entry into all the buildings, I don't think you'll need to leave C-building to complete your work."

Upon arrival, the four walked up a ramp to a formidable steel door without a handle, but a numbered pad on the wall. Burns punched in a six digit code, allowing the door to open silently, revealing a reception area and two uniformed guards, one seated at a desk facing a bank of TV monitors, the other standing in the middle of the room.

A third man waited off to one side. He jumped toward them as if spring-loaded, introduced himself as Dr. Seebring, then proceeded to let them know he held two doctorates, one in physics and the other in mathematics.

St. James silently sized the man. He saw a prissy little guy with a large head, and immediately conjured a mental image of an elf who had somehow escaped Disneyland to find himself at the JPL quite by accident. *As long as he knows his job*, St James thought, *I don't care how he looks or acts.*

Seebring shepherded them towards a metal barrier, explaining how they would have to place their identification cards on a glass plate mounted near the door, while holding their right thumb beside the card and pressing firmly.

"An optical scanner reads both the card's thumbprint and yours simultaneously for compatibility," Seebring explained, as if talking to children on a class tour. "It also reads the color-codes to make sure you have the required clearance to enter whichever building you're in. I helped invent the system," he added smugly.

"You don't say," McCandless replied, his voice dripping with a sarcasm totally lost on the little genius. McCandless rolled his eyes, and St. James nodded a silent agreement.

They entered a room marked simply with the letter "J" on the door, and as they took seats around a conference table, couldn't help but notice a machine taking up an entire wall with its impressive size. Two technicians sat before a futuristic console arrayed with lights, dials, switches, and two aircraft-styled joysticks.

St James forced a smile. "We've heard nothing but good things about the work you're doing here, Dr. Seebring."

"Well, I'm glad to hear my work is appreciated. Our Converter over there," he said, pointing to the obvious, "was six years in the making, and it's been a resounding success." He waved his hands in dramatic fashion as he spoke, his eyes flashing and darting from one to the other. "This machine's actual scientific designated name is such an impossible mouthful that it has come to be known as simply the Converter. But regardless, it's one hell of a machine," he said, then grinned, patently proud of the fact that he could cuss with the best of them. "Now, I've been briefed from Washington as to what it is you gentlemen need. So, first, I will have to take a sample of your film in order to run a spectrographic analysis in order to feed the information into the Converter's computer. You see, I'm going to have to write a unique program just for your film, but once I have it working, that's when we can really get down to business. Do you understand what I'm saying?"

"A little," St. James answered, and as McCandless unchained the briefcase from his wrist and handed the reel to Seebring, his jacket opened, allowing his holstered Glock to become momentarily visible.

"Oh, my goodness, you have a gun!" Seebring said, jumping back a pace.

"Have to, Doc," McCandless answered. "It's just not safe in Washington for decent folks anymore. Everyone carries heat there, right Mr. St. James, Mr. Scott?"

In a silent answer, both men unbuttoned their jackets and flashed their weapons.

"Oh, my," was all Seebring could say. It took their best efforts to keep from laughing out loud.

Seebring walked over to the technicians seated at the console, while continuing to explain the process he would follow. "They will read the film, in a manner of speaking, then ready my program for the computer. That should take about three hours. So, can I take you gentlemen for some coffee, and maybe a tour of our fine facility while we wait? You would be bored staying here."

"How many men are going to work on this film, Doctor?" St. James asked, visibly concerned at the thought of leaving it with strangers.

"As many as I deem necessary, Mr. St. James," Seebring snapped back.

"Not quite, Doctor," St. James replied, picking up the film cannister from a startled technician who hadn't even had the chance to glance at the first frame. "I think you and I need a talk so that I can lay the ground rules."

"Now, just a minute, sir," Seebring exploded, "you will do as I say. We were told to help you in every way, but here, I'm in charge, Mr. St. James, and don't you forget it!"

It took all of St. James's control to keep from pounding the little Napoleon into a heap. Instead, he grabbed Seebring's arm and led him to a corner and out of earshot, while still cradling the film cannister in his free hand.

"Look, you little shit," he began, his tone deliberately threatening, "I've had all the frigging nonsense I'm going to take from you. I was sent here by the President of the United States to do a job, and that job will be done under my terms, not yours." As he spoke he squeezed the thin arm to drive home his point. The look of pain and shock on Seebring's face told him the scientist was a good listener. The message was being absorbed. St. James continued. "This film is some of the most important footage that has ever come into the possession of our government, and it will not be viewed by every clown you decide to sneak in to have a peek at it. So, here's what we're going to do," St James said, loosening his grip. "Is it necessary for you to have the entire footage in order to formulate a program?"

"No it's not," Seebring whispered through quivering lips, sounding as if he were about to cry. "Random sampling throughout the length of the celluloid strip will suffice, as long as we can get good spectrographic readings."

St. James nodded that he understood. He called McCandless over. Seebring must have thought he was to be the executioner because he shrank back as the CIA giant approached.

"Elliot, the good doctor and I have decided to edit out only those three parts of the film we're interested in. Would you please follow Dr. Seebring to an editing machine and remove those frames from the footage?"

McCandless nodded and looked at Seebring expectantly.

"Don't you think that I should do that Mr. St. James?" Seebring said in an unexpected, newfound authoritative voice. "If this film is as important as you say, then an expert should be handling it."

"Dr. Seebring," St. James began, "this gentleman just happens to hold a doctorate from MIT. I think we can trust him to do an adequate job. Now stop wasting the time that I don't have, and let's get on with the job at hand."

Ten minutes later, McCandless had removed the three needed segments of film and handed them to Seebring.

St. James looked at the scientist. "Pick out which man besides yourself is to remain and run this analysis from beginning to end. The other must leave, and no one else enters until we're finished."

With McCandless hovering beside Seebring, they began running the test required to create the new computer program. For the next two hours St. James and Justin kept each other from going stir-crazy with small talk.

"So tell me, did you ever meet J. Edgar Hoover?" St. James asked, referring to the fabled FBI director who had died of a heart attack only two weeks earlier.

"Several times, but like every other agent, I went out of my way to stay the hell out of his. Mr. H. was one tough hombre, and everybody in and out of the bureau was scared to death of him." Justin chuckled at the remembrance. "When I joined, you had to be either a lawyer or an accountant, and it was considered a real plus if you were

Catholic and Irish to boot. I was both: a Notre Dame undergraduate, and a Fordham University lawyer." He paused for a moment, then continued.

"At the present time there are no female agents at the FBI, so when we need decoys for a job, we simply "shanghai" them from the steno pool. But I'm hearing rumors that's all about to change, and the first women will come aboard and join us later this year. Everybody was afraid of the guy," Justin repeated, "including presidents. Mr. Hoover had the goods on all of 'em, and they knew it!" He shook his head in wonderment of the memories.

"I don't remember if you ever told me you're married. Is it even allowed?"

"It's damn near a job requirement. Hoover loved promoting the image of the family man even though he never got hitched himself. Yeah, I got married the week I graduated law school. Sally and I don't have any kids yet."

Every once in a while they wandered by to see how Seebring was doing. Finally, both he and McCandless beckoned them over.

"We have a program ready, Mr. St. James," Seebring announced. "Now, can you tell me what it is exactly we're looking for in these particular frames?"

McCandless spoke up. "Please give us a magnifying program so that we can point out what it is we're after."

When McCandless had the computer's magnifier program controlling the image on the screen, he placed the first filmstrip under a glass plate. He chose frame number 220A for initial study and zeroed in on the area requiring deeper analysis. "It's President Johnson's watch that we're interested in seeing more clearly," he explained, using a plastic pointer. "We need to bend this image in order to read the exact time off the watch's face. Right now, the present image falls apart and pixelates at magnification when viewed on a Veriscan," he added. "Now, it's important that the Converter also provides us with the frame number shown here," he added, pointing to the numbers and letters in the top corner of the picture, and it's an absolute must that we keep track of the numbering sequence on all three filmstrips. Any problems with that?"

Seebring studied the image, his left arm holding the right at the elbow, the index finger of his right hand resting on his chin. He contemplated the question for several seconds, then slowly shook his head. "No, there shouldn't be a problem providing you with the results you're looking for. We'll bend that image as far as the computer tells us we can go, and if the image on the watch face is latent, or even opaque, the Converter will retrieve it, and then enhance it. I promise, you'll be delighted with the results."

"That's great news, Doctor," St. James said with a friendly pat on Seebring's shoulder, letting the man know he harbored no grudge.

"Yes, well, let's get started." Seebring led his visitors to the computer terminal which was specifically designed to both read the photographic images, then convert them into electronic signals. As he fed the information into the computer, he explained what was taking place. "Of course, the actual conversion of the images into the binary code, then back into a picture again takes microseconds for the computer, but it's the development of the newly created image into a hardcopy which takes the Converter about five hours. It has to crunch a massive series of numbers. That's the tedious part of the process, but the results will be astonishing."

As soon as the last strip had been fed into the machine, he tapped on a series of buttons, then followed by placing his identification card on the glass screen while holding his right thumb beside it. With his left hand, he punched in another numerical sequence, then removed his card and clipped it back onto his lapel.

"I've locked the information into the computer so that no one can retrieve it from the Converter except me. If anyone would even try such a thing, the machine will shut itself down completely. We can safely leave the building now." He studied his watch. "Nothing will be ready until five o'clock this evening."

McCandless busied himself splicing the three film segments back into their original positions on the film strip, a process that took his professional hands mere minutes to perform.

"I think we could all use a quick bite, Doctor, then what we would really like is to get some sleep. We've all had a long night."

"Of course," Seebring replied. "We have cots you're welcome to use. I'll wake you at five."

Within minutes of his head hitting the pillow, St. James was sound asleep. It seemed as though only moments had passed until Seebring was shaking their shoulders.

"Time, gentlemen. Let's go see what chicks we've hatched."

Ten minutes later they trooped into the Converter room. Seebring went directly to the computer, placed his ID card and right thumb on the screen and again tapped a series of buttons with his left hand. "I've just unlocked the computer," he explained, while rapidly punching more buttons causing tapes to begin whirling rapidly in a bank of cabinets behind them. "Let's hope the Converter has done the job it was designed to do," he added, leading the trio to another terminal on the opposite side of the room. He donned cotton gloves, and after a few minutes began carefully extracting 8 x 10 color prints.

Twenty minutes later all the frames had been processed and delivered.

St. James found himself awestruck by the clarity of the images and the brilliance of the colors. It was hard to believe they had been taken off of 16mm film. The group began studying the prints. They found their first answer on frame 229A. St. James let out a low whistle, followed by one word: *"Bingo!"*

President Johnson's watch face was clearly visible, and even though it had been angled some 60° away from the camera's lens, the Converter had manipulated the image perfectly. The hands were frozen at eight-ten.

"Oh my God, would you just look at that!" St. James exclaimed in a hushed voice.

The remainder of the A-letter designation strip was scrutinized, but no other frame in the grouping showed the watch face. They turned to the next strip: frames 450C to 461C, and hit paydirt with frames 454C and 455C. Both clearly showed Johnson's watch face, and the time read eight oh-four. St. James was stunned. *According to the watch, for six full minutes Lyndon Johnson had seemingly traveled backward in time! It was a physical impossibility!*

The last of the frames were labeled 1214D to 1227D, chosen from close to the end of the footage. St. James found his answer on frame 1219D. The watch's dial clearly read eight-twelve. President Johnson's watch was running correctly again, *gaining eight minutes from start to finish!*

McCandless's hunch to use the Converter had paid off. They had cracked the secret of the film. It had indeed been skillfully doctored, but nonetheless was an obvious fake. They now held in their hands the irrefutable proof needed by even the most hardened skeptic.

"There it is gentlemen," St. James said, tapping an index finger on the stack of blowups. "What kind of a watch first clearly shows eight-ten, reverses itself for six whole minutes to land back on eight oh-four, then somehow miraculously runs properly again for eight minutes and ends up at eight-twelve?"

The others merely grinned their silent replies.

"*Correct. The answer is none!* There's not a timepiece made that can inexplicably begin to run backward, but especially not the expensive Rolex we see on President Johnson's wrist. This is all the proof President Nixon needs when he confronts Secretary Brezhnev in Moscow next week. What we've just proven beyond all doubt is that a crude attempt was made to try and blackmail President Johnson with a tampered piece of bullshit film, purporting to show him colluding with Ambassador Dobrynin to assassinate President Kennedy, and then place the blame squarely on the Chinese. It was a pretty slick piece of work by the KGB, but by having the Converter we've managed to stop those Soviet bastards cold. And I'll make one last point to further prove that piece of film has been fiddled with. We clearly heard President Johnson say that he had been with the ambassador for eight minutes and it was time for him to leave. But we all know this footage runs for only six minutes, so the million dollar question is this: What the hell happened to those crucial missing two minutes?"

St. James turned to Seebring. "And you, Doctor, are a genius for inventing that incredible machine. The imagery is better than perfect. None of this would have been possible without you," he said, again pointing to the stack of prints, "and I intend to tell President Nixon just that."

"I'm delighted to have been a help, Mr. St. James, and I apologize for my earlier boorish behavior. It was totally uncalled for."

"Likewise, Doctor," St. James answered. "Please accept my apologies." He warmly shook hands with the scientist.

Two hours later they were airborne, this time flying east, too flushed with adrenaline to sleep.

CHAPTER 30
WASHINGTON D.C.
MAY 15, 1972.

PRESIDENT NIXON WAS ALL SMILES as he studied the photographs. He kept nodding enthusiastically as St. James pointed out various features, explaining how the images had been retrieved.

Dr. Kissinger entered the Oval Office. He had been awakened at six-thirty by the White House switchboard with a request he go to the President's office immediately.

"Henry, look what we have here," Nixon called out, waving a glossy print in the air. "Our *Pegasus* has struck again, and this time he's scored a bull's-eye."

Kissinger winked at St. James as the President pointed out the salient features of the blowups. He had never seen Nixon happier.

After five minutes of oohing and aahing, the President turned to Justin and McCandless. "My congratulations and heartfelt thanks to both of you also for a job well done." Pivoting back to St. James, he added, "And I want you to remind me to write letters of appreciation for each of their files."

"Yes, sir, I'll do that gladly."

"Good, good. Now gentlemen, I must ask you to excuse us while we get on to other matters." He shook hands again, then said to St. James, "On second thought, *Pegasus*, I need you to stay, OK?"

Justin and McCandless left, leaving the President, Kissinger, and St. James alone in the Oval Office. It was now close to eight o'clock, and the White House staff was arriving for work.

The President led the way to the sitting arrangement in front of the fireplace as a steward entered, steering a food tray trolley laden with coffee and Danish pastries. This was the first time St. James ever had breakfast with the President and was tickled to admit to himself that he felt humbled and honored. He immediately formed a mental picture of his disapproving father and wondered whether he could finally admit to himself that maybe his son was not a failure after all.

"Now I can look Brezhnev and Kosygin squarely in the eye knowing I have all the proof needed to expose their diabolical attempt to blackmail President Johnson. And Henry, in light of the information has brought back from California, we're going to have to revise several topics on our agenda."

"That shouldn't be too difficult," Kissinger mumbled, after swallowing a mouthful of Danish. St. James had already deduced that Nixon and Kissinger must have eaten breakfast often enough for the President to know how much his National Security Advisor loved pastries. He had eaten three to Nixon's one.

President Nixon walked over to his desk, picked a print up at random, and came back. "You know, Henry, I've been thinking, the Soviets must have known they had just as much to lose as did Lyndon if they had ever decided to release that film. I mean, it clearly showed Dobrynin to be a co-conspirator. How would they have explained that to the world?"

Kissinger swallowed before answering. "Mr. President," he began, "they don't have to answer to the world. They live in a closed society, and their system does not rely on the goodwill of its people. I suppose if the heat was ever really applied, then they might be forced to recall Dobrynin and accuse him publicly of acting alone. But no matter what, when all would be said and done, President Johnson would be the only one to lose his head over the scandalous affair. The Soviets would come out winners, I'm afraid. Also, keep in mind, that as of this moment no one in the Kremlin knows we have a copy of this doctored film in our possession, so we should not be talking as if this is behind us. Brezhnev's plan might still be to drop a bombshell on us at an opportune moment, like maybe while we're in the final stages of negotiating an end of the war with the North Vietnamese delegation in Paris. It would dash all our hopes for signing a peace treaty."

President Nixon pondered that scenario for a long moment. "You could be right, of course, but I intend to convince him the game is over before it ever escalated that far. I'll be bringing with me the CIA's detailed photo analysis of the film, pointing out how the original had been amateurly sliced and diced to the extent that several of the early frames actually showed that President Johnson's watch was running backwards."

Kissinger patted his mouth with a napkin to remove some crumbs, then said, "And how could his so-called experts have allowed two whole minutes of the footage to vanish completely with no explanation whatsoever? I mean, we all saw President Johnson studying his watch while clearly saying he'd been with Dobrynin for eight minutes and it was time for him to leave."

"All that's true, Henry, Nixon said, "but just in case Secretary Brezhnev should stubbornly choose to brush aside what I tell him and threaten to make the film public regardless, I'll counter by asking how he plans to answer the millions of pissed-off Americans seeking revenge when they learn the truth about who really killed President Kennedy? Not to mention how Chairman Mao will react. No, he'll be left with only two options to choose from. He can either ignite World War III, or choose the path to peace and prosperity for his people."

Kissinger nodded, and saw this as his moment to change the subject. "Are you planning on conveying the good news to President Johnson any time soon?"

"Heck, yes, of course I am Henry. In fact, I'll do it right now." Nixon picked up the desk phone and asked the White House operator to call the LBJ ranch in Texas. In less than a minute, President Johnson came on the line.

Nixon activated his scrambler, and so did Johnson. After exchanging pleasantries, Nixon mentioned that Doctor Kissinger and Andrew St. James were present. He spent the next five minutes explaining what had been uncovered out in California, and it was obvious to St. James while looking at Nixon's face, the former President was greatly relieved by the news.

"None of us ever doubted your loyalty, Mr. President," said Nixon, "but I had to be able to offer irrefutable proof to any doubting Thomas what the Soviets were up to, and by God, we've done just that."

They spoke for a few more minutes, and as he was preparing to hang up, President Nixon winked at both Kissinger and St. James, then said into the mouthpiece, "Rumor has it that you might be running against me in November, Lyndon. You're still eligible for another term." He flipped a switch on the console so they all could hear Johnson's reply.

President Johnson guffawed long and loud at the suggestion, then a single "Never!" came his booming reply. "No, siree, I've served my time," he continued, "and I'm not crazy enough to want four more years of that punishment. It's all yours, Mr. President." The voice became somber. "You know, Dick, dad and granddaddy both died in their early sixties. Longevity is not in the cards for my family. It's no secret that I've already had a couple of serious heart attacks, and I really don't believe I have much time left. So, whatever future the good Lord sees fit to grant me, I plan on spending that time close to my family. Ladybird and the girls merit nothing less."

"And you have certainly earned a well-deserved retirement, Lyndon. All I ask is that I can continue to call on you for advice."

"Please do that, Mr. President," Johnson replied in his most formal voice.

Both said their goodbyes and hung up. There was a long moment of silence, then Nixon turned to Kissinger. "What do we do about Dobrynin? If there ever was a case for throwing an ambassador out of a country . . ."

Kissinger cut in. "The thought also crossed my mind, Mr. President, but my instincts tell me you should do nothing. Sure, we could banish him back to Moscow, but he would only be replaced with a complete unknown, and that could really bring on major problems. At least we can talk to Dobrynin, but he will definitely know the relationship has forever changed."

"You agree, Andrew?"

"I do, Mr. President. What's done, is done, and nothing we do now will change past history. We've learned an invaluable lesson from Mr. Dobrynin and his pals. While they smile their toothy smiles in our presence, under those masks are faces that say they want us all dead. To them, the end justify the means, and always will. President Kennedy paid with his life for opposing them, and as much as I hate to say it, Mr. President, you too could pay such a price. The Soviets are that kind of a foe."

Nixon just stared at St. James for a long moment, then nodded. "Alright, he stays. Now let's get down to work."

For the next two hours, they toiled on finalizing the agenda for the upcoming, historic journey to Moscow.

By Friday St. James was as ready as he would ever be. Justin was nominally in charge while he was away. With permission from the President, the two briefed the new Acting Director of the FBI, L. Patrick Gray, and his deputy Mark Felt, as to whom it was they had in custody at the safehouse in Alexandria. They also reached an agreement wherein the FBI would begin providing round-the-clock protection and coordinate with Justin on creating a new, permanent identity for Zakharov. The director also agreed that St. James and his team should continue to debrief the General, asking only that his agency be provided with manuscripts of the sessions. St. James assented with a silent nod, knowing that would be a nonstarter, unless President Nixon gave his approval.

That evening, he spoke on the phone with his boys, explaining how he was flying to Moscow with the President as his official interpreter.

"Gee whiz, Dad, that sounds cool," exclaimed Kevin, his oldest.

"Yeah, cool, Dad," echoed Chris on the upstairs extension.

"Will you get to take some photographs? Maybe of Mr. Nixon and the top Russian man shaking hands?" Kevin asked.

"All I can do is try, fellas," St. James said and laughed. "But as soon as I come back, we'll spend a few days together doing fun things. I promise. I'll also bring you both back a surprise. OK?"

"Super," was their joint reply.

"Bye, now, and be good boys for your mother." St. James hung up, vowing silently that come hell or high water, he would keep that promise.

CHAPTER 31
MOSCOW
MAY 22–30 1972

For the second time in three months, President Nixon found himself on the first leg of an historic journey. This time the destination was Moscow for a summit meeting with Leonid Brezhnev and Alexei Kosygin. The date was May 22, 1972, and as far as the American President was concerned, life could not be better. Both he and Kissinger had worked hard on the agenda, and in light of recent events, both men held high expectations. They had met twice in the past week with Ambassador Dobrynin, who had conveyed to the White House minor changes in a list of subjects suggested for discussion by his government. The changes were well-received on both occasions, and nothing in the President's behavior suggested that relations between their governments were anything but the best they had been in at least a dozen years. Dobrynin had tried to draw the President into a discussion of his recent trip to China, but Nixon adroitly sidestepped the issue after minimal conversation on the topic, explaining that his only interest at the moment lay in strengthening the fabric of peace between both of their countries.

While Air Force One was en route, the President decided to leave his private compartment and venture into the lounge area to chat informally with the news contingent on board. He was in a friendly, expansive mood, and engaged happily with the press corps that most time he went out of his way to avoid. Over the span of his public life, Nixon had not enjoyed a good working relationship with the press, so his relaxed approach now was regarded with downright suspicion by some, but with genuine surprise by all. Even his most vocal critics conceded that the prospect of four more years of Nixon in the White House was almost a sure thing, and they were trying mentally to prepare themselves for the continuing battle. But at this moment, Nixon was all charm and grace, and the majority decided to accept the extended olive branch, if only for the length of this trip.

The presidential party included Mrs. Nixon, Secretary of State Rogers, Dr. Kissinger, and other assorted aides, including Andrew St. James.

On May 22, 1972, President Nixon's entourage was greeted by Soviet President Podgorny at Moscow's Sheremetyevo Airport, then driven by motorcade to the Kremlin where they were met by an ebullient Leonid Brezhnev and a smiling Alexei Kosygin. All three behaved like long-lost friends for the world's cameras. After much light banter, the Nixons were escorted to an apartment inside the Kremlin, while all other officials were quartered in hotels nearby.

The first day was spent engaged in public functions for the benefit of the international press. President Nixon presented Brezhnev with a 1972 Cadillac Eldorado, much to his delight.

At ten o'clock the following morning, the two leaders met in a private session. A Russian interpreter accompanied Brezhnev, while St. James was on hand to do the honors for the President.

As the two men made themselves comfortable in the ornate chairs decorating the Secretary's offices, Mr. Brezhnev turned to St. James, and with a toothy smile asked in Russian, "Have you ever been to The Soviet Union before?"

"No, this is my first time, Excellency," St. James replied in flawless Russian. "I have worked in our Department of State for many years, but this is my first visit to your country. I am grateful for the opportunity to accompany President Nixon on such an historic occasion."

He had deliberately made his reply longer than necessary because he wanted the Secretary to know he could carry a conversation both well and fast in his language.

Brezhnev looked at St. James for a long second or two, the smile still frozen, but his bushy eyebrows had come together in a slight frown, as if trying to commit the American's face to memory. He turned to Nixon as the President began speaking.

"The last time I was in Moscow was back in March, 1967," Nixon said, all the while wearing a disarming smile. "Of course, I was just a private citizen then, but I do recall the visit as if it were yesterday. I remember especially how I wanted to see Mr. Khrushchev and pay my respects, but your government said no. And now he is dead." He continued smiling, but Brezhnev obviously sensed the American President was not amused.

"*What in the hell is he driving at?*" St. James also wondered, as he translated the President's words. He could see that the Soviet translator was rattled by Nixon's opening comments; it was not at all what he had expected to hear. He now remained silent as St. James continued with the translation.

"As far as I remember, Mr. Khrushchev was not in Moscow at the time of your last visit," Brezhnev replied lamely, stalling for time while trying to compose his thoughts.

"No, maybe not," replied Nixon diplomatically, knowing full well this was not the case. He took a few sips of mineral water before continuing. "Mr. Secretary," he began, "our agenda is full, and we have much to accomplish. But before we do, though, I would like to recount for your benefit what I consider to be the important highlights of my recent journey to Peking. It was really in the best interests of both nations that the meeting between Chairman Mao and me took place. And in large measure, it's you and your associates in the Politburo who were most responsible for my going there in the first place."

Brezhnev's face took on a bewildered look as he listened to his interpreter, not fully understanding what the President was saying.

"But getting to the point," Nixon continued, "while I was in Peking, I was shown a short film that I found very disturbing. It was apparently shot in the Soviet Embassy in Washington some nine years ago, and then, at some later date, edited here in the Soviet Union. This film purported to show how President Johnson had entered into a conspiracy with your Ambassador Anatoly Dobrygin to murder President Kennedy. I must admit, the editing was very convincing. Anyway, the film was duplicated, and a copy was then forward to Peking by a Chinese spy in the Soviet Union sometime in 1967. The Chinese, needless to say, have been extremely worried for the past few years over what they saw. They explained during my February visit how for many years they fully expected to be attacked by the Soviet Union and the United States working in tandem."

Brezhnev threw his hands into the air. "This conversation is not making any sense at all," he said, squirming spastically while acting thoroughly bewildered. His interpreter had beads of sweat glistening on his forehead and upper lip. He looked desperately to St. James as if pleading for help.

"In 1967, Premier Kosygin threatened President Johnson with this film during their summit meeting in New Jersey," Nixon continued, with St. James now translating for Brezhnev. "No, threatened is not the correct word, the proper wording I should use is 'threatened to blackmail.' Well, Mr. Johnson refused to bow to the pressure and chose not to seek reelection rather than do your bidding about Israel and see the United States torn apart after your lying film was shown to the entire world. I deliberately use the word *lying*, Mr. Brezhnev, because I have that Chinese copy of your film. It was given to me by Chairman Mao himself. So, whatever your game was, or maybe still is, know for a fact, it's one hundred percent done, over, finished, because I can prove beyond a shadow of a doubt that piece of film was doctored right here in the Soviet Union."

"I know nothing about any such film!" Brezhnev shouted at St. James, "and I can speak for the rest of the Politburo members when I say they also know nothing about any such phantom film as you describe. No, no, my friend, it's you who's been duped by the Chinese. I suggest they have cleverly tried to put a wedge between us so that in some devious way they can benefit from our dissension. America and the Soviet Union both are on the threshold of a new era of cooperation, and the Chairman knows this. I further suggest Chairman Mao would do anything and everything to sabotage our efforts."

President Nixon was having none of it. "Mr. Secretary, I have spoken at great length with President Johnson about this, and we have been able to reconstruct events as they truly happened that day inside Ambassador Dobrygin's second floor study in your Soviet Embassy. I'm talking about such trifling matters as the death of Soviet spies in the fall of 1963; the murder of the President of South Vietnam in the fall of 1963; and, of course, the assassination of President Kennedy, also in the fall of 1963." His tone was dripping with sarcasm. "You certainly had a busy few months back then.

"You manipulated international events so that President Johnson felt compelled to act as he did in Vietnam after Ambassador Dobrynin convinced him the Chinese were plotting to assassinate President Kennedy during his upcoming trip to Asia in early 1964. Of course, that lie was nothing more than a diversionary red herring because your Soviet assassins had already made their final preparations to execute the President in Dallas on November 22. Naturally, President Johnson later assumed China had upped the timetable. And knowing now the full circumstances of what was happening at the time, I can assure you I would not have acted any differently. But I digress. Your aim was to get the United States embroiled in a protracted and fruitless war in Vietnam, a war that could, and should, have been settled years ago. You wrongly thought that with America so deeply entangled, and with China wrongly seen in President Johnson's mind as the country responsible for Mister Kennedy's assassination, you would be free to march into the Middle East and create chaos, to the sole advantage of the Soviet Union. But your plan backfired because your spies misjudged the strength and determination of the Israelis. That was one expensive lesson to learn. And it was while you were still licking your wounds that you had Premier Kosygin brazenly attempt to blackmail President Johnson in Glassboro. But your scheme failed. The longer you could keep us bogged down in Vietnam while goading Hanoi to hold out in Paris with their impossible demands, the easier it would be for you to make power grabs in other parts of the world. Yet it didn't end there. We have irrefutable proof that your government has spent vast sums in the United States subverting our cities and campuses into a state of near-revolt, just as you were responsible for the uprisings that plagued Western Europe in 1968, 1969, and 1970. But the important upshot to all of this is that America has survived your onslaught. To put it bluntly, Mister Secretary, you have failed in your attempt to subvert the United States." Nixon paused, took a long drink of water, deliberately allowing St. James time to translate. When finished, St. James looked expectantly at the President, and waited for him to continue.

Nixon put down his glass. "Mr. Secretary, I recounted that long list of facts so that both of us know exactly where we stand. We can put this behind us and start afresh; I, for my part, am willing to do just that. The United States and the Soviet Union both have much to gain at this summit meeting, so I suggest we now proceed to do what we know is in the interest of both our countries. All of the cards are on the table, and there is nothing left to hide. We can and should proceed from here."

Secretary Brezhnev waited for almost a half-minute after St. James had completed his translation, then spoke. "Mr. President, I have no idea what grounds you have for any of the preposterous accusations you have hurled at me. You speak of some film and regurgitate a history rewritten for some unknown purpose to suit only yourself. You accuse the Kremlin of killing President Kennedy when your own American Warren Commission proved he was killed by an American madman. You blame us for somehow forcing America to send a half a million men into a country ten thousand miles from your borders, while you conveniently forget that your own Senate voted almost unanimously to support Mr. Johnson in his quest to conquer North

Vietnam. Am I to suppose somehow we in the Kremlin forced all but two senators to vote in favor of what has become known as the Gulf of Tonkin Resolution? And as to the Middle East, you dare accuse us of fomenting war? What a laugh! America has armed the Israelis to the teeth for years. To help evenly balance the power structure in that volatile area, we Soviets saw fit to help arm the impoverished Arab nations with only the bare necessities to defend themselves. History has shown that the Israelis are the real warmongers, bent wholly on the total destruction of their neighbors. If it were not for the small influence of the Soviet Union in the area, the Jews would control all the land from Tangiers to Tehran. Well, we do not propose to let that happen. That is why we will continue to help countries like Egypt and Syria when they ask for our help. No, Mr. Nixon, your charges are nothing but insults and lies, and only because there is so much at stake now, will I continue this summit meeting with you. You suggest that the past be forgotten and that we be guided in our discussions only by that which will benefit both our countries in the future. I will agree to do that, so, in a spirit of cooperation, I will put aside your accusations and promise never to mention them again."

St. James had to admire the Soviet leader as he listened, then translated for the President. Brezhnev had just proved he was an absolute master at thinking on his feet, deftly skewing historical events in an off the cuff rant to suit his purposes. St. James sized him up as a worthy, yet despicable foe.

Brezhnev stood and signaled his interpreter to open the office doors. "Now, I suggest we end this meeting and convene again in the afternoon for a fresh start."

Nixon and St. James rose in unison. Neither had been fooled or taken aback by Brezhnev's near-tirade amid his protestations of innocence. The President had very smartly given the Secretary a face-saving way out by saying he was willing to forget the past, and the Secretary had wisely grasped at the opening. Each now knew where the other stood, and to St. James's trained eye, President Nixon seemed confident that the summit would now produce historical results.

Nixon invited St. James to join him for lunch in his suite, along with Secretary of State Rogers and Henry Kissinger, where he recounted the morning meeting in great detail as to how the Secretary had reacted, looking to St. James every once in a while for confirmation of some point.

"I would say you did extremely well, Mr. President," said Kissinger. "There can be no doubt in Mr. Brezhnev's mind now as to where matters stand. I'm feeling we'll have accomplished all we could have hoped for at the conclusion of this conference."

Kissinger was proved right. By the time the President and his entourage was ready to return home, the two had signed the first of the Strategic Arms Limitation Talks (SALT), and the Anti-Ballistic Missile (ABM) Treaty. Publicly, both leaders announced that there was still much negotiating to be done in Geneva and Helsinki before a complete treaty could be signed, but both pledged to the world that such a treaty would receive the support necessary from each to make it a reality.

On the third day of the talks, Brezhnev and Foreign Minister Andrei Gromyko met with Nixon and Kissinger, and again, St. James interpreted. The topic was Vietnam. The President spent the better part of the first hour pointing out the benefits for both America and the Soviet Union in seeing the war come to an end with an honorable settlement. He told how the Chinese had committed themselves to helping the belligerents find a common ground for peace at their meeting earlier in Peking and suggested it was time for the Soviet Union to do the same. Brezhnev and Gromyko listened politely, and then Brezhnev replied.

"What you say has some merit, Mr. President. We have tried to persuade Hanoi to be less rigid in its demands, but it has chosen to ignore our pleadings so far. Now, I feel that maybe we can apply a more direct economic pressure to make the North Vietnamese government bend a little at the peace table."

As he was speaking, Gromyko interrupted and whispered rapidly into Brezhnev's ear. Brezhnev made a short, but harsh, whispered reply, and actually pushed Gromyko away. He turned to President Nixon.

"Andrei here has suggested that maybe the Soviet Union should do nothing, at least not until after the upcoming election in your country. He points out that it looks like Senator McGovern will be your opponent in November and that he has promised to end the Vietnam War in 90 days by removing every last American if he's elected. I told him that I seriously doubt that Senator McGovern will be the next President, and that I fully expect you to remain in office for the next four years."

"And I can assure you, Mr. Secretary, that I have every intention of doing just that," Nixon replied.

"So, here is my counterproposal," said Brezhnev. "We Soviets will do all in our power to bring this war to a close. But with conditions. The more emphasis you put on fulfilling your side of the proposal, the more emphasis we shall put on ours."

"And what is your proposal?"

"What we touched on yesterday. Our buying your wheat and corn this year. I speak candidly, when I tell you that our agricultural experts are predicting a poor harvest, which means we will need extra grains. But we're willing to pay a reasonable price. However, I must have an ironclad guarantee that you will agree to sell in the amounts we need. We will not know our exact requirements until later this summer, maybe in July, but I must have a signed agreement with you that the sale will go through at the price set here in Moscow and for the quantities specified."

President Nixon nodded his agreement. "Is there anything else?"

"That you persuade your Congress to grant Favored Nations Trading Status to the Soviet Union. You have much to gain in the way of raw materials from us, and we have much to gain in the areas of technical assistance from you. Both of us stand to gain, so really, how can you object to either proposal? The wheat and corn sales will mean a good market for your excess crops and at good prices. Is that too much to ask for peace in Southeast Asia, indeed, in the whole world?" Secretary Brezhnev sat back, obviously pleased with his plan.

"Mr. Secretary, I can say yes to your first proposal here and now," Nixon replied. "As to the second one, I will do all in my power to persuade the Senate to approve Favored Nation Trading Status for the Soviet Union. But I must make it perfectly clear that I cannot guarantee it will come to pass as soon as you would like."

"That is good enough for me. Your signature on a document agreeing to the terms for the sale of some wheat to help out in a time of a little scarcity is sufficient for me to begin to exert more influence on Hanoi. Your pledge of good faith in the trade agreement will be met with equal good faith on my part. We are agreed, then, yes?"

"We are agreed," replied Nixon. "I will have Secretary of Agriculture Butz make the necessary arrangements with our largest grain companies to expedite the sale."

That night, after a state reception, Nixon met with Kissinger, Rogers, St. James, and other close aides for a review of the day's events. After the President spoke for ten minutes, he turned to Kissinger.

"Henry, what did you make of Brezhnev's outburst, and his shoving Foreign Minister Gromyko over the McGovern running for president thing?"

Kissinger wore a smug look as he answered, "Mister Brezhnev was acting out a political charade, nothing more." The look turned into a loud chuckle, then he continued. "I wouldn't be surprised to learn that the two of them had prearranged that bit of theater strictly for your benefit, Mister President. It was meant to show you that Brezhnev has confidence you will be calling the shots in the White House for four more years."

Nixon mulled that over for a few seconds. "You could be right." Then he asked, "Do you see any deeper ramifications over the wheat thing he was pushing for so hard? Is there something there I'm not seeing?"

"No, they're just looking for a good deal, nothing more," replied Kissinger. "As you know, even the United Nations is forecasting poor harvests this year for the Soviet Bloc and also for Australia. Brezhnev is just preparing now. The bigger problem as I see it is the Favored

Nations Status they're seeking. I know how Senator 'Scoop' Jackson will react."

"No doubt Scoop will give me a giant headache on that one," said Nixon. "Anyway, we'll do the best we can. The Soviets have promised to help us with Hanoi, and I fully intend to have this war over before my inauguration come next January."

Before President Nixon left Moscow, he addressed the Soviet people on television, another historical first.

Aboard Air Force One high over the Atlantic, St. James stood next to Bob Haldeman, who was engaged in small talk with the President. "Mr. President, I'm convinced history will record your first administration as one of the finest in our country's history."

Nixon's face wore a serious look. "You could well be right, Bob, but I'll promise you both this: I intend for my next term to be even more momentous, to the point history will forever remember the name Richard Milhous Nixon."

The first order of business upon returning home was for the President to instruct Secretary of Agriculture Butz as to the desires of the Kremlin in the purchase of grains. The Secretary assured President Nixon he would get to work on the problem at once, and by the middle of June, he had reported back to the President. After meeting with the owners of the six largest grain companies, he was given an estimate as to how much grain could be sold abroad, while not undermining domestic reserves in the process. It was expected the Soviets would ask for approximately five hundred million bushels of various grains, the bulk, of course, being wheat. The Secretary saw no problem in meeting this request. Talks had already begun between the Americans and Soviets in earnest, and problems such as delivery schedules, payments, and shipping arrangements were being worked out, even though the finalized Soviet requirements as would not be known until the middle of July.

Speaking with St. James and Dr. Kissinger during a rare personal conversion several weeks later in the Oval Office, the President recounted exactly how he felt the moment Brezhnev had realized his attempt to blackmail President Johnson had failed so miserably, and that the true story behind the assassination of President Kennedy also died that day in the Kremlin, the same place it had started those many years earlier. Nixon had convinced himself the book was closed on the Soviet plot to subvert America.

How wrong he was, remembered St. James, many months later. *Indeed, how wrong we all were.*

CHAPTER 32

WYOMING – JUNE 1974

THE U.S. MARSHALS SERVICE in coordination with the FBI had done a praiseworthy job in providing the deep-cover identity transition of Mykel Alexei Zakharov into Edward Albert Tilden. Anyone checking his birth certificate, school records, IRS returns, Social Security Administration records, or his U.S. Army Retirement Folder at the National Personnel Records Center in St. Louis, would find that Edward Albert Tilden had been a model citizen since his birth in Bayonne, New Jersey, in 1919. Because of Zakharov's military background, it was decided that Edward Tilden should be a retired noncommissioned officer who, after serving twenty-nine years in uniform, had chosen to settle down on a recently purchased working ranch in Wyoming.

St. James had last seen Zakharov three months earlier, but a troubling telephone call had prompted him to fly west to take personal stock of the situation. His feelings toward the man hadn't changed a whit, yet he had to admit: Zakharov had been candid to a fault during his many months of debriefings, and every shred of information had checked out one-hundred-percent. This Soviet defector had earned his keep a thousandfold. St. James had indeed found himself angered to the depths of his being as he learned of events from ten years earlier, just as Zakharov had promised he would.

And President Nixon had agonized over what he should do with the information, until finally deciding that going public with the film from Chairman Mao, coupled with Zakharov's confession of Soviet complicity in the assassination of President Kennedy could well trigger World War III. He reached a decision. Nixon ordered St. James hand-carry the film, along with the Johnson and Zakharov debriefing tapes, and Edgar Snow's China diary entries, to a special sixty cubic foot presidential vault built inside the United States Bullion Depository at Fort Knox, Kentucky, by Franklin Roosevelt in February 1942.

The *Sitting President of The United States Access Only* was the required security clearance to enter the vault, assurance this package would never see the light of day unless resurrected by some future president. The *Warren Commission Report* would forever remain the definitive historical document of what happened that day in Dallas. St. James also instructed his team to forget everything they had learned from the Russian defector.

St. James rang the buzzer, and moments later Zakharov appeared behind the screened door. The Russian now wore a trimmed beard, but in the intervening ninety days his hair had turned completely gray. Zakharov removed an unlit cheroot from the corner of his mouth. "Good to see you, come on in."

Once inside, St James observed Zakharov at closer quarters. Even though he had seemed fit from behind the mesh, St. James now saw a startling change and, after a few minutes of requisite small talk, asked in a quiet voice, "How are you really feeling, Alexei?"

"The truth? Not so good. I have terrible stomach pains and I'm bleeding most of the time now."

St. James's mouth firmed, a sign he had reached a decision. "We're going to the hospital first thing in the morning. It could be nothing more than an ulcer, but we will get you better, I promise."

Zakharov smiled weakly. "I am grateful for how you've always treated me."

St. James shrugged. "I made a deal and I keep my promises. It's as simple as that."

Their appointment was for nine; and at eight-fifteen, they set out in his rental car. St. James was simply dressed in jeans, wool shirt, and a windbreaker. He was also armed with a .38 Smith & Wesson Special revolver and had brought along a new state-of-the-art Motorola radio capable of providing a secure satellite link with the White House.

As they drove on the all-but deserted road, St. James was trying his best to keep Zakharov's mind engaged with idle chatter, but glancing sideways every so often, he could see that the Russian was preoccupied.

"Did I ever tell you why I defected?" Zakharov suddenly asked.

"No you didn't, and I never pressed. I decided long ago you were entitled to a modicum of privacy. But while we're on that subject, you also never told me how you knew about me and my cover as *Pegasus*."

"I'll answer the why question first. It was because of my wife, Marie," Zakharov began, his voice breaking. "She and I never had children, and she was my world." He fell silent for several moments, then cleared his throat and unabashedly wiped his eyes. "Four years ago she was diagnosed with leukemia, and the news came as a terrible blow. My lovely Marie was only forty. I read all the literature I could on the subject and learned of a clinic in Switzerland that was having remarkable success in treating her type of cancer. I wanted Marie there, so I went to General Andropov, the head of the KGB, and asked him to secure permission from Secretary Brezhnev. He assured me he would. Well, nothing happened, and a few months later she withered away and died in my arms. I know she would have lived much longer had Brezhnev helped me in my hour of need. It was so little to ask in return for all my years of faithful service. Andropov later told me that Brezhnev had angrily refused my request, and cautioned him never to broach the subject again. Of course, Brezhnev attended the funeral along with President Podgorny and Prime Minister Kosygin, and all three offered their condolences and cried their crocodile tears. I pretended to accept their sympathy, but made a vow then and there that they would pay dearly for what they had done. I bided my time, and the rest you know." Zakharov turned silent and began staring out his side window.

Glancing in the rearview mirror, St James noticed that a rolling wreck of a pickup had tucked in behind him. After several moments of tailgating, the driver swung out to pass. As the clunker drew abreast, St James saw a grizzled old character hunched over the wheel, mouth set and eyes fixed as he coaxed the last ounce of speed from his worn-out engine. St. James smiled.

When the pickup had pulled ahead by a quarter of a mile, its right rear tire unexpectedly blew apart inside a cloud of white smoke. The now out-of-control truck careened crabwise across the two lanes of blacktop, bounced up onto the opposite shoulder, and shuddered to a stop amidst a shower of gravel and dirt.

Coming alongside, St. James saw that the wheel rim was buckled and the tire in shreds.

The left door swung open and the driver slid out, his left leg in a grungy cast encasing the foot from knee to ankle, but leaving five dirty toes exposed. Grabbing ahold of a crutch, the geezer hobbled back to survey the damage.

"Wait here," St. James said to Zakharov, noting there was no spare tire on the battered truck. He walked up to the old man.

The man wore a sheepish grin then spat a long train of tobacco juice into the dirt.

St James had to laugh. "The Indianapolis Five Hundred race was last month," he said while bending down to inspect the damage.

A harrumphing sound was followed by another tobacco-laced stream. "Can you fix it, son?"

"With what? You don't have a spare."

"How about using yours until we get into town?"

"Can't, they're different sizes."

"Damn!"

"Tell you what, though" St James said while rising. "I'll get a wrecker to come and help you." He turned and called out to Zakharov. "Ed, would you bring me the radio?" He turned back and looked closer at the ruined tire. His brow furrowed. Something was odd. The car door slammed, and he heard Zakharov's footsteps crunching on the gravel.

As he leaned lower the furrows deepened. The stench of burnt rubber and a hint of cordite forced him to hold his breath. And then he spotted several dangling electrical wires that had no business being there.

"*Andrewwww!*" It was a bloodcurdling shriek.

The hairs on St. James's neck rose in an atavistic response. Something was horribly wrong! *Zakharov had never addressed him by his first name.*

"*Andrewwww!*" Zakharov screamed again at the top of his lungs. "*It's Romulus, President Kennedy's assassin. He's found me!*"

Christ, I've been blindsided like some frigging amateur! St. James began to rise, his eyes now glued on the old man. He watched in slow motion as *Romulus* pointed his crutch at Zakharov and pulled a trigger. A .45 caliber hollow-point tore into the Russian's head.

"Goddammit all to hell!" St. James roared, his words rolling across the desolate landscape like a thunderclap. He already had a grip on his revolver, but its holster had become entangled inside his bunched-up windbreaker.

Romulus was unbelievably fast. Gone was the ancient cripple of moments ago. Pivoting a full 180 degrees on his good leg, *Romulus* swung his lethal crutch in St. James's direction and squeezed the trigger for a second time.

The bullet slammed into his chest, its kinetic force sweeping St. James completely off of his feet. He came down hard atop a mound of jagged gravel with all four limbs akimbo, then lay motionless. A searing pain exploded inside his thorax, and as he stared up into a cloudless, Wyoming sky, a still-conscious Andrew St. James waited for the kill shot that would end his life.

Who will warn the President we have a traitor inside the White House? That was his last thought before the world turned mercifully black.

THREE DAYS LATER

Slowly it dawned on St. James that the moaning was coming from within. The sound was followed by a flurry of activity, then everything turned blissfully quiet and black again. This happened two or three more times until he was finally able to open his eyes and keep them open. His nose told him he was in a hospital, and from what little he could see, tied to every machine, bottle, and tube in the place. A hazy face appeared.

"Can you hear me, Mr. St. James?" a female voice asked from afar.

He nodded.

"How many fingers am I holding up?"

"Six?" he whispered.

"Really?"

St. James concentrated. "Three?"

"Much better, now go back to sleep."

A week later they unhooked the machines and removed most of the tubes. A team of specialists visited twice a day and with each examination affirmed he would be as good as new in no time. Meanwhile, the staff was abuzz about the patient with the around-the-clock FBI detail guarding his room. There was also a rumor that President Nixon was calling daily for updates on his condition.

St. James woke from a fitful sleep to find Justin Scott seated beside him.

"How's it going, Boss?" Justin asked in a low voice, then got up and shut the door. "You sure had a close call, but I guess you know that. *What in the hell happened?*"

"How's Zakharov?"

Justin shook his head. "The man never stood a chance."

"It was *Romulus*," St James said feebly after thirty seconds of silence.

Justin looked puzzled. "What do you mean, it was *Romulus*?"

"*Romulus*, the assassin who killed President Kennedy. Zakharov screamed a warning to me that *Romulus* had found him. Those were his last words. It's now obvious the Soviets had known where to find him." St. James placed a worried hand on Justin's arm. "Which means there's a leak inside the White House. Has to be. It was an internal setup."

"Holy shit!" Justin whispered in reply.

"God only knows why he didn't finish me off," St. James said a full minute later.

"Because he's a professional, and his orders were to only kill Zakharov. You were a nuisance, nothing more, so he let you live. *Romulus* is no psychopath, Andrew. He's simply the best, and that's why it's a safe bet for me to say he'll never be caught."

Another minute passed and St. James gasped as a wave of pain rolled through him. He finally managed, "The principal players are all dead. Kennedy, Johnson, De Gaulle, Snow, and finally Zakharov," he said, "but I'm thinking our problems are far from over."

The expression on Justin's face told St. James that he wasn't making much sense.

"Follow along with me for a minute," St. James continued in a weak voice. "President Johnson's been gone since January; a patriot dead at age sixty-four from a massive coronary brought on in large measure by a Kremlin troika that had visions of blackmailing him on their way to ruling the world, or at least a huge chunk of it."

"And Major General Mykel Alexei Zakharov met a similar fate simply because the KGB refused to believe he had perished in that Italian plane crash back in '72," said Justin.

St James nodded. "You know, he had time to tell me the reason he defected. It seems his motivation was a combination of anger, grief, and an all-consuming hatred for Brezhnev and Kosygin. The anger was brought on by the inconsolable grief he was suffering over his recently deceased wife. He discovered Brezhnev had refused to allow her to leave the country for cancer treatment at a Swiss hospital known for making miracles happen to patients with her condition. She died in his arms several months later. He said, and I quote: 'It was so little to ask in return for all my years of faithful service.' Zakharov decided to bide his time and then defect to America, bringing with him the most powerful of bargaining chips: the true story behind President Kennedy's assassination."

St James stayed silent for several seconds, then added, "He was getting ready to finally tell me how he came to know who I really was and why he would only defect to an American agent he knew simply as *Pegasus*. But it was too late. He was killed and the secret died with him."

St. James looked away and changed the subject. "I suppose our traitor could be someone with the Marshals Service," he said in a wistful voice, hoping against hope that the turncoat would not be found inside his own diminutive ranks.

He slowly closed his eyes. "I'm really beat, Justin. How about coming back in a couple of hours? I've got some instructions for you to take back to Washington."

Seconds later the door closed, leaving Andrew St. James alone with some very dark thoughts for company.

EPILOGUE

THE PRESENT

JUSTIN PRESSED THE STOP BUTTON and looked over to his wife. Paula raised both hands to chest level in a sign of silent surrender. She shook her head to signal her husband that she wasn't ready to talk—at least not yet.

"I understand," Justin said in a sympathetic voice.

He had made the decision to bring Paula aboard when St. James had said that he would be recounting in minute detail the entire sequence of events that had taken place in the Nixon White House, beginning with the defection of General Zakharov on May 8, 1972, and ending at noon on August 9, 1974, when the President had resigned from office in disgrace.

For a full five minutes Paula sat in silence, trying to make sense of what she had learned over the several sessions of listening to the discs. Finally, she looked at Justin, seeing him for the first time in a different light.

"To think that I never knew what your job really was during those days at the Nixon White House," she began. "In all the time I worked with you at the FBI; and even after you retired and I followed you into your new venture as a private investigator for the city's coterie of rich and powerful trial lawyers, never once did you speak of those years.

And even after we got married and really retired, you still said nothing. Now I know why."

"I'd also forgotten most of what we've just heard," Justin replied. "Remember, it was fifty years ago, hon; a time when our small team of secret agents were literally uncovering the worst crime ever committed on American soil. We had no idea how far the cancer might have spread, or whom we could turn to for help. Not only was Mr. St. James almost killed by that same Russian assassin, but the country was deep in the throes of the Watergate scandal. It was June 1974, and President Nixon was barely functioning. He was a physical and mental wreck. For all intents and purposes Alexander Haig was acting-President. I know for a fact *Pegasus* never trusted Haig; he saw the General as a power-grabbing megalomaniac, and that's why he kept him in in the dark regarding our Russian defector."

Paula glanced at the grandfather clock as it chimed nine times. "Let's hear what Mr. James has in the way of instructions for you, then we'll call it a night. I know I'm beat; you must be exhausted. That way we'll be fresh in the morning."

Justin returned to his seat, pressed start, and a moment later St. James appeared on the screen, lying in the same hospital bed.

"Justin, I'll be brief. First, the key. It's to Unit 201 at the CubeSmart Self Storage in Alexandria, Virginia. It's actually been rented under your name, paid in advance for two years, and the lone package inside has been there since January this year. It contains duplicates of all the original material: the Johnson–Dobrynin Soviet Embassy film, Edgar Snow's China diary entries, President Johnson's taped meeting with President Nixon in the White House in 1972, and of course, all of the debriefing sessions we conducted with General Zakharov. This next part is important," St. James said, then paused, and winced. He murmured something to an off-screen presence, and a man replied by clearly asking if he wanted the dripline increased. St. James shook his head, and Justin and Paula waited a full minute for him to proceed.

"Justin, I've stamped the word 'UNCLASSIFIED' on every page and every item in the package. I'll tell you why. The Soviet film was not produced in the United States by any of our intelligence gathering services, which means a U. S. security classification does not automatically apply. Remember also, none of this material was ever in the official hands of any governmental agency. Even the original file stored in the Presidential Vault at Fort Knox does not carry any classification, due in part to all of the confusion in the White House at the time of the Watergate brouhaha thing. In normal times it could easily have been classified *Top Secret–Eyes Only*, if Nixon had so wanted. It was his decision, and his alone to make, just like all Presidents have the ultimate authority to declassify any document at any time. But the last days of the Nixon White House were anything but normal times, and he remained silent on the subject, which means you will not be breaking any laws pertaining to the handling of top secret material. The information you have on the discs, and what's in the storage locker, is simply the unvarnished truth as to what happened in Dallas on November 22, 1963, and in the years immediately following that awful tragedy."

Paula signaled him to hit the pause button. "Could what we've just heard from *Pegasus* be true, Justin? I mean, about any level of secret classification not applying here. Somehow it doesn't sound right. I remember how careful we had to be especially when handling the top secret stuff at the FBI. Or am I just being an old worrywart?"

Justin reached over and squeezed Paula's hand. "And that's why I love my girl," he replied, "but in this instance, Andrew St. James is one hundred percent correct. The man was a genius. But to be absolutely sure, he held all this under wraps for more than fifty years, waiting for the Kennedy Files to be as fully declassified as possible before making his move. Talk about having the patience of Job."

Paula was relieved, and it showed. "Then let's find out where you're supposed to deliver the package," she said, as Justin started the disc.

"Justin, write this number down," St. James said from beyond the grave. "I recommend storing it in your phone under the name 'Concierge Service' because that will be easy to remember. 1-800-881-1963. You will hear a recorded message asking you to leave your name, and a cellphone callback number. A live person will return your call within the hour, and will provide you with everything you'll need to complete your task. And, Justin, you will be well compensated for all your troubles."

Justin watched as St. James began a fruitless struggle to sit up straighter. Within seconds, a pair of arms came into view and tenderly helped the dying man into a more comfortable position. St. James smiled a silent thanks toward the unseen assistant, then turned back to face the camera, the smile still affixed.

"Justin, I've long considered you a special friend," he began, his voice reflecting a profound tiredness, but strong enough to be heard clearly. "I saw something exceptional in you the first day we met and decided soon after to make you a member of my elite band of brothers at the White House. It was an easy decision, and you proved me right. And even after your White House assignment was over and you'd returned to the bureau, I followed your career from afar, including your post-FBI adventures where you were so instrumental in solving several international crises which would not have ended well without your intervention. You've made me proud to have been an early mentor."

St. James took several short, shallow breaths, and Justin saw tears well up in his eyes. "And now the time has come for me to say goodbye, Justin," he said in a barely heard whisper. His right arm slowly appeared from under the covers, and with all the strength he could muster, St. James raised the arm to his temple and rendered one last salute, holding it for several seconds. "Goodbye, my friend," he mouthed silently into the camera lens, then slowly brought the arm down.

Justin's call to the unknown phone number set multiple wheels in motion. True to the recorded message, a man retuned his call within twenty minutes and politely asked if Justin was prepared to come to Washington.

"Yes, but I'll be traveling with my wife. We both have lots of friends there, so our plan is to spend a couple of days visiting after completing a task for Mr. St. James. I'll be making our plane reservations and hotel booking as soon as we hang up."

"That won't be necessary, Mr. Scott. I've arranged your transportation and have booked you into a suite at the Four Seasons Hotel."

Justin laughed. "Well, thanks, but that's a little rich for my blood, if you get my drift . . ." He did not get to complete the sentence.

"Please, sir," the voice interrupted politely, "this was all taken care of by Mr. Andrew St. James before he passed. Pegasus Industries will dispatch a company plane to your nearest airport, which I believe is Witham Field in Stuart, Florida."

☆   ☆   ☆

Three days had passed, and Justin, now seated in a luxurious, multi-functional Moroccan Leather chair, reached out for his wife's hand. Paula smiled from an identical twin seat, entwined her fingers with his, and returned the slight squeeze.

They were en route from their home in Jensen Beach, Florida, to Washington DC in a Gulfstream G650ER cruising at 38,000 feet. Its black and gold livery reflected an understated elegance, as did the plane's customized registration number, N2263PI, and a winged logo galloping across the tail. Even the uninitiated observer would know immediately this was the property of a very wealthy individual.

"Justin, I've been thinking: Could it be possible the Chinese decided way back in 1967 when they first obtained that film that they would need to build a mighty country in order to never again be in the position of being held hostage by a Superpower?"

Justin pursed his lips, lost in thought. Finally, "You could be onto something. The premise certainly gives a compelling reason for them working so feverishly for the past five decades to become such an economic and military juggernaut." After another long interlude, he added quietly, "On second thought, I *know* you're right. Good job, honey, you have all the makings of a crackerjack FBI agent. You would've done old J. Edgar Hoover himself proud, though he never hired a single female agent in his almost fifty years of running the joint."

Paula flushed at the high praise and squeezed Justin's hand all the tighter as she looked at him, his eyes now closed.

He's still a heart-stopper, she thought, as she studied Justin's strong, lean, no-nonsense face and stylishly cut, mostly graying hair. He was dressed in French cuffed shirtsleeves, his expensive slacks held fast by crimson suspenders. His weakness for clothes went as far back as she could remember, and he often joked that in this one regard he was worse than most women he knew.

They had married a decade ago. Her first husband had been killed in an airplane crash; their only son, a West Point honor graduate, was now an Army colonel currently stationed at Ft. Bliss, in West Texas.

Still studying Justin's face, her mind flew back over the intervening years. Where had they gone? And so fast! He, and his now-dead first wife, Sally, had had no children. Over time they had slowly drifted apart, remained friends, but never divorced.

Lucky me, she thought, as she squeezed his hand a little tighter. *He's been a wonderful husband, everything I could have ever wished for.* She closed her eyes, fully content just to be in the moment.

By two p.m. they had checked into their suite at The Four Seasons. The process had only taken a few minutes. They were invited to merely sign for anything they needed while guests, and told the final bill would be paid by the party making the reservations, namely, Pegasus Industries. They were handed keys to a rental Lexus which had been delivered an hour earlier.

Justin looked at his watch. "How about we go over to the storage unit and take a look at the package?"

"Good idea. Then we'll be free to do whatever we want."

"Like enjoying these sinfully luxurious digs."

Forty minutes later they were standing in a small concrete cubicle, eyeing a single box on the floor already wrapped for shipping, an address label affixed. There was an envelope lying atop. Justin opened the unsealed flap, saw two pieces of paper, took out the first, put on his half-frame cheaters, and began to read.

Justin, the box contains the whole story. You will notice it's addressed Attention:

Curator. The Richard Nixon Library & Museum, 18001 Yorba Linda Blvd, Yorba Linda, California. 92886. *Included on the label are the words:* Perishable Printed Material. Open Immediately. *I suspect the whole world will finally know the true story of President Kennedy's assassination within days of the package's arrival.*

Thank you, ASJ

PS. *Send it by regular U. S. mail. If the Post Office was entrusted by Harry Winston to deliver his gift of the $250 million Hope Diamond wrapped in plain brown paper to the* Smithsonian National Museum of Natural History *in D.C., from his store in New York City in 1958, then I confidently choose to do the same.*

PPS. *Justin, should you balk at accepting the attached gift—and I sincerely hope you don't, feel free to donate it to your favorite charity. ASJ*

He handed the note to Paula. As she read it, he pulled out the second piece of paper. His heart skipped a beat. He blinked, looked again, then silently passed it to his wife.

Paula studied the small sheet for a long moment, then whispered, "You think it's real?"

"It's real alright," Justin whispered back. "You'll notice it's a cashiers' check, which means it can be cashed or deposited at any bank, anywhere."

"But it's for a half a million dollars."

"Yeah, and that's Chase Bank paper, which happens to be our

bank. Andrew thought of everything." He chuckled. "This will clear easily."

Paula let loose a small giggle. "Then let's run to the nearest branch right after we've been to the Post Office."

★　　★　　★

Early next morning, Justin told his wife he had one last piece of business to attend to.

"We need to visit Arlington National Cemetery for me to pay my final respects to Andrew. I discovered on the Internet that's where he's buried."

At ten o'clock they found themselves standing in front of a white marble tombstone in a row of similar grave markers halfway up a grassy incline. It bore a simple Christian Cross at its top, and directly underneath, engraved USAF Pilot Wings.

ANDREW ST. JAMES
1LT USAF
AUG 22 1935
JAN 16 2023

Justin Scott came to attention and saluted. "I return your salute, Lieutenant Andrew St. James." He held it for ten seconds, then whispered as he lowered his arm, "Rest in peace, Andrew. *The Pegasus Directive is finally closed.*"

The End

AUTHOR'S NOTE

REGARDING THE ACCURACY OF HISTORICAL EVENTS AS DESCRIBED IN THIS STORY.

All major events that the author has described in The Pegasus Directive are historically correct and easily verified by the reader.

1. In 1972 the ARPANET system was a top secret, computer-driven, communications network used by the Department of Defense. Years later it would evolve into the Internet.

2. French President Charles de Gaulle did contact President Nixon in 1970 regarding opening a dialogue with Communist China. He died before the initiative bore fruit.

3. Mao Tse-tung told Edgar Snow in 1970 that he would welcome work to begin on a normalization of relations with the U.S., and asked the author to so inform President Nixon. This overture helped pave the way to the historical meeting of the two leaders in 1972. Edgar Snow had died in Switzerland six days earlier as described by the author.

4. In September 1971 British Intelligence uncovered a
   Soviet spy network, and subsequently expelled 105
   Soviets. Oleg Lyalin was the low-level KGB agent in
   London who turned traitor, just as described by the
   author.

5. On the night of May 5, 1972, Alitalia Flight 112
   crashed into Mount Longa, near Palermo, Italy. There
   were no survivors.

6. President Johnson and Premier Kosygin did meet at
   Glassboro, New Jersey, 23-25 June 1967.

7. Lee Harvey Oswald showed up unannounced at the
   Soviet Embassy in Mexico City, on September 27, 1963,
   and stayed until October 3, 1963, just as described by
   the author.

8. The tragedy that took place in Dallas, Texas, on
   November 22, 1963, is a part of our history and needs
   no further explanation.

9. The Second Vatican Council, Part Three, was in session
   from September to December 1963. Select clergy from
   all over the world attended workshops and participated
   in various panels by invitation. The Council provided
   the perfect cover for the two Soviets to re-enter Europe
   via Rome disguised as priests, then continue their
   journey on to Moscow.

10. The "Converter" is described in the story as being at
    the JPL in Pasadena and used by NASA to finely detail
    maps of the moon's surface in preparation for Neil
    Armstrong's historic Apollo 11 lunar landing, as well
    as "bending" the images of President Johnson's watch.
    It was the author's fictional "precursor" to the James
    Webb Space Telescope (JWST) which was launched
    in December 2021, and began sending its incredible
    images of the universe back to earth in July 2022.

11. In 1942, President Roosevelt secured a special sixty cubic foot vault at Fort Knox to store priceless U.S. government documents during WWII. He personally visited the fort on April 28, 1943 to see for himself that it was as safe and secure as promised. This is the same Presidential Vault where The Pegasus Directive was "buried" on directions from President Nixon.

ABOUT THE AUTHOR

IAN A. O'CONNOR is the author of *Point Option – A Military Thriller*, the 2022 Silver Falchion Award winner for the year's Best Thriller.

Ian is a retired USAF colonel. He is a recognized expert in the field of national security management, a qualification which serves him well as the foundation for his novels. He is the author of *The Seventh Seal* and *The Barbarossa Covenant*, both Justin Scott Thrillers. *Kirkus Reviews* wrote in high praise of Ian's work: "The end result fits nicely into the Tom Clancy-meets-Dan Brown canon." His co-authored book *SCRAPPY: A Memoir of a Fighter Pilot in Korea and Vietnam*, published by McFarland Publishing Company, remains a favorite of the international military aviation community. It recounts the amazing career of Colonel Howard "Scrappy" Johnson, the 1958 Collier Trophy winner for the year's most meritorious flight.

His thriller, *The Twilight of The Day*, a harrowing tale of Vietnam pilot-POWs, was awarded a bronze medal by the Military Writers Society of America in 2018. Copies of both books are found in the United States Naval Academy, and the United States Air Force Academy libraries. Ian is a member of Mystery Writers of America. He lives on Florida's Treasure Coast with his wife, Candice.